PRAISE FOR KATE WHITE

THE SECOND HUSBAND

"Intricately plotted and suspenseful. *The Second Husband* is a terrific book, packed with surprises and a nail-biting conclusion."

—Sarah Pekkanen, *New York Times* bestselling coauthor of
The Golden Couple

"Immersive, spellbinding thriller about a woman questioning everything—including her husband. In Kate White's perfectly plotted novel, it's impossible to predict what will happen next."

—Samantha Downing, international bestselling author of
My Lovely Wife

"*The Second Husband* is suspense at its most addictive. The pages turn in a blur. You won't put this one down."

—Michele Campbell, international bestselling author of
It's Always the Husband

THE FIANCÉE

"A tense, simmering, fast-paced mystery, Kate White's latest captivating thriller explores the secrets that lurk just under the surface . . . . ced through this story about a . . . . ring at an idyllic estate that qu . . . . ept me guessing until the very e . . . . re the danger was hiding."

—. . . . . *York Times* bestselling author of
All the Missing Girls and *The Last House Guest*

"Kate White's *The Fiancée* is exactly what we all need right now: a fast-paced, perfectly woven murder mystery, with a hearty dash of family drama. This one must not be missed!"

—Aimee Molloy, *New York Times* bestselling author of
The Perfect Mother and *Goodnight Beautiful*

"Kate White's newest thriller *The Fiancée* is a perfect poolside or beach read, as this psychological thriller has everything a great summer read needs! Told in an almost locked-room style, as we are secluded at a wealthy family's sprawling estate, this mystery looks at what appears to be a picture-perfect family. . . . The constant threatening feeling in the air propels this psychological thriller to a truly surprising climax."

—*Nerd Daily*

"A twisty family drama."

—*Library Journal*

"A skillfully constructed page-turner. . . . Expert pacing, characters readers can love to hate, and an intelligent heroine make this a winner. White consistently entertains."

—*Publishers Weekly*

BETWEEN TWO STRANGERS

ALSO BY KATE WHITE

FICTION

If Looks Could Kill

A Body to Die For

Till Death Do Us Part

Over Her Dead Body

Lethally Blond

Hush

The Sixes

Eyes on You

The Wrong Man

So Pretty It Hurts

The Secrets You Keep

Even If It Kills Her

Such a Perfect Wife

Have You Seen Me?

The Fiancée

The Second Husband

NONFICTION

Why Good Girls Don't Get Ahead but Gutsy Girls Do

*I Shouldn't Be Telling You This: How to Ask for the Money,
Snag the Promotion, and Create the Career You Deserve*

The Gutsy Girl Handbook: Your Manifesto for Success

BETWEEN TWO STRANGERS

A Novel of Suspense

KATE WHITE

HARPER

NEW YORK · LONDON · TORONTO · SYDNEY

HARPER

BETWEEN TWO STRANGERS. Copyright © 2023 by Kate White. All rights reserved. Printed in the United States of America. No part of this book may be used or reproduced in any manner whatsoever without written permission except in the case of brief quotations embodied in critical articles and reviews. For information, address HarperCollins Publishers, 195 Broadway, New York, NY 10007.

HarperCollins books may be purchased for educational, business, or sales promotional use. For information, please email the Special Markets Department at SPsales@harpercollins.com.

FIRST EDITION

Designed by Jamie Lynn Kerner

Library of Congress Cataloging-in-Publication Data has been applied for.

ISBN 978-0-06-324736-9 (pbk.)
ISBN 978-0-06-332290-5 (library edition)

23 24 25 26 27 LBC 6 5 4 3 2

BETWEEN TWO STRANGERS

1

Now

THE CALL THAT ENDS UP CHANGING EVERYTHING—NOT ONLY MY present and future but the past, too—comes late on a Friday afternoon. At the sound of the ringtone, I shoot a glance at my phone screen, but once I see it's from a number I don't recognize, with a 914 area code, I just let the phone ring. I never pick up if I don't know who's on the other end, and sometimes even if I do. It's probably spam, anyway, some automated voice warning me I need to renew my vehicle warranty, though I haven't owned a car in over a decade.

I return my attention to the pile of items on the worktable in my tiny East Village studio, but I'm interrupted again moments later when a sound alerts me that the caller's left a voice mail.

My breath catches. What if it's Deacon, the jerk I last saw a few weeks ago? During the brief period I'd known him, he'd phoned a couple of times just to chat, and since I've deleted his name and number from my contacts, it would show on my screen only as digits. But the number doesn't seem familiar, and based on how our last date ended, there's no way it could be him.

I tap the voice-mail icon and play the recording, feeling nervous anyway.

"Ms. Moore, my name is Bradley Kane," a male voice says, deep, firm, and serious. "I'm an attorney in Scarsdale, New York, and it's important that I speak to you about a private matter. Can you please give me a call at your earliest convenience?"

The second I hear him say "attorney," my stomach twists. There's something about that word that always triggers a rush of dread in me, like when I notice one of those K-9 unit German shepherds at an airport and wonder if I swallowed a half dozen cocaine-packed condoms earlier in the day without remembering it.

I tell myself to relax, that although a call from a lawyer seems ominous, I can't be in any kind of legal trouble. I've never broken the law to my knowledge, except smoking weed in college before it was legal. The only debt I'm carrying is on my credit card, which, if anything, the bank seems delighted with, and I don't have a sidewalk someone could have slipped and cracked their skull on. I've also never even been to Scarsdale, a suburb north of the city, or heard of anyone named Bradley Kane.

But then my heart suddenly skitters. Could this have something to do with my recent work? For the last three years—four if I count the twelve or so months it took me to finally summon enough psychic energy simply to gather supplies—I've been making collages with all sorts of odds and ends and "found objects," like snippets from magazines and catalogs, scraps of fabric, Polaroid photos, torn-off pieces of maps and packages, images I paint myself, and sometimes even 3-D stuff, too. Though I've never had the specific goal of offending anyone, it's happened. A year ago, I used a book jacket as part of a piece that was exhibited in a downtown Manhattan street fair. The self-help author somehow got wind of it, wrangled my cell number from the organizers, and lit into me over the phone.

Okay, his book cover had been glued between a Polaroid of a disembodied doll's head and a gauze bandage, but I'd convinced myself that if the author ever happened to see the piece, he'd be amused by the irony. Well, he wasn't. He threatened to sue me for disparaging his book and possibly impacting sales. There was no way his sales would have been affected by my artwork, and I was pretty sure I was protected under the "fair usage" defense, which allows artists to use copyrighted material in their work, but I couldn't afford to consult with a lawyer for peace of mind. So just to be on the safe side, I removed the jacket and filled in the gap with something else.

Though the revised piece ending up selling later for four hundred and seventy-five dollars, it didn't seem nearly as good as the first incarnation.

I don't have any collages on display at the moment, but several are featured on the website I just redesigned for myself. Is it possible I've inadvertently ticked someone off again, and this time they have good reason to sue?

My heart does a second skip as another possibility enters my mind. A few hours ago, I received a message from Josh Meyer, the art dealer who's giving me my first real show at his gallery on the Lower East Side, asking me to call him back when I had a moment. I've put off doing it, figuring he wants to nudge me about the piece I promised him after he decided the exhibit would look best with a tenth collage. The opening, after all, is a week from Tuesday. But maybe Josh was reaching out because he'd gotten a call about me from the same lawyer.

I pull a long breath and try the gallery instead of the law firm; Josh happens to answer the line himself.

"Hey, Skyler," he says. "Thanks for getting back to me."

"Of course. Everything okay?"

"Yes, fine, I just wanted an update on your last piece."

I breathe a sigh of relief. "Right, right, thanks for checking. I'm actually staring at it right now."

"Excellent. Can I have one of my guys pick it up tomorrow?"

"*Tomorrow?*" I exclaim, feeling anxious all over again. I've been working hard on the piece, but I've also had to make time each day for the graphic design work I do to pay the bills, and at the very least I need the weekend to finish it.

"I thought you said it would be ready Saturday."

"Sorry, I must have misunderstood. Uh, would Tuesday morning work? I can deliver it myself."

"I know I didn't give you much time, but that's going to be cutting it close," he says. I envision him grimacing on the other end of the line and running a hand through his thick brown hair. "What if we say Monday afternoon? The gallery's closed for business then, but some of us will be here."

My gaze flicks back to the collage in progress. I like the individual elements I'm playing with—none of which I've settled on yet—but so far they're not coming together as a whole. If I have any hope of finishing the collage this weekend, it will mean begging for an extension on the graphic design job that I promised a client would be delivered Monday.

"Okay, I'll drop it off at the end of the day." I just have to pray I'll be done.

"Great, and while I've got you, I wanted to mention that we're getting a ton of RSVPs for the party. My guess is that we'll end up with close to a hundred people."

Please no, I think, as panic foams through my entire body. When Josh tracked me down six months ago saying he'd been following me on Instagram and wanted to discuss exhibiting my collages, he mentioned that there would, "of course," be a small opening night reception. Though I loathed the idea of a party, I told myself I would have to grin and bear it. I figured there'd be thirty people tops, and most of them would be present to see the work of the photographer being featured at the same time. I never once anticipated the guest list going into triple digits.

"Um, oh. Wow. But just checking, I'm not expected to say anything, right?"

"Not if you really don't want to. After enough people have arrived, I'll do a welcome and talk a little about your work and Harry's, too."

That won't be a problem for Josh. He grew up on the Upper East Side of Manhattan, the son of a legendary gallerist, and he's a smooth, polished fortysomething-year-old guy, probably totally at ease in front of a crowd.

"You'll want to say *something* when I'm done," he adds, "but it can be short and sweet. Though maybe as we get closer, you'll change your mind and want to say more."

"Sure, I'll let you know."

But I won't change my mind. I suffer from a form of anxiety that, for more than a decade, has left me a wreck in most social settings. Though I'm hardly what you'd call dazzling in situations with only a couple of people, I do okay; it's when I'm in a group of five or more that everything goes to hell. My heart races uncontrollably, my head throbs with a weird fizziness, and I generally end up blushing, sweating, and stammering. The few times I've met with Josh, it's only been the two of us with the gallery assistant hovering in the background, so he hasn't a clue.

"Thanks, Josh," I say. "Um, was there anything else?"

"Nope, that's it. And I can't wait to see the piece."

I tell him goodbye and sign off. Though I'm freaked out about the new deadline for the collage and the potential size of the party, at least he hadn't been calling to report a legal issue.

I glance at the time on my phone. It's close to four, meaning the law office will surely be closing soon. If I don't want this weird voice mail to eat away at me for the entire weekend, I need to return the call *now*. Steeling myself, I tap the number. A secretary or receptionist answers with the name of the firm—something, something, Harrison, and something—and after I tell her my name, she says she'll transfer me to Bradley Kane right away. While the hold music plays, I glance out the studio window and across Second Avenue. The October sky has already darkened like a mottled bruise, and I'm suddenly ambushed by an intense sense of unease.

"Ms. Moore, thank you for returning the call," Kane says when he picks up. "I have some information of importance to you, but for security purposes, I need you to verify your identity first."

I exhale, feeling my tension release as I realize I have nothing to worry about—it's a scam. Like those people who claim to be calling from someplace like Social Security and are trying to trick you into revealing personal data they can use to hack into one of your accounts.

"I bet you need my iCloud password, don't you?" I say, letting the sarcasm drip from my voice.

"Pardon me?"

"How do you people even look in the mirror?"

"Ms. Moore, please, all I need is for you to do is confirm your address."

"Oh, so now you want to break into my apartment?" I say facetiously.

"I can understand your hesitancy, and please forgive me for calling before I mailed you an official letter."

I start to lower the phone to end the call when he tells me, "Please, it's essential that you hear this, Ms. Moore."

I hesitate. Because if I *am* in some kind of hot water, I need to know what it is.

"Thank you," he says when it must seem apparent to him that I'm still on the line. "Ms. Moore, a client of mine passed away recently, and the purpose of my call is to inform you that you've been left an inheritance by him."

Before I can stop myself, I experience an involuntary swell of giddiness. An *inheritance*. Maybe there really is a God, and things for me are about to take a turn for the better. It's possible I've been named in the modest will of some long-lost relative of my father's. My dad died of a sudden heart attack when I was only five, two years after my mother, Margo, left him, and though it's been forever since I was in touch with any of his relatives—a wayward brother and several cousins—one of them might have bequeathed me a little something.

"What was your client's name?" I ask, and then hold my breath.

"Christopher Whaley."

The name draws a total blank in my mind, meaning there's clearly been a mistake. I feel a gush of disappointment as reality smacks me back down to size. Whatever inheritance Christopher Whaley left will certainly not be going to me.

2

Now

'M SORRY ABOUT YOUR CLIENT," I SAY TO KANE, "BUT I DIDN'T
know him. There must be a mix-up of some kind."

Even as I utter these words, though, I'm ransacking my mind
to see if the name Whaley is burrowed deep in there. Could he be a
distant relative on my *mother's* side? I know she has cousins with the
last name *Wheeler*, but no Whaleys, I'm quite sure.

"You're certain of that?" Kane asks.

"Yes. You've confused me with another person."

"Ms. Moore, I assure you I haven't. Do—"

Okay, this *is* some sort of con. "Look, I don't know what your
game is, but I'm really not interested in playing it."

"Allow me to make a suggestion," he urges. "Hang up the
phone, take a minute to google me and my law firm—Abood,
Kane, Harrison, and Wong—and then call me back at the number
listed on the website."

I have this overdue collage staring me in the face, and every
second I spend on the phone with Kane is a second that I'm not

devoting to it, but . . . what if I *am* the right person? Blowing him off feels a bit like failing to respond to one of those chain letters I got emailed as a teenager, the kind asking for something like a prayer or a dollar. A tiny part of me always worried that if I didn't respond, I might live to regret it.

I don't do as he tells me, not at first. As soon as I disconnect, I google "Christopher Whaley, Scarsdale" instead, and an obit surfaces immediately. With a quick skim I discover that Whaley passed away of pancreatic cancer a week ago.

There's no photo included, but based on the details in the obit— age forty-nine, Scarsdale resident, business executive, married, two children—I'm now even more certain that this man and I never crossed paths, though it's hard not to be a little saddened at what this must mean for his wife and kids.

From there I google the three names of the law firm that I've managed to recall and immediately find a link to its website. It appears to be a legitimate, boutique-sized outfit in Westchester County, New York, with trusts and estate planning as a specialty. There are photos of the major players, including Kane, who looks to be in his late forties, too. He's one of those older preppy types, with light brown hair, dark eyes, a chiseled jaw, and a pricey-looking tie.

I call him back at the main number. He and his firm might be legit, but this has to be a screwup.

"Thank you, Ms. Moore," he says. "Now if you don't mind indulging me on one additional matter. As I mentioned previously, for security purposes I need to verify your identity. Can you please provide me with your address?"

Even if there *is* something fishy about this whole business, Bradley Kane is probably not going to show up at my walk-up, also in Manhattan's East Village, and make off with my three-year-old laptop, my thirty-inch flat-screen TV, and the sad little pair of fake diamond studs I keep in a Ziploc bag. I rattle it off for him.

He thanks me again and then tells me he's sure there's no mistake, that Mr. Whaley intended for me to be the beneficiary.

"Beneficiary of what?" I ask. "Do you mean actual dollars and cents?"

"Unfortunately, I'm not allowed to share the exact details quite yet."

I sigh in frustration. "Can you at least explain why you think I'm the right person? What was the reason he gave for leaving me anything?"

"Mr. Whaley didn't share the reason for the inheritance, but he did provide your address and background information about you. You were born and raised in West Hartford, Connecticut, graduated from Tufts, worked at the Wadsworth Atheneum Museum of Art in Hartford before attending one year of an MFA program at Boston University, and you've been living in New York for over a decade, currently working as a graphic designer and artist, correct?"

"Right," I say, my guard still up. It feels creepy that he has all that info at his fingertips, but I guess he could have gotten most of it from LinkedIn.

"Obviously there's no mistake. I'm hoping then that you're free to come to my office in Scarsdale on Monday at eleven, at which point I'll share the details with you."

"Is that the reading of the will?"

"No, this is somewhat different. Are you able to come then?"

"This is starting to sound *very* complicated."

"Please, Ms. Moore. I know it's an inconvenience, but it's essential that we speak in person."

I think for a second. The collage will have to be done by then, anyway, and I can deliver it to Josh once I return to the city in the afternoon.

"Will it just be the two of us?" I ask. I'm certainly not going to subject myself to a room full of people.

"Just one other person will be joining us. I simply ask that you bring your license or passport so I can verify your identity."

"Okay, I guess I can be there."

He wraps up the call by offering directions to the building from the Scarsdale train station, but I don't bother to write them down, figuring I can always rely on GPS. Besides, despite what I told him, I'm not a hundred percent sure I'm going to show up. I need to think it through some more.

Not right this second, though, because I've got bigger fish to fry. Before tossing my phone aside, I shoot an email to the creative director who assigned me the graphic design job due Monday, begging for an extension. After pouring myself a glass of water from a jug I keep, I return to my studio worktable and stare long and hard at what I've done so far. The nine other collages for the show aren't specifically part of a series but they could be, since each one has to do with an aspect of being female, and each also involves a startling, perhaps even disconcerting juxtaposition of images. The new one has to have the same degree of impact, but so far that isn't happening.

My eyes wander to the window. Lights have begun to blink on here and there in the buildings across Second Avenue, and from where I'm sitting, I can see three enchanting-looking wooden water towers dotting the rooftops.

Maybe I need to play with *three* of something. Three is the smallest number that can create a pattern, and even simple patterns of three, if done right, can be intriguing and charged with meaning. I grab a pencil and begin doodling in my notebook. When that gets me nowhere, I page through a small stack of the old photography books I've bought for dirt cheap at the Strand Bookstore and tear out a few pages that speak to me.

When I finally close the last book and push it aside, I notice how quiet the building is—no footsteps or chatter coming from the corridor outside. Checking my phone, I see that it's after seven, later than I realized and past the time when most people on my floor—other artists and various freelancers—seem to split for the day. Though I don't interact with the other tenants working in my part of the building—unless you count the occasional hello with a Mexican artist named Alejandro who rents space two doors down from me—I feel safer when they're around. The building doesn't have a security guard, or even CCTV.

I stuff a few things into my messenger bag, kill the lights and lock up, then step into the wide, poorly lit hall. There's not a soul in sight, and the only noise is from the honking horns and revving car engines eight floors below. After what seems like an endless wait, I take the elevator to the lobby.

I live just a few blocks away, on Seventh Street between First Avenue and Avenue A, and I cover the distance quickly, making a brief stop on the way at a deli for a few cans of Diet Coke and some tea. Once I've reached my redbrick walk-up, I let myself in and climb the stairs to the fourth floor. As soon as I open the door to my apartment, Tuna, the calico rescue cat I was gifted three months ago by my half sister Nicky—who clearly thought I was desperate for companionship—scurries toward me and rubs her silky body back and forth against my calves a couple of times. I stoop down to stroke the top of her head, but a few seconds later she darts away and reassumes her perch on the back of the couch. Tuna often treats me like a roommate she was forced to recruit from Craigslist after her landlord doubled the rent.

After unloading my stuff, I dump a can of wet food into Tuna's bowl, do my best to resuscitate a head of lettuce under a stream of cold water, and then make a salad with the lettuce, two hard-boiled eggs, a few cherry tomatoes, and some asparagus spears left over from last night's dinner. Once I've splashed olive oil and vinegar on it, I carry it and a Diet Coke to the small wooden table at the end of my living room, grabbing my laptop on the way.

Once I've taken a few quick bites, I pull up the obit again, and this time I read it more closely. Christopher J. Whaley grew up in Scarsdale, it says, and attended Bowdoin College and the University of Michigan Law School. He was employed for the past fifteen years as a senior executive, not a lawyer, for the Delancey Pharmaceutical Company in Westchester County and in his spare time liked to sail and mountain climb. His survivors include his wife, Jane; a son, Mark, and daughter, Bee, both twenty—obviously fraternal twins—as well as a mother in Scarsdale and a brother residing in Buenos Aires.

The obit contains a link to the funeral home, and when I follow it, I find the same obit, though this one has a photo. The man in the shot appears to be in his late forties, so it must be recent. He's attractive, with a strong nose, full mouth, and high cheekbones—and almost totally bald. I wait for a jolt of recognition, but none comes. It doesn't help that his eyes are partially obscured by the black frames of his glasses, yet I'm pretty darn sure I've never seen him before.

I grab a pencil from the mug on my desk and jot down key words from the obit on a scrap of paper, hoping if I stare at them long enough, one will trigger a memory. The one person I know who went to Bowdoin is a girl from my high school in West Hartford whom I haven't seen in years, and though I've met a few people who attended Michigan, they were undergrads, not law students. I have never set foot in Scarsdale or heard of the company Whaley worked for.

And even if I had a wide social circle, which I certainly don't, I doubt it would've overlapped with his. Not only is he the type of guy I generally only cross paths with when I'm passing through the business-class section of an airplane on my way to economy, but he was eleven years older than me.

Next, I google "Scarsdale." I'd been vaguely aware that it's fancy, but I quickly learn that it's apparently the richest town on the East Coast and second richest in the US—with an average household income of $450,000. *Jeez.*

A thought begins to gel. According to his lawyer, Christopher Whaley knew I was an artist. What if he'd been an art lover, even a collector, who decided to become a benefactor when he learned he was dying of cancer, leaving me and other artists financial gifts to help foster our work? It might mean as much as ten thousand dollars—maybe more. I mean, doesn't stuff like that actually happen sometimes?

And it could really help me. I might finally be able to turn down some soul-crushing graphic design gigs and spend more time on my collages. It could also be a cushion to guarantee I've got the rent each month for my art studio, a space that might be tiny and shabby but has helped me kick-start my art career after an eight-year hiatus.

A small windfall could also allow me to spruce up my apartment. I moved in a decade ago, before the East Village was as trendy as it is today, and though my rent, thankfully, has stayed reasonable by Manhattan standards, it doesn't allow me to even *browse* on a home decor site like One Kings Lane. I've tried my best to make the place charming, using eclectic fabrics and displaying quirky flea market finds, like the painted wooden mushroom on top of my bookshelf and African stone bracelets hung along one wall. But everything's been bought on the cheap, and it shows. What would it be like to set a drink on a side table made of wood instead of particleboard, paint the walls something other than the sad, flat white they came in, and light Diptyque candles in scents like "fig tree" or "feu de bois"? It would be fabulous, that's what it would be.

But as much as I'd love to add some small luxuries to my life and have much more time for my art, there's something I want to do with the money more than anything else: get pregnant.

For the past few years, I've had a case of baby fever that I've been unable to cool, even with rational thoughts like, *This will be impossibly hard*, and *You're almost thirty-eight, so why don't you just let it go*. It's not so severe that I have to take to my bed after seeing a woman with a baby bump, but being around infants and toddlers sets off a yearning in my heart that hurts as much as a hand slammed in a door. Maybe I've had no luck winning over a rescue cat, and maybe there are people who view me as gloomy, someone who never sees the glass half-full, but I know that I'd be a good mother. I'd love and cherish a baby, devote myself to his or her care, and though it would be brutal to be a single mom, it'd be worth it to me.

And unlike the grinch who stole Christmas, my heart won't have to grow three sizes in one day to handle it. Because it's big enough and always has been.

There are major hurdles, though. Lucas, the only guy I've actually loved in the past dozen years, is long gone (him: *As much as I care, Skyler, it's just too hard with you*). Even if I had a male *friend* who I could strike a please-get-me-pregnant-and-you-won't-have-to-do-a-damn-thing bargain with, I wouldn't want to be tied to him even indirectly. This means that to make a baby, I have to go the insemination route using donor sperm.

Which is going to cost me a bundle. I've already had a consultation at the Dobson Fertility Clinic, a place I found after an online search, and where I learned that a single intrauterine insemination, IUI, procedure costs close to a thousand dollars. And it's only about 10 percent effective in my age category, which means that if the first few attempts fail, I might have to seriously consider going with IVF, in-vitro fertilization, which is far more expensive.

And then there's the cost of raising a baby in New York, a place I feel I need to be if I'm going to have any chance of making it as an artist. According to the research I've done, a baby will set me back over twenty grand the first year alone, and that only includes stuff like formula, food, diapers, medical expenses, and basic part-time childcare, not even extras like crib mobiles and Baby and Me classes. Because of my age, I have to act *soon*, but there's no way I can swing it financially right now.

All that could change in an instant with a gift of ten or, God, twenty grand.

I fish my phone out of my purse and tap my sister's number. Maybe she can enlighten me a little.

"Hi, everything okay?" Nicky says, and I understand the anxiety in her voice. Despite our seven-year age gap, I don't know what I'd do without my younger sister in my life, but she's almost always the one who initiates our phone calls.

"Sorry to bother you on a Friday night," I tell her, "but I have a weird question. Does the name Christopher Whaley mean anything to you?"

There's a pause as she seems to rummage through her memory. "Gosh, no. Why?"

As soon as I tell her about the call from Kane, she's full of her typical unbridled enthusiasm. "Oh my god, Sky, that's incredible," she says. I picture her blue eyes going wide and her fingers twirling a tendril of the long blond hair that frames her pretty, heart-shaped face. The idea of a scam has clearly not popped into that trusting brain of hers, which is no surprise. Unlike me, my half sister sees the world through rose-tinted glasses.

"And as far as you know, we don't have any distant relatives with that last name?"

"Not on Mom's side, I don't think. But maybe on your dad's?"

"Not from what I recall."

"Mom might have an idea."

"Since neither of us recognize the name, it's probably *not* a relative," I say, changing the subject, as my mother is the last person I can talk to about this. "So I've been thinking it might be a guy who's seen my art somewhere and wanted to support my career after he died."

"Oh, wow, maybe."

"I guess I won't know any more until I show up at the lawyer's office on Monday. . . . Wait," I say, quickly mapping out the distance between Scarsdale and West Hartford, where Nicky and her husband live in a new house not far from my mother and stepfather, David. "Want to come with me? It would be about an hour-and-a-half drive for you—but I'll buy lunch."

As soon as the words are out of my mouth, I realize how stupid my request is. Nicky's a full-time physician's assistant who works nine to six during the week.

"Gee, I wish I could, Sky, and I actually took the day off, but it's to help Mom."

I feel a prickling sensation in my stomach. "Is everything okay?" I ask.

"Yes, fine—but that's when we're going to be prepping for the tag sale next Saturday."

I can't help but flinch. When I was home over Labor Day weekend, I'd heard my mother tell Nicky that she was hoping to hold a yard sale this fall to unload small furniture and tchotchkes before she and David downsized to a town house in late November, and I assumed she'd fill me in once a date was confirmed. Not only would I have been more than willing to help in the effort, I also wanted the chance to grab a few mementos from the suburban house I'd more or less grown up in. But she's never said a word.

"No, I hadn't heard."

"Uh, I'm sure Mom didn't want to bother you. I mean, it's going to be kind of tedious—going through closets and the basement, and, you know, putting stickers on stuff. Mostly Mom just wants to get rid of it all."

Nicky's gone into overexplaining mode, something she does when feeling self-conscious.

"Got it, and no worries," I reassure her, then promise to call her with an update.

Poor Nicky, I think, as I drop the phone on the table. Once again she's caught in the middle, and I know she's probably feeling bad now. Slumping back in the chair, I glance in Tuna's direction. She shoots me an inscrutable look but then resumes licking her fur on the couch, in a way that could put me in a hypnotic trance if I stared too long. Though I never wanted a cat, I think I could warm to her if she only gave me half a chance.

I clear my plate and utensils from the table and set them in the kitchen sink, toying with the idea of calling my mother and asking her point-blank why she didn't ask for my assistance with the tag sale. But I don't have the nerve, and she'd only lie, anyway, probably say she had no idea I'd want to give up a workday, especially with my show at the gallery coming up.

But the truth is my mother doesn't want me there. More and more she seems to find ways to distance herself or reasons to keep me out of the mix with her, David, and Nicky. Because she still blames me for what happened to my half sister, Chloe, which basically ruined my family's life. And maybe she has a right to.

3

Twelve Years Ago

"DO YOU WANT TO COME, TOO, CHLOE?"

I was on the phone with my younger sister, inviting her to a party being given by a grad school classmate of mine. Purely by coincidence we were studying in Boston at the same time, me getting an MFA in painting at BU—after a couple of years working and saving while I lived at home—and Chloe finishing her third year at Emerson, with hopes of eventually becoming a Christiane Amanpour–style war correspondent, or news anchor, or host of her own TV show, or whatever was guaranteed to bring the most fame and fortune.

But the minute the words were out of my mouth, I wondered if I'd live to regret them. I loved Chloe, I did. And despite the four years between us, we mostly got along, laughing at the same jokes, watching Netflix together, and sometimes even trading foot massages on the couch. But though I loved her, I didn't always *like* her.

Chloe, you see, could be careless. Thoughtless, too. She craved attention, which meant she tended to get sulky and irritable when the spotlight wasn't planted firmly on her, or if life wasn't going her way. There were repercussions at times to that kind of behavior, and though she never seemed to mind them—I once watched her smile and say, *Thank you*, to a woman who'd called her a bitch for cutting into a line—I didn't enjoy seeing them unfold in front of me.

That Friday morning in late April, however, I felt I had no choice but to throw her a lifeline. My mother had mentioned to me recently that Chloe was on the outs with the in-girl crowd she'd befriended her freshman year and was having a tough time as a result. More and more I sensed my mother needed regular reassurance that the life she had with David was better than the one she'd left behind with my dad, and part of my role in that was looking out for my younger half sisters.

"Who's going to be there?" Chloe asked.

"A bunch of kids from my program. And apparently my friend's younger brother will be there, too, along with some kids he knows from MIT. He's a senior, I think."

Silence followed, and I assumed she was still making up her mind.

"It might not be too exciting, though," I added, giving her an out. "Probably just thirty or forty people, and there won't be a keg or anything like that."

"Skyler, I don't know where you got the idea that I'm into *keg parties*. No, it sounds like fun, and it means we get to spend some time together."

Since the party was twenty or so miles outside the city in Dover, and I was the one with a car, I offered to pick her up. *Be out in front at 7:30 sharp*, I'd told her, but she was nowhere in sight when I pulled up to her building, and the text I sent elicited only an all-lowercase reply of coming. I was about to circle the block for the third time when Chloe sauntered out of the lobby, flung the door open, and burst into the car, nearly choking me with the overwhelming floral scent of her perfume.

As usual, she looked gorgeous. She'd recently cut her wavy, buttery blond hair to shoulder length, and the result was stunning. It was, she'd told me, in preparation for her internship at a Hartford TV station that summer. She was going for a more professional look, so she'd be seen as "assignment ready" in case some sort of a virus felled most of the reporting staff.

And her outfit was perfect—tight jeans, cute boots, and a blue ruched top that matched her eyes and emphasized how perfectly in shape she was.

"You look pretty," she said to me after checking her reflection in the visor mirror. "I love your hair like that."

"Thanks."

I knew I wasn't in Chloe's league, but I'd made a real effort that night, styling my light brown hair in a sloppy topknot, applying a full face of makeup, and wearing my best low-cut jeans with a tight pink cashmere tee. A guy from one of my painting classes, Carson, whom I'd been lusting for all semester, had mentioned that he was going to the party. I couldn't tell if he'd done it purposefully, but I wanted to put my sexiest, un-oil-paint-spattered foot forward and see what might unfold. I'd even stuffed a few condoms in my purse just in case.

Chloe sighed. "What's your friend's name and how come she lives all the way out in Dover?"

"Jamie Bolton. And she doesn't live there, her parents do. But they're away."

"I see. This should definitely be fun, then."

"Yeah, hope so."

And please, I thought, taking in her outfit again, *if you end up flirting with anyone tonight, let it be Jamie's brother or one of his friends and not a guy from my MFA program.* With my luck, Carson would be hopelessly dazzled by her and forget all about me.

As I pulled away from the curb, Chloe seemed unusually subdued.

I asked how she was doing, and she said fine, she was pretty sure she'd make dean's list this term, and she was getting psyched for her internship. Nothing about the friend problems, though, and I didn't press. Had she made a play for a pal's boyfriend? I wondered. That wouldn't have been out of the realm of possibility, but I still felt sorry for her.

In my experience Boston drivers were notoriously bad, and so I concentrated on not rear-ending another car as I navigated the tight streets. As the city fell away behind us, we both grew quiet, and once I glanced over to see that Chloe had her head pressed against the window with her eyes closed. She looked really sweet at that moment, and also the tiniest bit vulnerable, summoning a memory of the little girl I once knew. When she was a baby, I'd been so smitten with her and had to be constantly reminded not to squeeze her too hard. Once she grew into a doll-like, golden-haired two-year-old, nothing pleased me more than to have her toddle after me, babbling semi-intelligibly, or curl up in my lap in the den. But that seemed like light-years ago.

Finally, Chloe stirred, as if sensing we were nearing our destination, and soon enough the GPS led us to the end of a dark, tree-lined road. I'd heard rumors that Jamie came from money, but I was stunned by what was in front of us. The house was really more of a mansion, a huge limestone structure that looked like it must be a century old, though it had probably been built in the last thirty years. It was set far back from the road, with a rolling lawn in front and what appeared be a huge stretch of woods in the rear. I knew Dover was a very affluent town, but this was over the top.

"Holy shit," Chloe said, taking it in herself as I parked behind a long row of cars on the road. "I'd throw a party too, if our family had a place like this."

I'd predicted thirty or forty people, but all the cars suggested more than that, and sure enough, the second we stepped inside I saw that the crowd was at least fifty strong. Jamie greeted us at the door, dressed in a cropped sweater, tiny skirt, and tights and with her raven hair piled high on her head. She shook hands with Chloe and introduced us both to her younger brother, Rob, who was lingering nearby. He was an attractive guy, tall and slim with hair the same color as his sibling's and scruff to match, but he wore a vaguely smug look on his face.

"Bar's in the kitchen," he told us. "Help yourself."

"But, please, no selfies," Jamie urged. "I don't want my parents seeing their house on someone's Facebook feed."

Rob stepped away to greet another new arrival, and Chloe announced she was going in search of a drink.

"Wow, you two are *sisters*?" Jamie said once it was just she and I. "You don't look at all alike."

"Different fathers," I explained, used to comments like hers. I was five seven and lanky, Chloe was five three and voluptuous, and her facial features were more delicate than mine. The only thing we had in common were our almond-shaped light blue eyes.

There was no sign of Carson yet, but it was amazing to be in the immense house, which turned out to have five fireplaces on the ground floor alone, including a huge limestone one in the front hall. Rihanna was singing on the sound system, and in addition to white wine and bottles of beer, there was a vat of Mexican cheese dip on the kitchen table, along with bags of tortilla chips. After grabbing a bottle of beer, I located a few of my BU buddies and hung out with them, laughing and doing a postmortem on the semester. All of us were pretty giddy because summer was around the corner.

Like me, some of the guests seemed to park themselves in a single spot and never move, while others joined the steady flow from one room to the next, a river of people that circled endlessly through the house. Though it was typically cool for late April, I saw through a window that a group had gathered on the patio at the rear of the house, next to an enormous swimming pool.

Chloe seemed to be having a good time, but then why wouldn't she? Whenever she wandered into the same room as me, I noticed guys eyeing her, some of them bold enough to chat her up.

About an hour after we arrived, she snaked through the crowd in my direction, holding an empty beer bottle.

"You about ready?" she asked.

I lifted my own beer, half-empty at that point, and shook my head. "Thanks, but I'm only having one tonight. I'm driving, remember?"

"No, I mean ready to go."

"*Go?* We practically just got here, Chloe."

It would be rude to take off so soon, and though Carson hadn't shown up yet, I was hopeful he still would.

"Well, when do you want to leave, then? The house is great, but most of these guys are nerds," she said under her breath.

I rolled my eyes. "You have to give me at least another hour, okay?"

She shrugged, looking miffed, and moved off again. About twenty minutes later, I spotted her drinking from a red party cup, with what appeared to be a guy's dark green sweater knotted around her waist. Okay, she'd apparently found someone to keep her amused.

Before another hour had passed, though, the allure of the party began to fade even for me. For one thing, it had become clear Carson wasn't going to materialize, and I was disheartened by what it might imply about his lack of interest in me.

Beyond that, the still-ballooning crowd had started to feel off. At some point during the evening, a group of cocky-looking alpha-male types—at least five years older than most everyone else—had begun to infiltrate the scene. One of them was Jamie's cousin, apparently, who worked in finance in Boston, and the rest were friends of his and friends of *those* friends. They all seemed to wear Ralph Lauren polos or cobalt-blue dress shirts with the sleeves rolled to the elbows, as if they'd come straight from the office.

Soon the rooms seemed to be pulsing with an edgy kind of energy, a *tension* really, almost like this new group knew something that the rest of us were completely oblivious to. I kept wondering if someone was going to be shoved through a plate glass window or one of the younger nerdy-looking guys would end up thrown in the pool with all his clothes on.

Shortly after ten, I was formulating an exit plan when a guy I vaguely knew from my oil painting class wandered over to me.

"Hey, Skyler," he said. "Having fun?"

"Yeah," I lied.

"You're friends with Carson, right?"

I nodded. This was interesting. "Uh-huh. How come?"

"He said if I saw you tonight to say hi. He was going to come but he had a family emergency and had to drive to New Hampshire."

Okay, this dude had been at the party since I'd arrived, and he was only telling me this *now*? But I felt a rush of excitement that Carson was interested enough to send a message.

Wanting to leave on a high note, I set off looking for Chloe, making a big loop around the first floor of the house, but I came up empty. I retraced my steps in case I'd somehow missed her and also checked out the patio, but there was no sign of her. I wondered if she might be searching for me at the same time, so I changed direction and made a counterclockwise sweep, but still no luck.

By this point I was starting to get annoyed. I'd told her "an hour," and she was on her phone enough that she must know what time it was.

As I stood in the front hall trying to figure out my next move, I noticed a red-haired girl coming down the staircase, and so I decided to check upstairs. I climbed to the second floor and made my way down the wide, dimly lit hall. There was no one in view, and I couldn't hear any noise coming from behind the closed doors, but just to be sure I took a peek behind each one, getting a glimpse of five massive bedrooms. All of them were empty. Maybe the redhead had just been snooping around.

Turning to go back downstairs, I jerked in surprise. One of the older, alpha male types was standing in my way, having obviously come up the stairs without me hearing him.

"Looking for me?" he asked. He was wearing a pompous grin and reeked of beer.

"No, I wasn't," I said curtly.

"Really?

"Yeah, *really*." He laid a hand on my arm, but I shoved him aside with an elbow and hurried downstairs.

Now what?, I wondered, feeling a sliver of concern mixing with my annoyance. As I returned to the crowded living room, I spotted Jamie leaning against a wall and sharing a joint with a guy whose hair was dark and shaggy.

"Hey, Jamie, have you seen my sister by any chance?" I asked, approaching them.

She stared at me blankly, her olive-green eyes unfocused.

"What?" she asked after a second.

"The girl I came with, Chloe Severson," I said, raising my voice above the noise. "Have you seen her?"

"I know who you mean," the guy announced, sounding more lucid than Jamie. "She split a little while ago."

"*Split?*" I repeated, totally flabbergasted. How could she have left without fucking telling me? Besides, I was her ride.

"Yeah, about twenty or thirty minutes ago," he told me. Now that he'd angled his body toward me, I saw that he was wearing a black T-shirt that said, I HAVE PEOPLE IN BOSTON, in white letters and I remembered him being introduced earlier as a childhood friend of Jamie's from Dover.

"Are you sure we're talking about the same person?" I asked.

"The hot blonde in the blue top? I heard her talking to a couple I know who were getting ready to drive back to the city, and she asked them for a ride."

"Did you actually see her leave?"

"Yeah, I was under the portico out front, and I watched her get in the back seat of their car."

Shit. My concern had now turned to indignation. I dug out my phone from my purse, expecting to see a text from Chloe apologizing profusely, but there was nothing. I muttered a thank-you to Jamie's friend and stepped away to call my sister's cell. All I got was her voice mail.

"Chloe, where the hell are you?" I demanded. "Someone told me you *left*. Call me as soon as you get this."

I wanted nothing more than to take off that minute, but just in case the guy had been confused as to what he saw, I hung around another thirty minutes. As I nursed a Diet Coke, I kept my eyes peeled and repeatedly checked my phone to see if I'd missed the ping of a text because of the music, which was now louder than ever. Finally, after one more fruitless search through the house, I realized Chloe had really left, and I headed to the door. Before I could open it, Jamie came up from behind me and tapped me on the shoulder.

"You're still here," she said. Her eyes looked a little clearer.

"Yeah, but I'm going now. Thanks for a great party." I had to force myself to smile as I said it.

"Sorry to miss your sister. Tell her I said it was nice to meet her, okay?"

"Of course. I'm sure I'll talk to her later tonight."

If only I'd known how hollow those words were.

4

Now

On monday morning I'm at Grand Central by 7:10 for a 7:42 train to Scarsdale, far earlier than I need to be, but it's better than sitting at home trying not to jump out of my skin.

I'm wearing the exact same outfit I put together for my first meeting with Josh, the gallery owner—a long black faux-silk shirt, black leggings, and stacked black suede ankle boots, along with my camel-colored sweater coat. Maybe I should have chosen something dressier, but I don't *have* anything fancier, and if the so-called inheritance has anything to do with me being an artist, I figure it's fine to look the part.

Most of my stress today is about the meeting with Bradley Kane, about finally being able to learn—after two days of constant ruminating—what this inheritance thing is all about. But I'm also still agitated about my mother's upcoming tag sale, silly as it feels. I keep deliberating whether I should call or text her to wish her luck with it—just to be nice—but she might think I'm being passive-aggressive, that I'm letting her know that I'm onto the fact she hadn't included me in the preparation or the actual sale itself.

It's always so hard to read her. Sometimes I think I'm not paying enough attention to her cues and other times that I'm paying too much.

After trudging up the stairs from the subway, I make my way to the dining concourse on the lower level and treat myself to a coffee for the train. From there I head up the wide marble staircase to the main part of the terminal. When I travel a few times a year to Hartford to visit my family—Thanksgiving, Christmas, and a weekend in the summer—I take the Amtrak train from Penn Station, so it's been ages since I've been in Grand Central, and the noise and crowd are overwhelming. Commuters are darting in every direction, many glued to their phones, and in imminent danger of a collision.

Miraculously, the track number for my train has already been posted. Since I've bought a ticket online, I hurry to the platform, where I board a car and grab a seat in an empty row. I help myself to a few sips of coffee, but then rest the cup on the floor, sensing that additional caffeine will make me even more wired.

The train begins to fill up quickly, so I shift my bag from between my feet to the space beside me. It's obnoxious, yes, but the seats are small and close together, and I don't want anyone pressed against me right now. A couple of passengers eye my bag with disapproval as they snake down the aisle, but I hear them sliding into seats behind me. It's not like I'm making anyone stand.

A minute behind schedule, the train jerks to a start, and we move through the dank, gritty tunnel beneath Park Avenue, until we emerge aboveground in Harlem. The knot in my stomach tightens with each block we pass heading north. What in the world am I getting myself into? Should I have tried to convince Bradley Kane to explain more over the phone?

A small part of me still wonders if this is all a crazy scam, that I'll get to Kane's office and find out his team is trying to sell me a time-share in Key West or lure me into some kind of cult, like the one a few years ago that promised to empower women but ended up branding them on the ass instead.

Or maybe Kane has it all wrong; perhaps Christopher Whaley intended to leave an inheritance to someone named Skyler Moore, just not *this* Skyler Moore.

And yet despite my lingering doubts, every couple of minutes I'm almost knocked over by a swell of giddiness again. What if Whaley really *was* some kind of patron of the arts, a guy who decided on his deathbed to sponsor starving artists? I did additional calculations over the weekend and realized that with a gift of, say, twenty thousand dollars, and the sale of even a few of my collages at the show, I'd be able to kick off a schedule of IUIs and get on the road to motherhood.

The trip is only scheduled to take forty minutes, but it feels interminable, thanks in large part to the asshole a few rows ahead, barking into his phone about a deal in Hong Kong that's about to blow up on him. If there's any justice in the world, it will. Finally, an automated voice announces, "The next station stop will be Scarsdale." I grab my bag and, holding on to a few headrests for balance, make my way to the door. I'm finally here, about to learn my fate.

I order an Uber as soon as I step off the train, and by the time I exit the mock Tudor-style station, the gray Honda Accord is already waiting for me. According to Google, the firm is only a short distance away, but it's a long enough drive to give me a taste of Scarsdale. Almost every structure in the town center is mock Tudor, too, though when we reach Kane's building, it's actually a sleek glass and steel tower, about eight stories high. I'm so tense that I scramble out of the car without remembering to thank the driver.

Abood, Kane, Harrison, and Wong is on the fifth floor, and as I press the button for the elevator, I notice that my palm is wet with sweat. I wipe my hand on a tissue and pray there really will be only two other people at the meeting.

Though the building is super modern, the door to the law office turns out to be made of a heavy dark walnut, and as soon as I push it open, my worries about a scam begin to fade. Everything about the reception area—furniture, carpeting, window treatments—looks expensive and classy, and it seems pretty obvious I'm in a legit law firm office.

Even the middle-aged receptionist is elegant. She's wearing a white satin blouse with a pussy bow, and her grayish-blond hair is coifed into a perfect French twist. This is not a woman who's going to be snacking on a big bag of Cheetos at her desk while you stand there trying to grab her attention.

"Have a seat and I'll tell Mr. Kane you're here," she says pleasantly after I give my name. "He's expecting you."

I've barely made my way to a chair when I hear carpet-hushed footsteps, and seconds later, a man steps into the reception area, wearing a navy suit and carrying a tan folder.

"Ms. Moore? Good morning, I'm Bradley Kane."

He looks exactly like the picture on the website, as if it was taken yesterday.

"Hello," I say, offering a wan smile and thankful he doesn't attempt to shake my hand—because it's already sweaty again. *I can handle this*, I tell myself. The very worst that could happen is that I've come all this way for nothing.

"Why don't you follow me?" he says in a neutral tone, then leads me down a long, quiet hallway. Though he'd kept his eyes on my face in the reception area, I catch him giving me a discreet head-to-toe once-over as we walk. And why wouldn't he? He's apparently as clueless as I am about how I ended up here.

Halfway down the hall, he directs me into a conference room, with a sleek long table surrounded by about a dozen butterscotch-colored leather chairs, the ergonomically correct kind. After closing the door behind us, he pulls out a chair for me, and then he takes a seat at the end of the table, diagonally across from mine. He sets the folder in front of him on the table along with an expensive-looking fountain pen, making sure they are perfectly aligned. I slip out of my sweater coat, scrunching it onto my lap along with my purse.

"How was your trip from the city?" he asks. His high, smooth forehead overhangs his eyes a bit, giving the false impression that he's the tiniest bit cross-eyed.

"Fine, thank you."

"Good to hear. Would you mind sharing your ID with me now?"

"Uh, sure," I say, extracting my license from my wallet and sliding it across the table in his direction. After briefly studying the front, he glances up at my face, then returns it to me. Our hands never touch.

"Is it just going to be the two of us after all?"

"No, someone will be joining us, but I thought it would be good for you and me to speak alone first."

"Is the other person who's coming an artist, as well?"

Kane narrows one eye, as if someone's blown smoke in it. My question has clearly confused him.

"No, we'll be joined by Mr. Whaley's mother, Caroline."

"His *mother*?" I say, startled. "But I thought you said this wasn't the reading of the will."

"It's not. That took place the day after the funeral. What this involves is a trust set up by Mr. Whaley's grandfather to benefit Chris's father, who later exercised his power of appointment to make Chris the beneficiary. That power of appointment then passed to Chris. As he and I were consulting about the trust, he indicated that he wanted his mother to learn how he'd exercised his own power of appointment because he knew it might affect what she decides to do with the trust his father assigned to *her* upon his death."

Nothing he just said made much sense, but my heart skipped

when he used the word *trust*. Aren't trusts generally a big deal, something rich people set up for their kids?

"Um, okay."

"Before we start, let me ask if you've had a chance to mull things over since we spoke on Friday. Perhaps by now you've recalled meeting Mr. Whaley."

I shake my head. When I wasn't working like crazy on my collage over the weekend, I did nothing *but* mull over the name Christopher Whaley and all the details in his obit, and yet none of them spurred a memory of how I might have crossed paths with him.

"I'm almost positive we never met," I say. I realize I'm rubbing the yarn of my sweater between my thumb and forefinger, like it's a security blanket. "But since you mentioned that he knew I was an artist, I've been wondering whether he'd seen some of my work online or at one of the street fairs I've exhibited at and decided he wanted to support me in some way—you know, as a kind of patron."

Again, the narrowed-eye thing.

"I'm sure that's not it," Kane says after a beat. "From what I know, C.J. wasn't into art."

It doesn't come across as a dig exactly, more a suggestion that Whaley was one of those guys who might have looked at an Agnes Martin or a Jackson Pollock and said, *A fifth grader could have done that.*

I shift in my chair, feeling a fresh blister of unease. Why am I sitting here, then? Why has Christopher Whaley deemed me worthy of an inheritance?

As Kane continues to study me, I realize that his last comment about Whaley has begun to burrow into my brain. And not simply because it means that my art patron theory has been debunked and the idea sounded stupid to Kane. No, it's because the nickname he used—C.J.—is ringing a bell.

For a few seconds those two initials hover just out of reach, but then, finally, a memory explodes into view, and my heart jolts.

Almost a dozen years ago, I met a man who called himself C.J. and spent an electrifying night in his Boston hotel room. And then I never set eyes on him again.

5

Then

BY THE TIME I LET MYSELF INTO MY APARTMENT AFTER THE party, I was fuming and nursing a nasty headache. I'd called Chloe once more on the drive back to Boston, and also texted her, but she never responded.

And there was still no word from her when I woke up Saturday morning. I figured she was sleeping in and would surface by midday—and decided that when she did finally make contact, I would let her have it.

I spent the entire morning working on an oil painting in one of the campus art studios on Comm Ave., and then headed back to my Brookline apartment on foot. I used the walk home to catch up by phone with my friend Tess, who had a few minutes of downtime at her job. She'd been my freshman-year roommate as an undergrad at Tufts and happened to be in Boston now, too, working as a desk clerk at a fancy boutique hotel called the Kensington until she figured out what she really wanted to do with her life.

"I can't believe it," Tess said after I described the situation with

Chloe. "I mean, how long would it have taken her to type the words, *Got a ride home*."

"Exactly."

"Do you think she wanted to try something kinky—I mean with the couple?"

"*Kinky?*" I exclaimed, as the MBTA trolley screeched to a halt on the tracks in front of me. "I doubt it. I think Chloe was just itching to leave, and when I refused to go at the exact moment she wanted to, she decided to bum whatever ride she could find."

Arriving back at the apartment, I found a note from my two roommates, Adam and Colton—a couple who shared the larger of the two bedrooms—saying that they'd decided to host an impromptu prefinals dinner party, had gone out to buy food, and would love to have me join them tonight. I let out a groan. I really liked my roommates, and Adam was a phenomenal cook, but after last night, I was in the mood for a quiet evening in. Since I didn't have plans outside the apartment, though, there didn't seem to be an easy way to extricate myself from the dinner.

After making myself a quick lunch, I tried Chloe again. It annoyed me to still be wondering about her whereabouts, but I wanted to be sure everything was okay. Maybe she'd ended up having too much to drink and had hitched a ride because she felt sick or tipsy. Sometimes my mother checked in with me on Saturdays, unless she was doing a weekend shift at the eye doctor's office where she worked as an optometrist, and she'd be less than pleased if I told her I had no clue where Chloe was.

But once again, my call went straight to voice mail.

A small swell of unease that I'd done my best to tamp down began to rise again. There was nothing incredibly out of the ordinary about Chloe going off without telling me and not bothering to follow up. After all, we'd had years of her borrowing my clothes

without permission, breaking promises, being late to meet somewhere, and once not even showing at all. But since Chloe lived on
her smartphone, it seemed odd she wasn't answering it. I scrolled
through my addresses until I found the number for her roommate,
Kim, which I'd acquired once for some reason I couldn't remember.

"Hey, Kim, it's Skyler. I'm looking for my sister," I said as soon
as she picked up. "Is she around, do you know?"

"No, she's gone out already," Kim told me.

So Chloe was up and about but hadn't had the basic decency to
check in with me. I felt the urge to throttle her with my bare hands.

"Do you know where?"

"No, sorry," Kim said. "I didn't get up till nine thirty and she
was already gone, and then I went out myself."

"Are you positive she was there earlier? I mean, did you see her
come in last night?"

"I didn't actually. Her door was closed when I got back after
midnight, so I just assumed she'd gone to bed. Uh . . ." I sensed Kim
hauling herself up from a chair or couch and starting to move with
the phone pressed to her ear. "That's funny. I realize now that there's
no sign of her in the kitchen. She usually makes a green juice and
leaves the blender in the sink."

Hmm. "So she might not have come home last night?"

"Give me a second." I heard her footsteps again, followed by the
creak of a door. "It's hard to tell. Her bed isn't made and there are
clothes everywhere, but I'm thinking it looked this way when she left
last night."

There was a chance, of course, that Chloe had arrived home
from the party around eleven, crashed, and gone out this morning
before Kim was up, but not a big one. The last time my sister had
risen super early on a Saturday morning was probably when she took
the SATs.

No, it seemed more likely that she hadn't been back to the apartment at all.

"Do you think something's the matter?" Kim asked, breaking the silence.

"No, no," I said. "We were at a party together last night, but she left with someone else." I wondered suddenly if Chloe had split abruptly because she'd made plans to hook up with some guy back in Boston. That might even explain why she'd been pressuring me to leave. "Do you think she could be with Taylor?"

I was referring to a ruggedly handsome BU hockey player Chloe had been dating earlier in the year, though according to our mother, she'd recently grown bored with him.

"It's possible. But I don't think she's been seeing him that much."

"Do you have a number for him?"

"Sorry, no," Kim said with a small chuckle. "She doesn't release that information to *anyone*."

"No worries," I reassured her. "I'm sure she'll turn up soon enough."

"I'll check in with a few of her squad if you want, though she hasn't been hanging with them so much these days. If I hear anything, I'll let you know."

Despite what I'd told Kim, I felt my anxiety mushroom as soon as we hung up. Chloe had left the party without telling me, hadn't returned my calls, and apparently hadn't gone back to her apartment last night. Something didn't feel right. And suddenly I didn't care about all the times she'd borrowed my clothes without asking or made me circle the block in my car. All I wanted was to know she was all right.

The surest way to put my mind at ease, I decided, was to track down the couple who'd driven Chloe back to the city and find out where they'd dropped her off. I wandered out to the kitchen, chugged a glass of tap water, and then called Jamie.

"Hello?" she croaked out, and I could practically hear her hangover pulsing through the phone. I quickly explained that I couldn't locate my sister, that she had left last night with a couple, and I needed to get a phone number for one of them so I could check on her. I added that the shaggy-haired guy she'd been smoking a joint with would know who they were.

Jamie seemed to have no clue whom I was talking about. Trying not to sound irritated, I slowly described the guy in the black T-shirt.

"Oh, that was Ryan," she finally said. "Let me track him down, and then I'll call you back after I figure out who those people were."

I felt myself relax a little. Even with a hangover, Jamie was a responsible pal, and I knew she'd get back to me before too long. I spent the next thirty minutes tidying up, changing my sheets, and folding the clothes that had piled up around my bedroom. As I was dumping the contents of my wastebasket into a black trash bag in the kitchen, my phone rang with a number I didn't recognize and I quickly picked up.

"Hey, this is Ryan from the party," a guy's voice said. "I heard you're worried about your sister."

"Not worried exactly, but I'd like to know where she is."

"Well, she hasn't been abducted, if that's what you're thinking. I called the guy who gave her a ride—his name's Kurt—and he said your sister had him drop her at a triple-decker on Carton Street in Allston—at 745 or 747, he thinks, with shingles—and she went into the apartment on the lower level. She told them she was spending the night with some guy she just started seeing."

Ah, a booty call, like I'd surmised, but something still felt off to me and I found myself jotting the address down on a scrap of paper. "It's weird she hasn't let me know, though."

"That's probably because her phone's not working. She borrowed Kurt's girlfriend's phone because she'd spilled beer on hers."

Okay, now things *were* starting to make sense. Chloe certainly didn't have my number memorized.

"Got it, thanks," I said. "I appreciate you tracking down these people for me."

"No problem . . . Hey, she's your younger sister, right?"

"Yeah, by four years. Why?"

"Maybe cut her some slack. You know how little siblings can be."

"Yeah, I do. Thanks again."

Of course, I would cut her some slack. That's what I always did with Chloe. And though part of me was annoyed, a sense of relief overpowered my irritation.

As soon as we hung up, I texted Kim, letting her know Chloe was fine. She said she was relieved, too, since her calls had turned up nothing and she'd started to stress herself.

Seconds later, as I heard Colton and Adam burst through the front door of the apartment, my phone rang again. Tess.

"Your sister materialize yet?" she asked.

"Yeah, she's apparently fine, but her phone's broken so we still haven't talked." Though I'd wandered back to the bedroom by now, I lowered my voice. "My next challenge is figuring out how to get out of the last-minute dinner party my roommates are throwing. I don't have anywhere to go, and it would be weird to hide in my room, faking a migraine."

"Want to stay here?" she asked.

She didn't mean her apartment. Occasionally, when the Kensington wasn't fully booked, she'd offer me a room simply so I could sleep for a night between high-thread-count sheets and have a marble bathroom with fancy soap and free cotton puffs all to myself. I gave it two seconds' thought before telling her yes.

As soon as I signed off, I stuffed a duffel bag with a few clothes and toiletries, explained to my roommates that I had to decline their invitation because a friend "needed a shoulder to cry on," and headed for the nearest T stop.

TWENTY-FIVE MINUTES LATER, I ENTERED THE KENSINGTON'S SMALL but elegant lobby, with its vaulted ceiling and curved marble staircase. Tess was working the front desk with another clerk, and I shot her a discreet smile before assuming a place in line behind a couple of other people checking in. It was nice to be back in this luxurious space, with the intoxicating scent of lavender that was always in the air.

As it worked out, I ended up reaching the head of the line when the other clerk became available, but since he had no clue about my special arrangement, I motioned for the guy behind me in line to go ahead. He was in his mid- to late thirties, I guessed, tall and sandy-haired with a confident air. I felt myself grow oddly flustered as his deep blue eyes met mine.

A minute later, the guest Tess had been dealing with moved off, and I strode toward the counter, greeting her politely as if the two of us were strangers. While she checked me in, I found my eyes wandering down the counter toward the guy I'd waved ahead of me. He was in profile now, and I saw that he had what an art teacher of mine called a Roman nose, strong with a little bend at the bridge. He was dressed in nice jeans, a crisp white dress shirt, and a navy blazer, and his only luggage was a pricey-looking black roller bag with a crocodile leather luggage tag. Based on the fact it was Saturday night, I guessed he was in town for personal reasons, though maybe he'd tacked on the weekend to a business trip that started Monday.

Unexpectedly, he turned in my direction and caught me staring. His eyes locked with mine again for a couple of seconds, then he returned his attention to the clerk in front of him.

Okay, that was weird, I thought. I wasn't in the habit of checking out men his age, and it was hard to believe a guy like him—

polished, sophisticated, maybe even a little arrogant—was looking twice at a lowly grad student dressed in jeans and a fisherman knit sweater. Surely, he couldn't be interested.

But several hours later, I'd see it differently. Because by then, I was in his hotel bed, lying naked beside him.

6

Now

BRADLEY KANE KNOWS SOMETHING'S UP. IT'S CLEAR FROM HIS EXpression that he's spotted the flicker of recognition in my eyes.

He cocks his head.

"What?" he asks quietly, perhaps fearful that if he pounces, I'll clam up or lie to him.

And my first instinct actually *is* to lie, to say, *Nothing*. I mean, why should Kane be apprised of details about a one-night stand I had over a decade ago? But I quickly switch gears, realizing that being less than forthcoming with him could backfire somehow, screw up my chances of walking away with the promised prize.

"Is there any chance you have access to a picture of Christopher Whaley when he was younger?" I ask. "From around a decade ago, or a little longer? Because—because I once briefly knew someone with the nickname C.J."

Kane nods slowly, clearly processing this development, and then looks up to the right, as if trying to remember. A second later he slides a phone from his pants pocket.

"Believe it or not, I do have a photo of him from that far back," he says, beginning to scroll through. I notice he's wearing a wedding band, an extra-thick one. Is that supposed to show that he's more committed than most guys?

"You were friends?"

"More what you'd call acquaintances. We both grew up here in Scarsdale and by chance ended up going to the same college, and though we weren't ever close, we were in the same extended group. This is from a regatta a bunch of us sailed in about fifteen years ago."

He finally stops dragging and flicking his thumb over the screen, an indication he's found what he's looking for. "The photo's a little out of focus, but it captures him pretty well. He's at the end on the right."

He slides the phone faceup across the table to me, and I take a look. There are five guys in the photo, standing on a weathered dock and dressed in shorts and T-shirts or polo shirts. All are in docksiders, the brown leather boat shoes I learned in college that preppy dudes favor. My eyes dart immediately to the guy at the end, the one with thick, sandy-colored hair and a sly smile. Though my memory takes a couple of seconds to catch up, I soon realize beyond any doubts that it's him. *C.J.* The man I slept with that night.

But this whole thing is making even less sense to me now. Why in the world would Christopher Whaley leave me anything? We'd spent fewer than twelve hours in each other's company and never connected again. I hadn't even known his last name, nor he mine, though he obviously figured it out. Had he rummaged through my purse when I was sleeping?

I glance back over at Kane. "Yes, this is the C.J. I met. I only knew his nickname."

Kane maintains a neutral expression. "Do you mind my asking the circumstances?" he says.

I hesitate again but decide that it's probably smart to be forth-coming. "It was about a dozen years ago. We met in the bar of the hotel where he was staying during a business trip and spent the night together."

Once again, Kane doesn't bat an eye. He's probably assumed there was some kind of carnal connection between Whaley and me, and given the way I just summed it up, he might even wonder if I used to be one of those college-girl escort types. But he knows better than to slut-shame me in this day and age, I feel sure.

"And you're saying it was only a single night?"

"Yes—that's why I didn't recognize him from the photo in the obituary. And also because he looked so different back then with all his hair and without the glasses."

"But . . . you must have had some kind of contact with him after that night. By phone, or mail, or something?"

"No, none at all."

Kane tilts his head slightly, looking skeptical.

"I swear I never spoke or corresponded with him again," I add. "Just because I slept with him didn't mean we were destined to be pen pals."

I pass the phone back to him. He seems poised to ask another question but is interrupted when the door to the conference suddenly swings open, and the receptionist enters. She murmurs something in his ear, eliciting a nod, and immediately departs.

"Caroline Whaley is here and is eager to get the meeting started," Kane tells me. "I'm having her brought in now, and you and I can continue our discussion afterward."

He rises to his feet. Seconds later the receptionist opens the door again and stretches out her arm to wave Caroline Whaley into the room. She's in her midseventies, I guess, and her appearance is a surprise. When Kane mentioned she'd be joining us, I'd immediately imagined an older woman with gray hair, perhaps heavyset, and dressed in a skirt and sweater set, a look I've seen on older suburban women in West Hartford—but how shortsighted of me. This woman is super stylish and arresting. Her short strawberry-blond hair is brushed sleekly back from her forehead and tucked behind her ears, and though none of her features are themselves remarkable, they've come together to create a striking face punctuated by lips she's painted a bright, fiery red. She's wearing slim navy pants, a crisp cornflower-blue shirt—with the collar popped self-assuredly—and a chunky beaded necklace in the same shade of blue as the shirt.

But despite her chic look, it's clear she's grief-stricken. The muscles in her face are taut, as if she's been trying for days, including right now, to maintain composure.

Kane introduces us to each other as Ms. Moore and Mrs. Whaley, and I do an awkward half rise out of my chair.

"Please don't get up," Caroline Whaley says in a husky voice. Her tone isn't what you'd call warm, but there nothing's hostile in it either. Still, I feel my unease flare a little, and I have to remind myself that this is as big as the group will get. Three people, that's all.

"I'm very sorry for your loss," I tell her. It's feeble, of course, but I know from my own experience of grief that nothing I say would make a difference, anyway. Her eyes, I notice, are a very deep blue, the color of wet slate, and I suddenly recall being struck by C.J.'s eyes. I think they might have been the exact same shade.

"Thank you," Caroline says. As she settles into the chair across from me, a scent wafts off her, something both fruity and woodsy. "And I'm sorry to rush you two along, but I do need to get to another appointment."

"No problem, we were just finishing up," Kane says, sounding eager to please. "I was explaining to Ms. Moore why Chris thought it important for you to be here, that it's key for you to learn where things stand."

"Yes, exactly," she says to Kane. Abruptly her head swivels in my direction and she meets my eyes. "But before we start, Ms. Moore, I hope you'll be courteous enough to answer a few questions for me."

"Uh, I'll try," I say, immediately flustered.

"I assume you had an affair with my son. Was it still going on at the time of his death?"

I gulp, not having expected her to be so blunt. Instinctively I slide my eyes toward Kane, wondering if he'll offer a hint about how to reply, but his face is blank. I look back at Caroline.

"We didn't have an affair. I—"

"Please," she says, her tone even. "There's no reason not to tell me the truth." Her eyes suddenly brim with tears. "In fact, there's nothing I'd like more than to think Chris was with someone who truly cared about him during the last year of his life."

Sounds like a dig at his wife, if I'm getting her meaning right.

"If he was in a serious relationship with someone during the past year, it wasn't me," I say. "As I told Mr. Kane, I spent just one night with your son. That's all."

I don't try to offer any defense of my actions by saying that I didn't know he was married—because at the time I hadn't bothered to find out one way or the other.

She purses her bright red lips, clearly surprised by my answer. She must have assumed she'd be meeting her son's lover today, and now she's left wondering, like I am, why on earth I'm benefiting from his death in any way.

"Let's get on with it then," Caroline says, abruptly turning her attention back to Kane.

He nods and flips open the folder he's laid in front of him on the table to reveal a thin stack of papers inside. After briefly skimming the top page, he looks directly at me.

I hold my breath. *Please*, I think, *just give me enough fucking money so that I can have a baby.*

"I'm going to skip the legalese and get right to the point," Kane announces. "As I mentioned to you earlier, Christopher Whaley was the beneficiary of a financial trust set up by his late father, and with that trust came power of appointment, which means that he could in turn assign the trust to whomever he wished. He came to me six months ago and asked that I draft an agreement making you, Skyler A. Moore, the beneficiary of the entire trust upon his death."

My heart stops beating at the words *entire trust*, and it only restarts when I force myself to take a breath.

"He's left me the whole *thing*?" I say.

"With several stipulations, however," Kane responds. "If you have a child or children one day, you can choose to appoint the trust to them upon your death, but the trust cannot be appointed to anyone else, including a spouse or partner, before or after your death. If you die childless, Mr. Whaley's descendants, if they're still alive, become the beneficiaries of the trust."

"So--so how much is this trust worth?" I sputter. It's an awkward, greedy question to ask in front of C.J.'s mother, but I can't bear waiting any longer.

Kane shifts a little in his seat. Is he about to clear his throat and tell me *One dollar*? Isn't that the kind of joke the dead sometimes play on the living?

"The trust," he says, "has a total value of three and a half million dollars."

7

Now

FOR A MOMENT I'M TOO STUNNED TO MOVE OR SPEAK. IT CAN'T possibly be true, it just can't be.

"Three and a half *million* dollars?" I say finally, my voice squeaking.

"Yes, that is correct."

On the train ride I'd let my mind toy with certain dollar figures, but I never came close to imagining an amount this high.

"But I don't get it," I say, shaking my head. "I don't get it at all."

"You know what *I'd* suggest, Ms. Moore?" Caroline Whaley interjects.

I almost forgot she was here. As I turn to look at her again, I notice that she appears almost sanguine, and there's even a hint of a smile on her face. This must not be a total shock to her. She would have known the amount of the trust and also that some strange woman was coming in today and would be awarded at least part of it. I stare at her blankly, waiting.

"Take the money and run," she says. "Mr. Kane told me you're an artist, and I'm sure you'll be able to put the funds to good use.

It's obvious that no matter how brief your encounter with Chris was, you meant something to him, and he felt a need to express his gratitude." She sits up even straighter and looks at Kane. "Now if we're done here, I'll be on my way."

As she rises from her chair, I instinctively start to stand as well, but Kane asks me to wait behind while he sees her out. I murmur a goodbye as she departs the room.

In the minute I'm alone, I replay what's happened so far. Is there something I'm missing, or not remembering? Or is this a crazy dream I'm about to wake up from?

"You okay?" Kane asks me when he returns and slides into his seat. His tone is the first indication that he's aware of how over-whelming this must be for me.

"No. I mean, yes, I guess. . . . This-this is going to change my whole life."

"I imagine it will."

I shake my head, still having trouble gaining purchase on the events of the last twenty minutes.

"Please," I say, not even bothering to hide the pleading tone to my voice. "You must have *some* idea why he did this. You have to tell me."

"As I said on the phone, I have no clue."

"Christopher Whaley just showed up one day and asked you to set this in motion without any explanation?"

"More or less. He came to me shortly after his diagnosis, and it was clear he wanted to move quickly because he wasn't sure how much time he had left. I tried to probe a little, but he made it clear he didn't want to discuss anything beyond getting the paperwork out of the way."

Okay, so maybe he's clueless. But someone somewhere must know the reason.

"Do you feel his mother meant it when she said for me to take the money and run?"

Kane adjusts the pen in front of him, realigning it perfectly with the folder again.

"Caroline's a smart woman, and a powerful one," he says firmly. "Until a few years ago, she ran a very successful real estate agency in Westchester County, and I doubt she says much she doesn't mean. Now, there's more for us to touch base about, specifically the transfer of assets, but I'm afraid we'll need to do that by phone tomorrow or Wednesday. I have another meeting in a few minutes, and I'm also waiting for certain details from the trustee you'll be dealing with. That's the person who holds the purse strings, not me."

I still have so many questions, but the meeting is clearly over.

"You'll call me?"

"Yes.

I start to push out of my chair again, but Kane lifts a hand, palm forward. "Before you leave, there's one more thing I need to mention. This particular trust was in Chris's name and his name alone, which means that he could appoint it to whomever he wished, and the terms didn't have to be included in the joint will he had with his wife, Jane. Since I assumed she believed the trust would be going to her or her children, I felt obliged to inform her, as a courtesy, that her husband had decided to make other arrangements."

"She knows my name?" I say, my stomach clenching.

"No, no. I explained that I wasn't allowed to divulge who the beneficiary was. Just so you're aware, she's not taking the situation as lightly as Chris's mother is. To avoid any awkwardness or unnecessary drama, I would urge you to be extremely discreet. Tell as few people as possible about the circumstances of meeting him—or about the trust at all."

I nod. I have no intention of breathing another word about it.

"Is there anyone else who might end up being pissed?" I ask as Kane rises from his chair. "I mean, I saw in the obit that Christopher Whaley had a brother."

"I imagine Liam has his own trust from their father and wasn't counting on anything from Chris. From what I know, he's already returned to Argentina, where he's lived for many years."

Now that he's done with the last point, Kane herds me out into the hallway and back toward reception. I ask where the ladies' room is and inform him I'll see myself out the rest of the way. It's not until I'm in the anteroom outside the stalls that I realize how shaken I am. My pulse is racing, and my knees feel wobbly, like I've just come within inches of being mowed down by a passing car.

I sink onto a long chrome and white leather bench, take a deep breath and try to process what I've learned. As I surmised when I first walked in the door, it seems pretty clear that this isn't a con. I'm here at a fancy-pants law office and I doubt they make extra money hoodwinking thirtysomething, calico-cat-owning single women living in crappy apartments in the East Village.

And as it turns out, I actually did know Chris Whaley.

But I don't have even an inkling about why he decided to leave me a fortune. Caroline says I must have meant something to her son, but *what*? Though we spent a sublime, erotically charged night together, it was only *one* night. Plus, I was a fairly inexperienced twenty-five-year-old, so I find it hard to believe he left me over three million dollars because he'd had the best sex of his life with me.

I finally give myself permission to start thinking about what this money means for me. First and foremost, the chance to try for a *baby*—and to raise my child without being in a constant state of financial anxiety.

But also enough to drastically reduce the number of graphic design jobs I undertake and instead focus on my creative work. Maybe even a better apartment down the road. A chance to travel a little.

As my eyes swell with tears, I rest my head in my hands. Is this really, really happening? Is my entire life about to change? Or could there be a hitch I'm not seeing?

"Is everything all right?"

I look up in surprise. The elegant receptionist is standing just inside the door, and something tells me she's come specifically to check on me. What does she think—that I'm planning to stuff rolls of toilet paper into a tote bag to take home? I should tell her that's a practice I gave up a couple of years ago.

"Just leaving," I say, and after hurrying out, I rush down the hall and grab an elevator to the ground floor. Disembarking, I decide on the spur of the moment to sit and have a cup of tea someplace rather than head directly to the train station. I need time to think, to get my head around this whole stupefying thing.

As I stand in the large marble lobby, searching on my phone for the closest Starbucks or coffee shop, I hear the clomp, clomp, clack, clomp, clack of approaching stilettos. Instinctively, I glance up. The woman sporting the black, pointy shoes is headed directly toward me with all the precision of a drone strike.

"Skyler Moore?" she demands as soon as she reaches me. She's in her forties, I guess, about my height, and though her brown hair is the same short length as mine, it's expensively cut and styled, with one lock falling slightly onto her face, which is part of the look, it seems.

"Yes?" I say warily.

"Don't pretend you don't know me. I'm Chris Whaley's wife."

My heart takes off at a gallop. How is this happening?

I try to make my face sympathetic. "I'm sorry for your loss," I say and shift position, starting to go around her.

"You should be sorry for a lot more than that. You were fucking my husband, weren't you?"

"No, I wasn't," I blurt out. It's the truth, at least in the present tense.

"Why don't you have the guts to admit it?"

I make another move to escape, but she takes a step to the right, blocking me.

"Let me by," I say, the words strangled.

She raises her chin, almost like she's pointing a weapon, and stares hard at me with brown eyes that are almost abnormally large.

"You're just a tramp, aren't you? You ought to be ashamed of yourself."

I finally brush by her, unable to avoid having our shoulders touch.

"Oh, please, go ahead, scurry away like a little mouse," she calls out to my back. "But guess what? You haven't seen the last of me."

8

Now

DON'T LIKE TO THINK OF MYSELF AS A COWARD, BUT AT THIS MO-
ment I'm the definition of one. Instead of telling Jane Whaley to
"go to hell," which I should, I do scurry away, like the mouse she
claims I am.

Just as I'm about to reach the door of the lobby, I notice that
we've aroused the attention of a couple, both college-aged, standing
against the far wall. They stare at me, their expressions pinched in
what seems like disapproval. A second later I see Jane Whaley join
them, and I realize they're not nosy passersby. They must be C.J.'s
twins.

I nearly burst out of the building and onto the street. There's no
way I can stop for tea now. What I need is to get back to the train
station, though I'm certainly not going to wait for an Uber in front
of the building and chance another run-in with the witchy widow.
I start walking fast in what I think is the general direction of the
station.

After checking behind me to make sure I'm not being followed,
I finally exhale, though I still feel rattled.

What did she mean when she said I hadn't seen the last of her? Is she planning to harass me about the money?

And something else is bothering me: Why she was standing in the lobby just now. Bradley Kane insisted she hadn't been given my name, but she clearly was, and she also knew when I'd be exiting the building. Could it have been Kane himself who tipped her off?

About two blocks away, I check behind me again, but there's no sign of her or the kids, just a few Lululemon-clad women with fancy shopping bags, ambling along the sidewalk. I slow to a stop, catch my breath, and after noting the address of the clothing boutique I'm standing in front of, I dig my phone out of my purse to order an Uber.

"Ms. Moore?"

It's a woman's voice, coming from the road on my right, and I nearly jump, thinking Jane Whaley followed me after all. I look up to see a black town car with tinted windows idling just beyond the row of parked vehicles along the curb. But it's not C.J.'s widow staring at me from the lowered window in the back seat. It's his mother.

"Do you have a minute?" she calls out.

"I'm sorry," I say, feeling a rising panic. "I need to catch a train."

"Please. Only a minute of your time. I'd like to speak to you one-on-one."

All I want is to be speeding back to New York right now, but my curiosity gets the better of me. Maybe she knows why C.J. left me the money and would be willing to tell me if we're alone.

I nod slowly. "Okay."

She slides out of the car without even giving the driver a chance to open the door. Now wearing a crisp black trench coat over her outfit, she flicks the back of her hand toward a cluster of tables outside a café a few yards down the sidewalk. "Why don't we sit over there for a minute?"

She strides toward an empty table, her posture stick-straight, and I follow. We take seats across from each other beneath an open blue umbrella. In the natural light, she looks even better, and though her skin is slightly waffled just beneath her eyes, it's otherwise as smooth as porcelain.

"I saw my daughter-in-law go into the building," Caroline says, her voice even. "Did she confront you?"

"Yes. She-she called me a tramp and said I hadn't seen the last of her."

Caroline chuckles, a deep and throaty sound. "Ah, poor Jane, she's never had much of a gift for words. Unfortunately, Chris was so dazzled early on by her self-possession and those too-big eyes, it took him years to notice she wasn't the brightest bulb in the chandelier."

"And . . . she didn't love him? You said in the conference room that—"

She shakes her head. "No, she didn't love him. Or if she did, she had a funny way of showing it."

"But your son stayed with her."

"When children are involved, parents often let their personal needs take a back seat. Chris was fiercely devoted to his kids."

How awful to have died in a loveless marriage and how alone her son must have felt toward the end of his. More questions run through my mind: Is that why he passed the trust to me? Was it his way of connecting, spreading goodwill to another person as he faced his mortality? Could he have kept track of me all these years, known I was a struggling artist?

"Do you think she meant what she said? That I haven't seen the last of her?"

She cocks her head, considering. "There's a chance she'll try to come after the money—Jane isn't one to take no for an answer—but she doesn't have any grounds. Chris was very ill when he appointed the trust to you, but his mind was clear. And besides, she'll be fine financially. She's inheriting all the joint assets—an expensive home, the stock portfolio, Chris's pension. The only thing she doesn't have now is the padding the trust would have provided, a way to pay for some of life's little extras."

Life's little extras. I wonder what Caroline would think if she knew the main thing I planned to do with the money.

A waiter approaches with two menus, but Caroline raises a hand to stop him. "Thank you, but I don't think we'll be staying. Can you give us a minute, however?"

He nods and retreats. There are only so many women in the universe who can pull off a trick like that: taking a prime seat at a restaurant table with no intention of ordering even an iced tea.

"What about your grandchildren?" I ask. "I think they might have been in the lobby, too."

"Yes, that was Mark and Bee." She pauses, as if gathering her words. "I'm sure they're annoyed about this wrinkle, but they'll be fine, too. They graduate from college in May, and Chris set up trusts that can be used for graduate school if they decide to attend. And one day, of course, they'll inherit from me."

Yeah, but still, it's over three million dollars that's *not* going into their bank accounts. Plus, they have to be wondering what my relationship with their father was, and that can't be much fun.

The sun has ducked behind a cloud, and I pull my sweater coat more tightly around me. This is all so awkward, sitting here with the grieving mother of a man I had a one-night stand with. But I can't leave without finding out if she knows the reason for the bequest—and so far she hasn't seemed inclined to volunteer it.

I take a deep breath and try to meet Caroline Whaley's eyes.

"Bradley Kane said he doesn't know why your son left me the money. Do you?"

She shrugs, lifting her Burberry-clad shoulders. "As I told you earlier, you must have meant something to him."

"But he never said anything to you?" I ask, realizing the pleading has returned to my tone. "Something that would help me under-stand this better?"

She shakes her head softly, then purses her lips, which are still perfectly red without a smudge in sight. "He did inform me before he passed that he wasn't assigning the trust to Jane or the kids and that he'd asked Bradley Kane to include me in the meeting with the beneficiary. But sadly, my son and I weren't as close as I would have liked, and that was all I could find out."

Her answer sounds authentic, but I have no idea whether I should buy it. Having run her own business for years, she must be practiced at only revealing what she wants people to know.

"Okay, thank you," I say, shifting restlessly in the chair. I'm not sure what she's getting out of talking to me, but I need to hightail it to the station so I can deliver my last collage to the gallery before five. "I'm sorry, Mrs. Whaley, but I can't stay any longer."

"Caroline, please."

"Caroline."

She rests both elbows on the table, steeples her hands, and taps them against her chin a few times. Her nails have been painted the palest shade of pink, a total contrast to her lip color.

"One final question," she says, lowering her hands. "One I didn't want to ask in front of Kane." Her eyes suddenly brim with tears, like they had in the conference room. "Did-did my son seem happy to you?"

I have no idea how to answer. Even if I'd occasionally allowed myself to entertain memories of that night back in Boston, how could I be sure my observations at the time were accurate? Plenty of us are brilliant at disguising how we really feel, even who we really are. No one in the world, not even Nicky, knows what gnaws at my heart every single day. Maybe C.J. was just as good at that kind of deception.

And then, without warning, a memory of him blooms in my

mind, something so small and faint that if it were a sound, it would barely be above a whisper. He's smiling at me at the hotel bar, not a creepy come-on, but a friendly, engaging grin from a man seemingly at ease in his own skin.

"Overall, yes," I say, feeling an urge to comfort his grieving mother. "He did seem happy."

She smiles wanly. "I want very much to believe that, you see. Like so many people, Christopher didn't end up with the life he'd hoped for, and I'd like to think that toward the end, he at least felt somewhat at peace. That there were moments of joy he could draw on."

"Mrs. Whaley, I can only address how he seemed during the one night we were together," I say, even though I'm certain this is going to disappoint her. "And it was such a long time ago."

Her eyebrows lift. "You mean your involvement with him wasn't recent?"

"No, it happened twelve years ago—when I was in grad school in Boston, and he was on business there."

The muscles in her face tighten, and looking off, she presses her index finger against her lips, smearing her lipstick a little.

"Goodness," she says, clearly taken aback. "That *was* a long time ago."

Briefly I wonder if she's going to break down and cry. She'd clearly thought my encounter with Chris had been recent, and that I might be able to tell her something significant, perhaps that he'd made peace with the idea of dying in those last months or weeks. But I have nothing at all to offer her.

"I'm sorry. I wish I had more to share. But I really should leave," I say, pulling my bag under my arm. "I need to spend the rest of the day in my studio and deliver a piece of art to my gallery."

She seems to recover her equilibrium and offers me a faint smile. "My driver will take you to the station," she says, sliding her phone from a slim, quilted Chanel bag, and typing for a moment, her thumbs moving expertly.

"No, please, that's really not necessary."

"I've just texted him. And it will give me a chance to sit quietly for a minute and order myself a drink. I think I need one."

I don't want to owe her anything, but this way I can get right to the train station without the risk of running into Jane Whaley again. "All right," I tell her. "Thank you so much."

"And please," she says, reaching into her purse again and withdrawing a business card. "Feel free to call me if you run into difficulty over the coming weeks."

"Thank you," I say, accepting the card. "And again, I'm so sorry for your loss."

I rise and hurry toward the town car, which is still idling in the road. I yank open the door and nearly lunge into the back seat.

"I'm going—" I say to the back of the driver's head.

"The station," he says without turning around. "Mrs. Whaley informed me."

We pull into traffic, and I grip the door handle, just for something to hold on to. The space, with its faint leathery smell and lingering scent of Caroline's fragrance, feels like a foreign country to me. How—no *why*—have I ended up here, in this car, in this Tudor-themed town that looks like a set for a movie about Anne Boleyn, in this entire situation? I want the money more than anything—I can *taste* how much I want it—but I also desperately need to understand why it's landing in my lap.

I rest my head back against the leather cushion and close my eyes. Another image of C.J. rises in my memory, almost as faint as the first. We're standing in the middle of his hotel room, still dressed, and his hands are cupping my face as he kisses me.

When I left his room the next morning, I had no idea I'd allow everything about him to go dormant in my mind. If anything, I assumed I'd be replaying those memories again and again, reliving the night I'd just spent. I'd not only felt completely relaxed in C.J.'s presence but also connected to him, despite the difference in our ages and status and where we were in life. And then there was the sex. It had been thrilling and intoxicating, and even, as corny as this sounds, *empowering*. I'd never been pleased by a man to that degree, never felt so sexually free myself.

But in the end, I had no choice but to dig a deep hole and dump those memories into it. Because there wasn't any way to separate that night in Boston from everything heart-rending that happened in the hours afterward.

9

Then

THE HOTEL ROOM MY FRIEND TESS ASSIGNED ME THAT NIGHT turned out to be "a classic" with a queen-size bed. It was decorated chicly in taupe and shades of cream and offered an enchanting view of Beacon Hill rooftops.

I set my duffel bag onto the luggage rack, unpacked my toiletries, and then flopped onto the bed, stretching out on my back. It was great to be avoiding the dinner party, but at the same time, I felt a little ragged, probably from a combination of fatigue and leftover anxiety about Chloe.

Had she thought at all about me today? I wondered. Had she worried that she hadn't been able to reach me, and that I might be really concerned? Probably not. It was always me worrying about Chloe, if she was doing okay, wondering if she wanted to share a pizza on a Saturday afternoon or if she would need a ride home for the holidays.

Part of me fantasized about telling my mother what had happened, just to let her see the thoughtless side of Chloe that she seemed oblivious to. But I could imagine what she'd say: *Oh, Skyler, your sister has so much on her mind right now* or *That's just Chloe being Chloe*. Since my little sister Nicky found Chloe enchanting, I always seemed to be the only one complaining.

I stripped off my clothes and took a long bath, something I never had the chance to do in my apartment, where we only had a standing shower. As I toweled off, I realized I was starving, but the idea of leaving the hotel and going out into the city to pick up take-out was totally unappealing.

The hotel bar, I decided. I'd been there with Tess a couple of times and recalled they served some reasonably priced bar bites like shrimp cocktail and blistered shishito peppers. I might be able to trick my stomach into thinking one of them was an entire meal.

By the time I exited the elevator on my way to the bar, Tess had been replaced at the front desk, so I texted her to say how much I was looking forward to the evening. The wood-paneled room turned out to be only a quarter full, a pleasant surprise for a Saturday night. I took a seat at the far end of the empty bar. In my jeans and fisherman sweater, I didn't think anyone would mistake me for a call girl, but I certainly didn't want to draw unwanted attention to myself.

There was indeed a shrimp cocktail on the single-page menu, and I ordered one with a glass of the cheapest rosé they had and asked the bartender if I could also have a piece of bread or some crackers. He nodded, though I could see him fighting off an eye roll.

The wine, when it came, was delicious and very cold, and I congratulated myself for my decision to come downstairs. It was good to be alone, scanning news headlines on my phone and no longer fretting about Chloe.

I was halfway through my wine—taking tiny sips since the bartender showed no interest in topping it off gratis, and one glass was all I could afford—when out of the corner of my eye, I saw someone take a stool several down from mine. Barely turning my head, I slid my gaze off my phone screen in that direction to see it was none other than the guy from the lobby. He was out of his blazer now and wearing a navy crewneck sweater with no shirt underneath. Though I'd practically needed neon wands and a reflective safety vest to get the attention of the bartender, this guy beckoned him over with nothing more than a small cock of his chin.

He ordered a Johnnie Walker on the rocks. And then, without warning, he turned to me and flashed a small smile, polite rather than flirty, the kind you offer strangers when you move into their space a little. I nodded pleasantly and returned to my phone.

But I couldn't help stealing brief glances at him now and then. He was as attractive as I'd thought earlier, but in such a different way than someone like, say, Carson, my crush from oil painting class. This guy was a *man*, emanating confidence and self-possession, the kind of guy who surely knew how to pick the perfect wine for a meal, change a flat tire without breaking a sweat, and get himself rebooked instantly after his flight was canceled. And if I started choking on my last piece of shrimp, he'd probably jump over and rescue me in seconds with a perfectly executed Heimlich maneuver.

For the first time I noticed that he wasn't wearing a wedding band. Which didn't confirm he was unattached to a wife or partner, but it meant there was a chance he might be single.

My glass was almost empty now, and the bartender asked if I wanted another.

"No thanks," I said, though I did.

He whisked the wineglass off the bar so fast you'd hardly know it had even been there, and then turned to ring up my bill.

"You sure?"

It wasn't the bartender speaking, but the guy a couple of stools down. I glanced back over at him. Could he be trying to pick me up?

"I have to leave in a minute to meet someone," he added before I could summon a response, "but I'd be glad to buy you a round before I go."

Interesting. He seemed to be saying that there'd be no strings attached to the drink, that he wasn't going to be hanging around and expecting me to hightail it up to his suite with him once I'd drained it. And this would mean I could chill at the bar a while longer.

"Um, sure," I said. "Thank you for that."

He asked the bartender to bring me another glass of rosé and shook his head when he was asked if he wanted another scotch.

"I've been to Boston only a couple of times but that was years ago," he said, redirecting his attention back to me. "Do you think I made a good choice with this hotel?"

"Well, you're right near Boston Common and the Public Garden, which are really nice to wander in. And there's a trolley stop close by, on the corner of Arlington and Boylston." I smiled at how stupid that sounded. "Though you're probably not planning to travel much on the T while you're here."

He smiled back. His eyes were blue like mine but appeared much darker, at least in the dimness of the bar.

"Hey, I *love* mass transit. . . . Are you in town on business, too?"

I chuckled. "Do I really look like a businesswoman?"

"If I were to guess, I'd say you're a tech genius working for a cutting-edge start-up."

"If only," I said, and smiled. "What if I told you I actually work for the National Board of Rosé Importers and part of my job is to travel around the country and make sure bars and restaurants are pushing our wines enough."

Now it was his turn to chuckle. His skin, I noticed, was a little bit weathered and his lips slightly chapped, like he might be someone who sailed as a hobby. I was pretty sure he didn't do anything outdoorsy for a living, though. No, he looked like the kind of guy who ran meetings and told people things like *Let's make it happen*—but not in a jerky way. He seemed too comfortable with himself for that.

"Ah, a rosé undercover agent," he said, clearly aware I was teasing. "That's the kind of job I might relish myself."

He drew a credit card from his wallet and laid it on the dark wooden bar for the bartender. *Please*, I thought, *don't leave right this second*.

"In all honesty, I'm in grad school at BU," I told him. "But my friend works at the hotel here, and she sometimes gives me a room when I need a break from my apartment mates."

"Nice friend."

"Exactly."

"Was she the one who was checking you in earlier?"

I liked that. He wasn't trying to pretend this was the first time we'd noticed each other.

"I'm going to plead the Fifth. And what about you? Are you a master of the universe or something?"

"Ha, no. I'm actually president of this hotel chain. We heard a report of staff giving away free rooms and I came to investigate." As soon as he saw my eyes widen, he raised a hand and smiled once more. "Hey, just kidding. Your secret is safe with me."

He turned and said something softly to the bartender, who'd come to collect his card, and a few seconds later he was scrawling his name on the bill. I felt a pinprick of disappointment.

"Enjoy the rest of your night," he said.

"You, too."

"And I hope you get a nice break from your apartment mates."

I trailed him with my eyes as he left. Would there be men like him in my life one day?

I ended up staying about an hour longer, nursing the second glass of wine and simply chilling. Surprisingly the bar got even quieter, as if something was going on somewhere and almost the whole world was there except me, but that was okay. When I went to pay, the bartender told me the guy had taken care of my entire bill. Wow.

The lobby was quiet, too. I strode to the elevator, pushed the button, and stepped in as soon as the doors parted.

And then there he was again, standing inside the elevator as if he had been conjured up by a magician. It took me a second to realize that when he'd returned to the hotel, he must have come in through the rear entrance, which led to a smaller lobby one floor below.

"Hello, again," I sputtered.

"Hello." He held my eyes with his, which really *were* deep, deep blue. "What is it they say? Third time's the charm?"

My heart skipped, and my eyes drifted to the shiny brass panel with the buttons for each floor. I could tell from the one lit button that he was going to the seventh floor, too, but I pressed the button, anyway, so it wouldn't look like I was planning to follow him back to his room.

The car stopped and he motioned for me to go first, and I stepped out into the sage green hallway. It was empty and silent, except for the whooshing sound of the elevator shooting back to the lobby.

"Well, good night again," I said, standing stock-still. My pulse was racing, and I felt desire I couldn't explain shooting through me.

"Good night. I'm C.J., by the way."

"Skyler," I said.

He stepped closer to me, cupped my face with his hand, and kissed me softly on the mouth.

And then we were kissing deeper, so close I could feel his heartbeat.

He asked if I wanted to go to his room, and I told him yes. Once there he explained he didn't have any protection but was happy to run out to a drugstore, but I told him I had condoms in my purse. We began peeling off each other's clothes, and his body turned out to be exactly how I'd imagined it might be. Strong, fit, the body of a man and not some college student.

The sex began kind of languorously at first, an erotic slow burn with deep kisses and an exploration of each other's body, but soon things became greedier and more urgent, like a fast-moving wildfire. He seemed so eager to please me, with both his hands and his mouth. I'd slept with one guy in high school and several in college, but none of them had come close to being as skilled as C.J., and at moments I had trouble catching my breath.

Afterward, as I lay in the crook of his arm, I felt almost high from the sheer pleasure of the past hour. I knew I should let myself savor the experience, but at the same time I felt sad that it was all *behind* me now. I wanted nothing more than to be going toward it for the first time again.

It wasn't until a few minutes later, when I got up to use the bathroom, that Chloe drifted back into my thoughts. I was still pissed that she'd left without saying goodbye, but if I hadn't been desperate to unwind after the stress of looking for her last night, I might have passed up Tess's offer of a room. Which means I would still be in the dark about how staggeringly great sex could be with the right man.

And then she was gone from my thoughts once more. I didn't think of her again until the next morning. Just before everything went to ruin.

10

Now

AFTER BOLTING OUT OF CAROLINE'S TOWN CAR AT THE STATION and climbing the stairs to the platform, I'm relieved to see there's a southbound train in only seven minutes. I pace back and forth on the platform, and briefly flirt with the idea of calling Bradley Kane to tell him about my run-in with Jane Whaley but decide I don't have the psychic energy at the moment.

The train seems to come out of nowhere, blowing a mournful sound with its horn and clicking over the tracks, and I end up in a half-full car where I'm able to snag a row to myself. I spend the ride rehashing the morning in my mind: the meeting with Kane; the ambush by C.J.'s widow; the unsettling conversation with Caroline. Is there something I missed today, something that could help me better understand why this has all happened to me? Though I've taken Caroline at her word that she has no clue why I'm the beneficiary, I'm beginning to suspect that Kane might be aware of more than he was letting on. But I don't know how to extract the information from him.

What if I simply let go of the need to understand the situation, and do as Caroline suggested: take the money and run? Part of me yearns to do exactly that, but it feels foolhardy to think there won't be a huge buckle in the road ahead, one that throws me on my ass. The last dozen years of my life could be a haiku titled "Other Shoe Dropping," so why should now be any different? Maybe Jane Whaley will come after the money at full throttle, or this whole experience will turn out to have been some massive misunderstanding.

It seems like no time at all has passed when the windows suddenly darken and the train begins to wobble through the tunnel into Grand Central. After exiting, I hop on the 6 train to Astor Place and start walking east. I'm tempted to stop off at my apartment to change clothes and decompress for a few minutes, but I need to get to my studio as soon as possible, so I drop in to a deli for a chicken wrap and then hurry toward Second Avenue. Approaching the building, I catch a quick glimpse of Alejandro departing with a large portfolio case, which means that at least one studio near mine will be empty, but as soon as I'm inside and on my floor, I pick up sounds of people behind a few of the closed doors. Though I don't want to interact with any of the other tenants, it's always nice to know they're around.

I let myself into the studio, drop my sandwich on the counter, and, still in my coat, turn my attention to the collage. Somehow, miraculously it had finally come together late yesterday, but I want to make sure the glue is dry and smooth out any rough spots, before I photograph and pack it up.

After thirty minutes or so of fussing, I snap photos with my camera, and then stand the collage on the counter, studying it as I finally wolf down the chicken wrap. I do really like the piece, I decide. Though it might not be as strong as some of the others in the show, it's got a certain style, and I sense it will not only look good in the mix but also hold up on its own.

At just after four, realizing Josh is probably wondering where I am, I dig out bubble wrap and brown paper from the cabinet where I keep them and secure the collage carefully with them. Twenty minutes later I'm in an Uber, pointed toward the gallery on the Lower East Side. It's my second of the day, an expense I don't need, but I don't want to risk any damage to the piece.

When I'm halfway there, my phone rings. It's Nicky.

"Is everything okay?" she asks.

"Yes, why?"

"I sent you a bunch of texts that you haven't answered," she says, a plaintiveness in her voice.

I sigh. "Sorry. I've been rushing to get a collage to the gallery and I haven't looked at my phone in hours."

"That's okay, I've just been in suspense. How did it go today with the lawyer?"

It isn't until she says the word *lawyer* that I even remember telling her about the inheritance—because I'd tried to wipe our last conversation from my mind.

"Oh," I say. "Well, it turns out I actually did know the guy, but it was years ago, so that's why his name didn't ring a bell at first."

"And did he really leave you something in his will?"

I adore my baby sister, and occasionally even confide in her, but right then I decide not to reveal the facts of the inheritance. For starters, I'm afraid that if I so much as *raise* the subject, it could jinx something that already feels as fragile as a robin's egg. I also don't trust her not to spill to our mother. I know Nicky means well, but Margo Severson is a master at prying top-secret information from her before my sister even knows what's happening.

"Yeah, but only a small stipend," I lie. "It turns out this guy was into supporting emerging artists, kind of a benefactor thing."

"Wow, that's great. Is it enough money to make a difference?"

"It's not clear yet. I'm waiting to hear more. But, hey, don't say anything to Mom, okay? I'm going to hold off telling her until I know more."

Actually, I can't imagine *ever* telling my mother—because she'd probably decide I didn't deserve any kind of glorious windfall from the universe.

"Uh, okay," Nicky says, sounding a little wary. "And, oh, today went good, by the way. We got almost everything for the tag sale stickered and into the garage, and we'll just move it outside on Saturday."

The words *tag sale* make my stomach churn, stirring up all the resentment I've experienced since I learned about it. I'm annoyed that she brought it up again, but I remind myself that Nicky is such a Pollyanna, she probably thinks that if she just keeps pretending there's nothing wrong, there won't be.

"Great" is all I say.

"I grabbed some things for you, too. Like those bird prints that were hanging in the upstairs hall."

My irritation dissolves a little with this news. The prints aren't worth a lot of money, but I was obsessed with them as a kid, and some of my earliest sketches were attempts to replicate them.

"Thanks, Nicky. That was so sweet of you."

"Want me to bring them when we come to your opening next week?"

"Hmm, I don't think I'll want to lug them home that night. Would you mind leaving them at Mom's and I can pick them up when I'm there next?"

"Sure," she says, just as I'm wondering if I even do want the pictures. I'm touched that Nicky remembered my connection to them, but my mother knew I loved them, too, and she hadn't thought to set them aside.

"Look, I'm just pulling up to the gallery," I say, though I have another block to go. "Can I give you a call later tonight?"

"Do you promise? I want to hear more."

"Of course."

I do my best to clear my mind as I tap on the door of the Meyer Gallery, and I even try to savor the moment. Not only am I having a show, one where people might actually purchase my work, but this is one of the galleries I used to wander into regularly when I first began to summon the nerve to create art again.

From the window I can see the gallery assistant, Nell, sitting at the reception desk, typing on a laptop. After several knocks, I manage to grab her attention and she's soon unlocking and opening the door. Nell's got short, jet-black hair, shaved on the sides, and silver rings in both her nose and her lips, and though she's at least ten years younger than me, I've felt ridiculously intimidated by her every time we've met

"Hey, Nell." I say, after clearing my throat. "Is Josh around?"

"Yup," she says, with her typical cool. "He's expecting you."

I follow her into the front room of the gallery and set the wrapped collage down on the floor, leaning it carefully against the closest wall.

Nell turns and apparently starts to go in search of Josh, but before she's gone far, he comes striding out from the rear of the gallery, with a day-old scruff and his longish, black-brown hair pushed behind his ears and away from his face. He's wearing tight jeans, a white shirt with a few buttons undone at the top, and an unstructured dark blue blazer, the kind of downtown-meets-the-Upper-East-Side look he usually seems to sport.

"Skyler, welcome," he says, grinning. "You made it!"

"Yeah. Sorry, it's a little later than I planned. Something came up this morning."

"I can't wait to see the collage." He flashes me a mischievous grin. "Are you hiding it behind your back?"

I smile a little and point my chin toward the brown paper-covered rectangle leaning against the wall. "No, it's over there."

"Shall we look together?"

I shake my head. "No, no, you can take your time. Besides, I need to run anyway." I can't imagine many things more excruciating than watching him assess it right in front of me.

Josh chuckles. "Okay, I'll wait until you're gone. Do you have one minute, though, to review the space for the exhibit?"

"Sure," I say, glancing around. "But isn't this it?"

"No, I decided that we'd hang all your pieces in the rear."

Though I had no reason to assume this, I just always pictured my collages hanging in the front area of the gallery. Is it bad that they're being herded to the back? I wonder. Is Josh regretting giving me the show?

"Follow me," he continues, and I trail behind him into the back area. He's tall, about six two, and obviously in good shape.

"Your collages will have a better chance to breathe in here," he says, coming to a stop in the center of the rear space. The walls are currently lined with abstract paintings, done in acrylics, which will obviously be coming down soon. "And because this room is larger, people will be able to step back and really see how they work almost as a series." He runs his gaze across the walls as he speaks.

"I see what you're saying," I tell him, though I can't help but wonder if he's just making this up to spare my ego.

Now he turns and looks right at me, his hooded brown eyes so dark they almost read as black.

"You know what else? The front exhibit next week will consist entirely of black-and-white photographs, and I love the idea of people seeing those first and then wandering back here and having their jaws drop when they get a look at *your* pieces."

"Thank you." I feel my cheeks redden. "That's so nice of you to say."

"The official opening of the show isn't till six, as you know, but I hope you can come by Tuesday morning and take a look at the collages once they're hung. Maybe at eleven, just after we open?"

"Oh sure, yes. I appreciate that."

We're standing really close to each other now, so close I can pick up the almondy scent of his soap, and I feel slightly flustered. I have little experience, at least these days, of being around guys as attractive and polished as Josh.

"I hope you realize how stunning your collages are," he says, "and I can't wait for people to see them. And speaking of that"—he starts walking again, slowly returning to the front room of the gallery—"a hundred and thirty people have now RSVP'd yes for the opening party."

Just hearing Josh utter *party* makes my pulse take off, and I have to fake a smile in response.

"Wow."

"Wow, indeed. I won't hold you up any longer. Thanks for coming by, and I'll see you Tuesday at eleven?"

He walks me to the door, where I say goodbye to him and give a little wave to Nell, who doesn't look up from her computer.

As I walk home from the gallery, my eyes watering a little from the crisp autumn air, I start to think more about the party, envisioning the sheer terror of being in a room packed with people. Even if I don't have to make a speech, I'll be expected to mingle and chitchat, to answer questions and comment articulately about my work. The last time I attended a cocktail party, which must have been over four years ago, my mouth turned so dry that every time I parted my lips, it felt like two pieces of Velcro being pulled apart.

But just as I'm about to start hyperventilating, I hear my phone ping with a text, and it's Josh saying he absolutely loves the new collage. Though he's obviously a killer salesman, his words seem sincere, and so did the comments he made about my art back in the gallery. As I continue my trek home, I can't keep a smile from my face, one seemingly born from a sudden rush of joy. Well, no, probably not joy, because I cut that emotion off at the legs years ago, but something close to it. When I started to make collages, it was initially to help dig myself out of a scary hole, because, like a line in a poem I once read, I'd "simply had enough of drowning." But in time I began to entertain the fantasy I'd had in my head when I set off to grad school, that I could one day make my living as an artist.

What if I really can? Maybe a bunch of my collages will sell next week, which will lead to future shows, and additional sales, and other shows after that.

I've flipped a switch to thinking positively, I realize, and I try to stay with it, fighting off any doubts before they gain more ground.

If only I could take the same approach with the other parts of my life, bring that same sense of hopefulness to them. I've been warning myself since I left Scarsdale that the inheritance from Christopher Whaley might be a bizarre mix-up, but it can't be a mistake, can it? He knew me, after all, and he was in his right mind when he decided to leave the trust to me. If I were smart, I'd start owning it. I'd even call the Dobson Fertility Clinic and schedule a full exam, the next step in the process on the way to becoming a parent.

But it's hard to own the idea of me as a newly minted million-aire, and mother-to-be, when I don't understand why it's happen-ing. Could C.J. have become smitten with me that night at the Kensington and have spent the next twelve years pining for me? I shake my head. It seems unlikely that someone as confident as he was would have let strong feelings go unspoken all that time.

About a few blocks from my building, I dart into the local su-permarket and pick up milk, a box of dried macaroni, and a slab of cheddar. I can't cook most things to save my life, but I make a decent mac and cheese, and I'm craving something carb-heavy and comforting given the coolness of the night. I grab a few more things

I need for my cupboards, as well as a couple of cans of premium cat food, the kind Tuna goes apeshit crazy for.

When I let myself into my apartment a few minutes later, it's after six, and I'm surprised to see that Tuna isn't on her perch on the back of the couch, waiting for her evening meal. Maybe she's sulking on the bed because I've been gone for so many hours. I give the plastic bag a couple of shakes, making a sound that generally piques her curiosity, but to my surprise, she doesn't come running. She must *really* be annoyed.

I shrug off my coat, put away the groceries, and dump the cat food into Tuna's bowl.

"Hey, Tuna," I call out. "Come on, I've got a surprise."

Still no sign of her. I trudge toward the bedroom, for the first time feeling how tense my muscles are from the nonstop stress of the day, but Tuna's not curled up on top of my duvet.

Nor does she seem to be anywhere else in the bedroom.

I head back to the living room and glance around again, also checking the two chairs tucked under the small dining table because she sometimes likes to curl up on the rattan seats. But there's no sign of her.

"Tuna," I call, louder this time.

I wait for her to crawl out from under the couch or from a hiding spot in the corner.

My stomach clutches as it finally hits me. My cat isn't anywhere in the apartment.

11

Now

TELL MYSELF TO RELAX, THAT TUNA HAS TO BE HERE.

Back in the bedroom, I do a more thorough search, looking for places she might have started napping without my knowledge: under the bed, on the window ledge behind the bamboo shade, and inside the closet. I check the bathroom, too, even behind the shower curtain, but still don't find her. I return to the living room, going down on my knees to check under the couch and poking my head behind the armchair and small bookcase.

By now I'm starting to worry, but I remind myself that every window in the apartment is shut and locked, so there's no way Tuna could have gotten out. She's probably playing an annoying game of wits with me.

And then, with my stomach sinking, I flash back to the hectic morning, when in a rush to leave, I'd stupidly left my phone tethered to its charger on the kitchen counter. I'd dashed back into the apartment to grab it, leaving the door to the hall ajar for several seconds, which means a fast-moving cat could have darted out when my back was to her.

Oh god. The cat barely seems to tolerate me, but I can't stand the thought of her out on her own—lost, scared, hungry, regretting her impulsive dash out the door. And to make matters worse, she doesn't have her collar on, since I only attach it when I'm taking her to the vet.

I stop and think for a moment. Though Tuna has managed to flee the apartment, the door to the vestibule on the ground floor of our building is always locked, and I can't imagine any of the other tenants letting her out onto the street. It's more than possible that she's still in the building somewhere, hiding in a corner of a hallway or having been welcomed in by a kindly neighbor. After locking up my apartment, I start by checking the corners on each floor, hoping Tuna is huddled in one of them. But still no sign of her.

I return to my apartment just long enough to grab my phone, and then, beginning on the sixth floor, I rap on each of the three doors, calling out, "Hi, this is Skyler Moore, one of your neighbors from the fourth floor, can I speak to you?" About half the tenants seem to be home and open their doors with the chains on, just wide enough to reveal half their faces and a whiff of the beef tacos or tom yum goong they've ordered in for dinner.

"No, sorry," they all say, some without even glancing at the photo I show them on my phone. After canvassing the whole building without any luck, I return to my floor, feeling frantic but unsure what else to do. Could Tuna be out on the street somewhere? The thought is crushing.

As I'm taking out my keys, the door next to mine opens, and my neighbor—a tall, light-skinned Black woman maybe eight or nine years younger than me—steps halfway into the corridor, wearing a white terry cloth robe. She moved in a couple of months ago, and though we've said hello to each other, we've never gotten past that and I don't know her name.

"Hi," she says, propping her door ajar with a bare foot. "Did you knock a little earlier? I was in the shower."

"Yeah, sorry to bother you. I'm searching for my cat. I think she must have bolted out of the apartment this morning."

"That's awful," she says, sounding truly sympathetic. "I was in and out a few times today, but I didn't see her."

"Did you notice anything weird today?" I ask. "People coming and going?"

"Oh, boy." She puts a palm to her forehead. "Now that I think of it, someone was moving in a couch, and they had the front door and vestibule door propped open for a while. Maybe your poor cat got out then."

Instinctively, I let out a loud groan. "How am I ever going to find her? She could be anywhere."

She shakes her head. She's stunningly beautiful, even without any makeup and with her super-short hair still wet from the shower. "She's probably very close by. When indoor cats escape, they never go far away. But they tend to hide really well, which means you have to look hard."

"Do you have a cat, too?"

"No, but I worked in a vet office part-time during high school. I have a bit more studying to do tonight, but if you want to search outside, I can help for a while."

"Uh, thanks," I say, touched by the offer, though there's no way I'm going to take her up on it. "Why don't I start on my own and see how I do."

"And be sure to go online. Cities all have sites where you can post about lost pets, and New York might even have them by neighborhood."

"Okay, that makes sense."

"I'm Mikoto Harris, by the way."

"Skyler Moore . . . and thanks again."

I let myself back into the apartment and take my laptop to the couch. Within a couple minutes of searching, I turn up a Facebook page for lost and found pets in downtown Manhattan, where I post the photo of Tuna, along with a written description of her, the area where she disappeared, and the promise of a seventy-five-dollar reward. But if my neighbor is right, Tuna hasn't gone far, and I might be able to find her myself. Since I'm still in my meet-my-fate outfit, I change into jeans, a sweater, sneakers, and fleece jacket, grab the one rinky-dink flashlight I own, and head down to Seventh Street.

Keeping Mikoto's advice in mind, I do a slow, methodical search of nooks and crannies, jabbing the beam into corners, around stoops, trash cans, and outdoor restaurant seating, and even under parked cars. After I strike out on both sides of the block, I cross Avenue A and enter Tompkins Square Park, where some dogs are still having their evening walk. I cover the whole park, using the paths but pointing my beam around bushes, tree trunks, chess tables, and playground equipment. Once I think I spot Tuna streaking behind a bench but realize with a sickening sensation that it's actually a rat, one big enough to eat Tuna for dinner rather than the other way around.

The temperature has dropped in the time I've been outside and I'm shivering now, but I force myself to keep going along Avenue A, then return to Seventh Street and search there again, as well as a stretch of First Avenue.

After an hour and a half of fruitless canvassing, I finally give up and return home. Though my teeth are chattering, my heartsickness makes me not mind the cold. Back in my apartment, I check online to see if anyone has messaged me through the Facebook page, but there's no response. I'm just about to start making a flyer to distribute in the neighborhood when there's a tap at my door, and I jerk back in anticipation, praying someone is standing on the other side with a squirming cat. But when I inch open the door, I find Mikoto, solo, on the other side.

"Any luck, Skyler?" she says as I open the door wider. She's wearing a luxurious-looking sweatshirt and a pair of pale gray yoga pants, and her hair has dried in a hip, spiky style.

"Nope," I say, hearing the catch in my voice. "But I've posted her picture online. And I thought I'd make some flyers, too, and pass them out to stores in the neighborhood."

Mikoto's eyes dart from my face and her brow wrinkles.

"You don't think flyers are a good idea?" I say, confused by her expression.

"No, I mean . . . your cat," she whispers, still looking over my shoulder. "She's right over there."

I spin around, and to my total shock, discover Tuna paused on the threshold between the living room and bedroom. As she eyes us inquisitively, letting out a plaintive meow, relief floods through me. I drop to the floor and put out my hand to Tuna, beckoning her to come close. Rather than simply offering me her usual resting bitch face, she scurries toward me and seems to greedily accept the strokes I offer her.

"Where have you *been*?" I exclaim, scooping her up. Has she pulled a disappearing act just to torture me for some reason?

"It looks like she's been in the bedroom," Mikoto says.

"But it's the size of a postage stamp—and I searched every square inch. This is so weird."

Mikoto smiles. "The crazy thing I learned about cats is that if they want to make themselves scarce, they can squeeze into the tiniest places. When I was working for the vet, these people found their cat hiding in an unfinished patio down the street, and some of the cinder blocks even had to be removed to rescue it."

"But Tuna's never done anything like this before."

"Has she been sick?" Mikoto asks. "Often, they hide when they're not feeling well. Or they're scared. Maybe it was all that noise from the guys hauling the couch up the stairs."

"She hasn't been sick, but, yeah, maybe it was the noise. Thanks again for your concern and for offering to help. I really appreciate it."

"Oh, you're so welcome. I've been studying most of the day, and frankly, this was a good diversion."

"Are you at NYU?" A lot of NYU undergrads and grad students live in the East Village, so it's a fair assumption.

"Yeah, I'm at the law school, in my second year. Are you a student, too?"

"No, I work. Mainly as a graphic designer, but I do some art of my own, too."

She glances over my shoulder, and I realize she's staring at one of my earliest collages, which is hanging on the far wall.

"You didn't do that one, did you?" she says, lifting her chin.

"Yeah. Collages are kind of my thing now."

"It's awesome." She looks back at me and winks. "Well, I should go and let the two of you have some alone time."

"Ha. And if she confesses where she was hiding all this time, you'll be the first to know. Good night—and thanks again."

As soon as I close the door behind my neighbor, I set Tuna down and then think to check her bowl in the kitchen. It's still full, which suggests that she didn't venture from her hiding spot until just now.

"What's going on with you, Tuna girl?" I ask. "Did all the noise scare you?"

No reply, of course. I scoop her up again and return to the living room, where I collapse onto the couch, and she begins kneading me gently with her paws. I realize suddenly that I'm starving and it's far too late to make the mac and cheese. While trying to summon the energy to assemble a peanut butter sandwich, my gaze drifts around the room, eventually settling on my desk. Since the apartment is so small, I try to avoid clutter, and I keep only a few items besides my computer on its surface. One is a yellow mug on the right-hand side that I use as a pen holder.

Except right now the mug is on the left side.

The back of my neck prickles. I'm almost positive I didn't move it—I'm right-handed so I always keep it in the same spot—and even if Tuna had jumped onto the desk at some point, it's hard to imagine she could have managed to nudge the mug all the way across the top.

I hoist myself up and begin circling the room, looking for other signs of disturbance, and I also open the desk drawer, where I store my checkbook and a couple of twenties. Everything is in its usual place. I hurry to the bedroom to find that the Ziploc bag filled with my costume jewelry is right where it should be, too, not that anyone would get much money for its contents.

I must have moved the mug myself and just don't remember doing so. I mean, my brain is pretty useless after everything that's happened today.

Food will help, I decide. I produce two slightly dry pieces of whole wheat bread from the back of the fridge and take down the jar of peanut butter. As I set to work on the counter, my eyes fall on the small mesh mail organizer next to the fridge where I store menus, odd pieces of snail mail, and flyers for events I might attend but probably won't. In the very front, facing out, there's a takeout menu from a nearby Indian restaurant.

But it wasn't the first item when I left the apartment this morning, I'm sure of it. Before I headed for Scarsdale, I wrote myself a reminder to buy milk for tea on the back of an envelope and then stuck the envelope right in the place where the menu is now.

I freeze, a slice of bread in my hand and a breath caught in my chest. Someone has gone through the papers and stuck them back in the organizer out of order. Which means that the real reason my cat went into hiding wasn't because of some noise in the hallway. She got freaked because someone was in my apartment.

12

Now

I BACK OUT OF THE KITCHEN AND SPIN AROUND. FOR A COUPLE OF seconds, I have this terrifying sense that whoever got in might still be here and is about to leap out at me, but I tell myself that's irrational. Given the thoroughness of my search for Tuna, there's nowhere anyone could be hiding.

Finally taking a breath, I walk to the door and, leaving the chain on, ease it open. There are no weird marks on the lock or the doorframe, but clearly someone must have jimmied the lock to gain entry.

I can almost *feel* their presence now.

But what were they doing here? Nothing of value has been taken, even though there was cash in the drawer and my Mac computer is sitting in full view. Did someone just poke around, perhaps looking for something specific that he didn't find or I don't know yet is missing? I grab my head in my hands and squeeze my temples. My day is starting to seem like a series of episodes of *The Twilight Zone*— "Dead Man's Money," "The Cat Who Wasn't There," and now *this*.

I think about who else has the key. Only the super, and yet he's a harmless-seeming guy who always gives me a heads-up if he has to be in the apartment for some repair-related reason.

Taking my key with me, I step into the corridor, close the door, and trot back over to Mikoto's apartment, hoping, since it's just after ten o'clock, that she hasn't gone to bed yet. I knock lightly.

"Sorry to bother you," I say when she opens the door, still in her yoga wear.

"No problem. Did you and your kitty get some bonding in?"

"Yeah, and I think what you said about her hiding because she was scared might be right. It looks like someone was in my apartment today."

"Whoa," Mikoto says, visibly concerned. "You mean like *broke* in?"

"Yeah, but it's strange. Nothing is actually missing—at least as far as I can tell—and yet a few items have clearly been moved around. My lock is still intact, so it must have been picked."

She shakes her head. "Jeez."

"You mentioned you were in and out today," I say. "Did you notice the super in the building?"

"No, and when I called him about fixing my bathroom faucet, he said he wouldn't be here until tomorrow."

My heart sinks. A part of me had hoped that he'd had to let himself in to check for a leak or a mouse infestation or *something*.

"I wonder if someone got in when the foyer door was propped open," she muses.

"Yeah, I'm wondering that, too. And maybe it was some kind of pervert, the kind who likes to go through women's things, which I can't bear to think about."

"It would explain why he didn't take anything." Mikoto bites her lip. "I know this sounds crazy, but—could it be someone you were dating? I've never had an ex break into my place, thank god, but one pretty much stalked me a few years ago."

There's no chance in hell it was an ex. Lucas, my old boyfriend, left town four years ago, and since then I've dated a mere handful of guys, all for just a short while, and I slept with only one of them for a grand total of two times.

I shake my head. "Not likely," I tell Mikoto. "I should let you get back to whatever you were doing, though."

"Are you going to call the police?" she asks.

"No. I mean, what would I say? 'Even though there's no obvious signs of someone breaking into my apartment, I'm sure someone was here because my favorite mug was moved, and my cat was so scared she tried to enter the witness protection program'?" I shake my head. "I'm going to have the lock changed, though."

"You have a chain, I noticed. But maybe you should put a chair or something against the door tonight. I think I might do the same."

"So sorry, I didn't mean to worry you."

"I'll be okay. Before law school, I had a regular salary and was able to swing a doorman building, but there's no chance of that now, and I'm pretty used to the security downgrade."

She wishes me good night and starts to close the door, but then tells me to wait. She grabs her phone from a little table next to the door and suggests we exchange numbers. I can't imagine why I'd call her and not 911 if anything happened, but I don't want to seem rude, so I rattle off my number.

As soon as I've returned to my apartment and made sure Tuna's still on the couch, I put the chain in place and drag over the small table I keep by the entrance. Finished, I spin back around, facing the room. Even with the barricade in place, I still feel unnerved, sick to my stomach about what this means. Someone got *in* here, without even having to hack down the door, and they went through my belongings.

I dig out a spray bottle of Lysol from under the sink, tear a wad of paper towels off the roll, and begin wiping down surfaces—the kitchen counter, the desk, the top of my dresser—as Tuna watches me from the couch. Then, even though I'm bone-tired, I change my sheets and throw the used ones, as well as my underwear and bras, into the hamper to be washed, just in case someone touched them as well.

My cleanup efforts have confirmed that there's nothing missing from either room, so the intruder has to have been some kind of nut who gets his kicks going through women's underwear drawers. As I stand in the middle of my bedroom, catching my breath, my mind returns to Mikoto's question. Earlier my kneejerk reaction had been to say it couldn't have been someone I know, because I couldn't imagine anyone being fixated on me. And yet there was that guy Deacon, the one I more or less ditched a few weeks ago and who left me with a really bad taste in my mouth.

We'd met one Saturday in the bookstore and gift shop of the New Museum on the Lower East Side, where we were both browsing through art books. He'd looked over at one point, smiled, and asked if I knew if membership included a store discount. It was a pretty lame line, but I told him it did, and we'd started talking about the exhibit we'd both just seen. Then he invited me for a coffee at a café nearby. I'd said yes, mainly because the thought of spending the rest of that gorgeous late summer day alone in my apartment seemed a little depressing.

He ran his own web design business, he told me over our cappuccinos, and loved to hike, and he asked a lot of questions, unlike most guys. He was nice-looking enough, too, with medium-length brown hair, a large but not unattractive nose, and light eyes, maybe gray but I don't recall. We met for dinner a week after the coffee date, after which he'd kissed me lightly on the mouth and asked me to dinner again.

I said yes, not sure how I felt about him, but a few minutes into our third encounter I realized that he was far too intense for my taste, with a tight smile that never went all the way up to his eyes. Yes, he asked questions, but instead of being keen to learn more about me, he seemed at times to be drilling me for answers he could challenge me on. There was no way I wanted to sleep with him, I realized then, or for that matter, spend any more time with him. I tried to pay for my half of the meal, but he refused to let me.

"*So*, what's next?" he asked as we walked out of the restaurant. I wasn't sure if he meant that night or in terms of the next date, but it didn't matter.

"I should get going," I'd said. "My life is about to become kind of crazy over the next weeks."

"You want to call me when you come up for air?" he asked.

"It's going to be a while," I lied. "I don't know when I'll have any time in the next few months."

He'd reared his head back, like a horse with a bit in its mouth. "Sounds like you're blowing me off."

"It's nothing personal," I said, fumbling a little. "It's just that I have a collage to finish for this show, and a bunch of paid assignments, too."

"Right," he'd said, the word dripping with sarcasm. "Well, good *luck* to you then." Then he turned on his heel and strode away.

I started to head in the other direction, my stomach clutching from the nastiness in his tone but relieved to be done with him. Suddenly a voice called out my name from behind me, and it took me a second to realize it belonged to him.

"Want to hear something that *is* personal?" he said as I twisted around, half facing him. He was now about ten feet away from me, and I just stared, not sure how to respond.

"You're a *cunt*."

For a second, I remained frozen in place, stunned by the viciousness of his insult. But then I turned back around and started hurrying away. It had taken me a few days to cleanse that exchange from my mind and forgive myself for not having his number the moment he'd spoken to me at the bookstore. He's just a garden-variety asshole, I'd told myself, a guy pissed about having nothing to show for two dinners and a couple of cappuccinos.

But maybe it's more than that, I think now. Maybe he's creepier than I realized, and still in a rage about being blown off. And he does know where I live. He'd insisted on walking me home after our first dinner, probably hoping I'd invite him up. It had been stupid of me, I realize, to let him see my building. But would he really have gone so far as to pick my lock and go through my possessions?

I try to chase the image from my mind as I wash my face half-heartedly and peel off my clothes, leaving them in a heap on the bedroom floor. Finally, I crawl under the covers.

Then to my surprise, I hear Tuna pad into the room. She leaps onto the bed, landing with a thud, and curls up right next to me, something she's never done before.

I'm tempted to put my arm around her, but don't want to come across as needy and send her scampering back to the couch.

Since it's chilly tonight, and the heat in the building is barely on, I pull the duvet up to my neck. As exhausted as I am, I can tell that I'm too keyed up to fall asleep. What if the intruder, having seen how little effort it took to break in, comes back? He won't be deterred by a cheap security chain and an IKEA end table.

Could it really have been Deacon? I wonder again. My stomach twists, thinking of him here, his toxic presence polluting my private space. I don't need this, especially right now, with everything else going on.

And then, as if out of nowhere, another memory of my night with C.J. surfaces: him stroking my hair after we made love, pushing it back a little from my face with almost hypnotic movements. I remember thinking at that moment how wonderful it would be if someone did that to me every night, that it would make it so easy to drift off to sleep.

I was actually a pretty good sleeper in those days, unless I was feeling tense about some of my coursework, but after that weekend I became a full-blown insomniac, sometimes taking hours to fall asleep and waking often during the night from bad dreams.

I flip onto my back and stare up at the cracks in the ceiling, which swim a little in the near darkness of the room. Though much of what happened that night with C.J. feels hazy to me, some memories are still hovering, ghostlike, around the fringes of my mind. What if within them there's a clue to C.J.'s motivation, something he said or did that appeared insignificant at the time but really wasn't?

What I've got to do, I realize, is summon as many of those memories as I can and comb through them for details—despite everything else that will be dredged up, too.

13

Then

AFTER WE'D HAD SEX, I WONDERED IF C.J. EXPECTED ME TO head back to my own room, and I asked myself if that's what I wanted, too. But when I came out of the bathroom a couple of minutes later, I saw him smile at me through the dimness and he asked if I was hungry.

"Um, yes," I said. "*Starving* actually."

He chuckled. "How about some lobster rolls then? I mean, isn't that what this town is famous for?"

"Well, beans too, I guess," I said, laughing. "But lobster will do."

It didn't take long for room service to arrive, and we devoured the rolls in bed, along with a bottle of San Pellegrino. I liked that he'd ordered sparkling water instead of champagne or wine, because it seemed to say our encounter wasn't something we'd simply done under the influence.

While we ate, I suggested a couple rounds of Two Truths and a Lie, a game I loved playing occasionally with friends. I sensed he wasn't interested in sharing much in the way of personal details, but I was curious to know more about him, and I figured that the game would be a way for him to divulge a few things easily enough—and without me seeming to pry.

"Sure, why not?" he said.

I did learn a few things about him, though they didn't add up to a whole lot: He'd climbed the Grand Tetons a few years ago. He was allergic to apple peel. And as a college student, he'd done a term abroad in Vienna.

When we'd finished our food, he took the plate from my hands and set it along with his own on the bedside table and then pulled me into an embrace. We made love again, this time even more intensely. Afterward, collapsing back onto the pillow, I thought again about returning to my room, but before I could summon the energy, I fell fast asleep.

I woke with a jolt at around five thirty Sunday morning. It was still dark out, with no light seeping in yet from the sides of the thick, silk curtains, and I realized after a moment that a dream had forced me awake. One about Chloe. She'd been whispering, saying something I couldn't hear or understand, and though I urged her to speak up, I still failed to make out her words. As I tried to replay the dream, my heart began to thrum. I loosened myself from the tangled sheets and sat straight up in bed.

A couple of things about Friday night suddenly didn't make sense to me. While I was asleep, my subconscious must have downloaded and sorted out details from that evening and was highlighting certain data in red. Though my sister's phone might be beyond repair, couldn't she have borrowed the cell phone of the guy she was with to make contact with someone on Saturday morning? She might not know my number by heart, but surely she knew our mom's landline.

And since she didn't know many numbers by heart, how was it she'd already memorized this new flame's digits and could call him from the car on the borrowed phone?

Panic began to swell in my chest again, like something that had simply been playing dead all night, and I could see that the only way I was going to calm it was by going to the apartment myself to make sure she was okay, dragging her out by her "assignment-ready" hair if need be. Too bad if I embarrassed her by showing up.

I swung my legs over the side of the bed.

"Everything okay?" C.J. asked, stirring with one eye open.

I twisted around so I was facing him. "Yeah, but I should get going now."

"You're welcome to stay for breakfast," he said softly.

"I'd really like that, but unfortunately, there's something I need to take care of first thing this morning." As I spoke, I tried to smile like I meant it—because I *did*. I was hoping that he'd suggest meeting up at least once more while he was still in Boston. I had no expectation of a potential relationship, or even a short-term fling, but I craved at least one more night together—because one didn't seem like enough.

Sliding out of bed, I located my jeans and sweater on the floor and slipped them on, then padded into the bathroom to wash up. In the mirror I saw that my hair was a mess, looking like an electric current had passed through my body, and I felt like it really had last night. As I splashed water on my face, a phone rang faintly from the bedroom. I startled, thinking it might be mine and wondering who would be calling at this hour. Could it be Chloe, finally making contact and in some kind of trouble? But as I reached for the door handle, the second ring was cut short. It must have been C.J.'s phone. He didn't talk for long, and he kept his voice low, though not so low that I missed the tension and exasperation in his tone. Was he actually married or involved with someone and the person was now calling, demanding why he hadn't been in touch? Could this be the moment when reality came crashing down on us?

I waited until I was sure he was off the phone before emerging into the bedroom. He was out of bed now himself, dressed in jeans and a moss-colored Henley.

"Do you have work due for your classes?" he asked. It sounded a bit perfunctory, as if he had other things on his mind now.

I sighed. "No, just some family drama I have to deal with."

"Nothing serious, I hope."

"I don't think so, but I can't stop worrying. On Friday night, I took my younger sister to a party with me—she goes to school here, too—and I haven't been able to reach her since then."

"So the last time you saw her was—?"

"At the party, at around ten or so. She was prancing around this huge suburban house with a guy's sweater around her waist—she's a pretty big flirt—and when I went looking for her later so we could leave, someone told me that she'd gotten a ride to someone's apartment back in the city. Supposedly her phone is broken, and that's why I haven't heard from her, but I woke up feeling a little—I don't know—unsettled, I guess."

It was probably much more than he wanted to know, a violation of the unspoken ground rules for a one-night stand, and I felt my cheeks redden. I turned quickly away and scanned the room until I located my mules and slid my feet into them.

"Has she done this kind of thing before?" C.J. asked from behind me.

"You mean is it just Chloe being Chloe? Maybe—I mean, she can be thoughtless at times."

My purse was all I needed now, and I spotted it on the floor, too, by the side of the armchair.

When I turned back to look at him, C.J.'s sleepy, handsome face was pinched. I appreciated his concern, but things felt suddenly awkward. The rumpled bed behind him and the bedside tables littered with dirty plates and glasses made it seem as if all the magic had now been sucked out of the room.

"I'm sure she'll turn up," he said. "Sounds like she might just be besotted with someone."

"I think you're right," I said. "Well, goodbye. Thanks for a lovely night."

"Take care, Skyler . . . And yes, it was very special."

He stepped forward, cupped one of my elbows lightly with his hand, and kissed me on the forehead before walking me to the door. His face was a total blank. It was now clear he had no interest in seeing me again.

When I reached my room, the corridor was still deserted, though as I unlocked the door, I heard the low drone of a TV from the room across from mine. Once inside I took a moment to brush my teeth and grab my duffel bag, then headed out. Thankfully, there was a coffee station in the lobby, and I filled a disposable cup before speed walking to the T stop, chugging coffee every time I paused at a crosswalk. I'd decided to take the train back to my neighborhood to retrieve my car. Traffic would be light on a Sunday morning, and if Chloe was ready to split, she'd probably want a ride home anyway.

The drive to Allston was quick, and once I reached Carlton Street, I slowed to a crawl, checking the numbers on the front of each building. The triple-decker at 747 turned out to be the only one on the block that had shingles—salmon-colored ones—instead of wood siding, which meant it had to be the place I was looking for, and miraculously I found a parking spot a few doors down. I slid out of the car and hurried back to the house, which, like every other triple-decker in Boston, resembled a layer cake.

After mounting the steps to the porch, I peered through the glass in the door. It offered a view to a small hall, with a door to the ground-floor apartment and stairs to the top two, so next I leaned over the porch railing and peered inside one of the bay windows as subtly as I could. All the lights were off, and there was no sign of movement.

Though it was ridiculously early, I was going to have to ring the buzzer. I found the one to the first floor and pressed, and even from outside I could hear a shrill ring pierce the quiet of the apartment. She's going to kill me, I thought, if I've interrupted some hot morning sex, but so what. All that mattered to me was seeing her face.

I didn't hear any noise from inside, so I leaned over again, squinting. Still no sign of life. I was just about to press the buzzer again when a back corner of the space flooded with light, as if a lamp had been switched on in an adjoining room. Okay, somebody was definitely home.

A few seconds later a girl with a bright blond ponytail emerged from a doorway at the rear of the living room, wearing what had to be a guy's T-shirt. *Chloe.* She moved toward the front of the house, eventually ducking into the hallway. When I leaned back and looked through the window in the door, I saw her advancing in my direction with a look of irritation on her face.

"What is it?" she called out, seeing me through the window in the door.

My knees went weak as I took in her face. A pretty one, framed by tendrils of blond that had come loose from her ponytail, but it didn't belong to Chloe.

"I'm looking for my sister, Chloe Severson," I said, raising my voice so she could hear me. "Is she here?"

"There's no one with that name living here," the girl said brusquely. "Try upstairs." She started to turn away.

"Wait, were you in Dover on Friday—at a party?" Even as the words came out, I remembered seeing her there, swaying to the music as she talked too loudly, as if in love with the sound of her own voice. And, in that moment I knew from the roiling in my stomach that this was the woman who'd hitched the ride with the couple back to Boston.

"What does that have to do with anything?"

"My sister is missing and might be in danger, and I'm trying to fucking *find* her." I'd raised my voice even louder but didn't care. "Someone told me she was dropped off here on Friday night, by a couple from the party. That she borrowed a phone because hers was broken."

The girl scrunched her face, now looking more concerned than irritated, and finally opened the door. "Some couple gave *me* a ride here from the party, and I borrowed one of their phones to call the guy who lives here. But there was no one else in the car."

Whatever came out of my mouth next was nothing more than a guttural response, not even actual words, and I staggered down the steps. As soon as I reached my car, I dry heaved once, before the contents of my stomach came hurling out onto the grass between the curb and the sidewalk.

I slowly stood up straight and wiped my mouth on the sleeve of my sweater.

If Chloe hadn't left the party when Ryan thought she did, if she hadn't been driven back to Boston and dropped off for a booty call, and if she hadn't sloshed beer on her phone, disabling it, then I had no idea where she was . . . and why she was unable to call or text me. Which meant that something very, very bad must have happened to her. I was going to have to call my mother—and the police, too.

14

Now

B Y NINE THE NEXT MORNING, THERE'S A LOCKSMITH STANDING in my apartment, a fiftysomething fireplug of a guy named Buddy, who confirms that yes, my lock was tampered with, probably with some kind of lock-picking tool because he can see the tool marks on the cylinder. What chills me even more: According to Buddy, this doesn't look like "your typical break-in." In walk-up buildings like this one, he says, burglars tend to hack off the lock or use a pry bar to bend the door away from the frame.

Tuna, I notice, has bolted for the bedroom. It seems like she's definitely got a thing about men she doesn't know, and that's what sent her into hiding last night.

"*Please*," I implore Buddy. "I need to make sure this never happens again."

"Okay, understood," he tells me. "But you're gonna need to upgrade."

He recommends a special maximum security dead bolt, which to my horror, is going to cost 295 dollars plus labor, but Buddy assures me it will offer the best protection. I agree to the price because I don't really have a choice if I ever want to sleep through the night again. And maybe I can harangue the building management company into paying for it, claiming that the original one wasn't adequate. Once Buddy has installed it and taken off, I turn the dead bolt back and forth a few times, trying to feel comforted by the heavy click, but it doesn't do enough to calm my nerves.

I have too much on my to-do list today—and too many issues to contend with—so I fight off the urge to curl up in a ball on the couch and instead make myself a cup of tea. After taking a few deep breaths, I place a call to the Dobson Fertility Clinic. Maybe it *will* help to act like the money is already in my bank account. The woman who answers quickly finds me in their system and, after confirming a few pieces of information, offers me their first available exam appointment, which is three weeks down the road.

"Right, yes, that's fine," I say.

She goes on to explain that the exam will include blood work, ultrasound, and a test for hormone regularity, and the doctor and I will also discuss whether I'm a candidate for medication to stimulate my ovaries. Thanks to my previous consultation at Dobson and the additional research I've done, I'm up to speed on what to expect, but I listen politely and thank her when she's finished.

As I hang up, my pulse is racing. Though I've spent the last few months canvassing the internet for anything I can learn about IUI and IVF, reading posts and essays by single moms, and having several consultations with clinics before deciding on Dobson, an exam will be a big next step. It certainly won't commit me to anything, and yet I suddenly feel so much closer to taking this leap.

It both terrifies and thrills me.

Next, I grab a notebook and set about the task I laid out for myself last night—to try to recall everything I can about my brief time with C.J. A few memories have already revealed themselves over the past few days, and I sense that if I sit quietly and prompt my brain, more will materialize. I start by scribbling down reflections about the images I *do* recall. C.J. in the lobby of the hotel where my friend Tess worked, looking dapper as hell. Him in the bar, where we first started talking. The two of us in his hotel room, peeling off each other's clothes.

I sketch a little, too, with colored pencils. His hand around a drink at the bar. The silk curtains in his room. The deep blue of his eyes.

And then suddenly a new image flickers in my mind. C.J. standing in the middle of his hotel room as I prepared to leave. His mood had shifted from the night before, and he suddenly seemed distracted, somber, even. I'd wondered if he was regretting the encounter, that it seemed tawdry to him in the near light of day, or it had been a wife or girlfriend on the phone call he'd taken when I was in the bathroom, and he was now feeling guilty.

I wait for something else, for a memory that will help me understand what's happened this week, but my mind stalls.

I spend the rest of the morning and most of the afternoon finishing the graphic design project I'd begged for an extension on, and the day passes without a peep from Kane. Though he mentioned that I might not hear from him until Wednesday, it annoys me he hasn't reached out today. All I want right now is reassurance about the money—until then, I can't relish the news. I'd be an idiot to do that before I have confirmation from him.

Around four, I end up calling his office. He's not available, I'm told by the receptionist I saw yesterday, but she promises to relay the message.

By dinnertime there's still no word, meaning I surely won't hear from him today. Is this a red flag, a signal that there's an issue with the trust? I thaw a frozen chicken breast in the microwave and, after a quick sauté, plate it with a small salad, but I'm so agitated I barely taste my food. As I'm clearing the table later, I hear someone out in the corridor, mounting the stairs to the next floor, and my whole body tenses. Even with the better lock, I still feel vulnerable. Though it's not even nine o'clock, I pull the table against the door again.

Out of nowhere, I feel a longing for my dad, a man I barely remember, except for the love and kindness he showed me on the weekends I went as a small child to stay with him before he died. How great it would be to call him right now and tell him everything.

THE NEXT MORNING, SHORTLY BEFORE NOON, I LUG A TOTE BAG OF cleaning supplies to my studio. I'm not planning to begin another collage until after the show, but I want to tidy up the space and inventory the materials I have for future pieces. I'm just opening the door when my cell phone rings. It's finally Kane.

"Excuse my delay in returning your call," he tells me, "but I needed to gather some pertinent information for you. Do you have a pen handy?"

"Um, yes, I've got one." I set down my supplies and quickly grab a pen and pad from the countertop.

As I jot down contact info for the trustee, a banker named Ava Wilcox, my hand trembles a little. My god, this really seems to be happening. I haven't been punked or conned, or hallucinated the whole thing.

"Do you have a sense of how long it will take for the money to hit my account?" I ask.

"Ms. Wilcox will have all that for you. And you'll deal with her directly going forward."

"Got it. Well, thank you. Is-Is there anything else I need to be aware of?"

He clears his throat. "Actually, yes, there's one additional matter I need to bring to your attention. It's about Chris's wife, Jane."

My heart skitters at the sound of her name. "I meant to tell you—she was waiting for me in the lobby when I left your office on Monday," I say. "Someone must have told her I'd be there."

He takes a moment to reply, making me wonder again whether Kane was her source. "Yes, Caroline Whaley informed me of that fact, and I'm very sorry about it. We're not certain who passed along the information about our meeting, but we're looking into the matter. Anyway, as I mentioned, she's not happy about the trust, and from what I've learned, she's looking to take some action."

"What *kind* of action?" I say, growing agitated.

Kane sighs. "There's no attorney-client privilege in this scenario, so I'm at liberty to share what I've heard. Again, it's just hearsay, but it looks like she's hired a law firm to contest the transfer of the trust."

How stupid of me to be lulled by Caroline's assurances that Jane wouldn't have a chance. I'd let myself believe she might not even try.

"But what grounds would she have?" I hear pleading in my voice. "That Chris was too sick to know what he was doing? His mother told me that wasn't the case."

"Not that, from what I've heard."

"Then what?"

Silence.

"Hello?"

"Yes, I'm here," he says, his tone even more serious now. "You said you and Chris never communicated after the night you spent together. I can only be of help to you if you're completely candid with me."

"I have been."

"There's no email or text history between the two of you?"

"No, nothing like that." Does Kane think I've been totally bullshitting him? "As I told you, I didn't even know his full name. Why? What difference would it make even if we *had* been in touch?"

Another pause, and this one feels especially ominous.

"There have been some cases lately—perhaps you've seen them in the news—of married men being extorted by women with whom they've had sexual relationships."

"Okay, but what does that have to do with me?"

"My understanding is that Jane is planning to claim that you're an extortionist and that you blackmailed her husband into leaving you all that money."

15

Now

I DON'T BELIEVE IT. BRADLEY KANE HAS JUST FLOATED THE IDEA
that I might be a blackmailer.

"Wait, you can't be serious," I exclaim. "As I've told you repeatedly, I never had any contact with C.J. after that night, and I'm
certainly not an extortionist."

"I'm not saying you are, but from what I've picked up, that's Jane
Whaley's story line. That you pressured Chris to give you money in
exchange for not revealing that he'd had a fling with you, and perhaps specific, even sordid details about your night together. Because
otherwise—and I assure you this isn't *me* speaking—why would he
leave his entire trust to you?"

That's the million-dollar question, isn't it, or should I say the
three-and-a-half-million one, and I don't have an answer for it. But
I certainly know it has nothing to do with me threatening to expose
our encounter.

"Thank you for letting me know," I tell Kane feebly. My heart's
racing hard now. "So—how do you think I should protect myself?"

"My advice, Ms. Moore, is to retain a lawyer, and I'd suggest someone in trust and estates who also is a litigator. I'm afraid I need to jump on a conference call at this moment. Let me know if you have any problems reaching Ms. Wilcox."

"Okay," I say, and he wishes me a good day, which almost makes me laugh out loud.

I toss the phone on my worktable, and pace the small studio, raking my hands through my hair. Jane Whaley told me I hadn't heard the last of her, but this is worse than anything I imagined. She's accusing me of committing a crime. What if this becomes public?

Kane mentioned recent cases of women extorting money, so I grab my phone again and start googling. Right away I find four or five links to a fairly recent story about a struggling actress who reportedly slept with several married Hollywood executives in exchange for help lining up auditions, but after she ended up with only a few bit parts, she texted each of the men hinting that there would be consequences—and those texts were eventually leaked. The resulting fallout: her career never went anywhere to speak of and the men all lost their jobs.

As I click through different links, I discover variations on the theme, including stories about men who engaged in online sexual activity with strangers who then threatened to send revealing videos to their romantic partners if they didn't pay up. The FBI even uses a specific word for this type of blackmail: *sextortion*.

God, wouldn't my mother love to see my name in the papers as a "sextortionist."

I have to hire a lawyer, I know. But I don't have a clue where I'd find one with the expertise Kane's suggesting, and whom I can afford right now.

My stepfather, David Severson, is a midlevel insurance executive in Hartford, and from what I recall, one of his pickleball buddies is a lawyer. Maybe that guy could recommend someone in New York.

But I dismiss that thought a second after it surfaces. Though David has always been kind to me, even after what happened to Chloe, engaging him would mean my mother would have to be in the loop about the inheritance, and I have no intention of telling her about it, at least right now.

Perhaps I should have asked Kane for a recommendation. It might even be good to have an attorney from Scarsdale representing me. But I'm not sure whether or not I can trust him after what happened with Jane Whaley.

I suddenly think of Mikoto. She mentioned she's a second-year law student, and though I certainly don't want to be beholden to her, she might at least be able to give me some names. I shoot her a brief text, asking if I can steal five minutes of her time.

And before doing anything else, I call Ava Wilcox, because it seems smart not to wait another second on that front. Isn't possession supposed to be nine-tenths of the law or something? It might help if I can secure the trust sooner rather than later.

She answers the phone herself, sounding possibly middle-aged and very no-nonsense. I start to tell her who I am, but she cuts me off. "Yes, how do you do," she says. "Mr. Kane mentioned you'd probably be getting in touch today."

"Thanks for taking my call. I was hoping that you could tell me what comes next. Is there something I'm supposed to do?"

"Yes, there's paperwork that has to be filled out on your end. If you provide me with your email address, I can have my office send it to you—though it might be at least a few days."

Her tone is on the cool side, and I wonder if that's simply her being a banker or if she's privy to the details of Jane's theory and has already passed judgment on me.

"And once I complete the paperwork, how long before I can expect the—the assets to be transferred to me?"

She clears her throat, and I swear she's tempted to say, *Not so fast, sweetheart.*

"That's going to take some time," she tells me instead. "First, we need to determine that the trust was properly exercised. We also need to receive releases from Mr. Whaley's descendants, since they are potential beneficiaries. It's critical to make sure that no one has plans to contest this."

The word *contest* makes my stomach clutch. I briefly wonder if I should tell her what's going on with Jane Whaley, but I decide not to put any ideas in her head.

"All right," I say, sounding far meeker that I'd like. "I'll wait to hear from you."

I smother a wail as I disconnect. The money is seeming more and more out of reach. I *have* to get a lawyer.

Feeling claustrophobic inside the studio, I'm tempted at that moment to lock up and leave. But my only options are to wander the East Village or sit at home and watch Tuna lick her way to a fresh fur ball, and neither will quell my unease. Better to stick with my original plan to clean. The physical activity might help me burn off some of my anxiety.

After wresting open both windows to let in fresh air, I start rounding up various art supplies—paint brushes, scissors, craft knives, and glue sticks—that I'd left scattered on every surface while finishing the last collage. Some go in plastic storage boxes, others into the couple of antique coffee cans I keep on the counter. Once I've finished tidying, I wash the worktable and counter with a sponge, Windex the windows, then clean the floor as best I can with wet paper towels.

Though the studio has a shabbiness that elbow grease can't fix, it's a relief to see it clean, to have turned down the volume of visual noise for when I start on my next piece. I fill the electric kettle on the counter and make a cup of tea, then I grab the plastic bin where

I store items I've collected for my collages. It's time to go through and curate.

There are some intriguing items in there, including a few that might work for my next project. Though my idea's still rough, I think I want to do a series about destinations I've dreamed of traveling to but so far haven't had much hope of seeing, and I want to make them even more exotic than the real thing, let my imagination completely off the leash. I grab a notebook and start sketching, playing with a few ideas.

I end up lost in my task, and when I finally check the time, I see that it's nearly six o'clock and I should head out. Mikoto still hasn't responded to my text, I see.

I store the items that might work for the next collage in a separate plastic box, return everything else to the storage bin, and pack up my cleaning supplies. Before departing, I make a run to the ladies' room down the hall, one of my least favorite places on the planet. With its grimy white subway tiles, ancient fixtures, and rusted sinks, it could get freelance work as a set for a film about a 1950s insane asylum. Per usual, there are no paper towels and I end up drying my hands on the sides of my jeans.

Returning to my studio, I spot my neighbor Alejandro squatting in front of the door of his studio, rifling through a messenger bag as if he's lost his keys. He glances up as he hears me coming.

"Hey, Skyler," he says, smiling. He's in his midforties, I've guessed, with short curly black hair and craggy but appealing features.

"Hi . . . Is everything okay?" I ask.

"Yeah, I was just making sure I packed my phone." He pats the outside of his bag. "By the way, a guy was looking for you a few minutes ago, trying your door."

My heart does a funny skip. No one ever stops by to see me unannounced. In fact, no one ever stops by to see me, period.

"That's really weird."

Alejandro rises to stand. "He said he was with your gallery," he adds. "My age, white, dark brown hair?"

I let out my breath. It sounds like it had to have been Josh, paying me an impromptu visit for a reason I can't imagine.

"Oh, okay."

"Maybe you can catch him," he continues. "He asked for the men's room, and I told him it was on seven."

"Right, thanks for letting me know."

"No problem. Have a nice night, Skyler." As Alejandro strides toward the elevator, I make a beeline toward the end of the hall, hoping I can catch Josh. As I reach the stairwell door, I feel a weird little flutter. Has he dropped by as a friendly gesture, curious to see my studio, or is it more than that? He's always been so attentive the few occasions I've met him, and for the first time I wonder if he might even be interested in me romantically, though the chances of that seem infinitesimal.

But then my thoughts veer in another direction. What if he really hated the new collage and wanted to break the news to me in person?

The stairwell is as dank and smelly as I remember from the one other time I used it, and I hold my breath as I hurry down the stairs and shove open the door to the seventh floor. It's completely silent. I guess many of the tenants on this floor don't hang around after six o'clock either.

I cover the length of the corridor and turn left onto a shorter one, at the end of which is the men's room, right below the ladies' one flight up. I pause a few yards away, so if Josh emerges, it won't feel like I'm intruding on his privacy. Maybe he's already left, I think, but the silence is suddenly broken by the sound of running water from inside the bathroom. A couple of seconds later, pipes clang forlornly and then stop. So does the running water.

I wait. A minute. Two minutes. It's going to be embarrassing, I realize, when he emerges and discovers I've been lurking out here the whole time. I probably should have stayed upstairs and phoned him from my studio. I back up a few feet and call out his name, so that he'll assume I came downstairs only seconds ago.

Another minute passes, and then another, and no one exits the bathroom. I've clearly missed Josh, meaning the sounds must have been emanating from the bathroom on the floor above or below. Or some guy *is* in the bathroom but isn't coming out for some reason.

The whole thing is starting to make me uneasy, and I take off back to the stairwell entrance, then mount the steps two at a time. Once I'm inside the studio, I snatch my phone off the counter and tap Josh's number.

"Ah, there you are," he says over the sound of traffic, indicating he's on the street already.

"Sorry, I must have just missed you," I say. "I looked for you on the other floor, but you were already gone."

"Wait, I'm not following, Skyler."

"My studio neighbor told me you dropped by, so I went to look for you."

"Hmm. I tried your cell a minute ago, but I didn't come by the studio. It must have been someone else."

16

Now

WITH THE PHONE STILL PRESSED TO MY EAR, I STEP TOWARD the studio door and quickly turn the lock so that the dead bolt's in position. If it wasn't Josh, then who was at my door?

"Could it have been someone else from the gallery?" I ask. "My neighbor said the guy told him he worked there. He was in his early forties, brown hair."

"I think your neighbor must have misunderstood," Josh says. "I'm the only one at the gallery who fits that description, and I wasn't there today. Anyway," he adds, "the reason I called you is that I've got great news. A reporter from *ArtToday* is doing a feature on contemporary collage artists, and he wants to talk to you."

"Oh, wow, that *is* good news," I say, smiling. This will be the first time I've had any public recognition for my artwork—and though *ArtToday* is online only, I know it's widely read.

"Do you have time this week for an interview?"

"Definitely. I'm wide open."

"Great. His name is . . . wait, where did I put it? . . . oh, James

Tremlin. I'll give him your phone number and have him reach out directly. He can't make the opening, he said, but he's going to drop by the gallery later in the week."

"Thanks so much, Josh."

"More to come. See you Tuesday."

I let the good news wash over me for a second, but as soon as I'm off the phone, my thoughts fly back to the mystery visitor. Who do I know who would just drop by on the spur of the moment? My life might not be boiling over with friends, but I'm on pleasant enough terms with a few of the people who assign me design work, even if it's mostly by email and Zoom. There's a guy named Trevor, for instance, who regularly gives me jobs and has suggested that we grab a drink together—just in a friendly way, I think. He knows the studio address because he had to messenger me something here once. But he never would have said he worked at the gallery or anything vaguely similar that Alejandro could have misinterpreted.

I suddenly recall the way Alejandro worded it: the guy wasn't knocking on my door, he was *trying* it. Even if it was a person I know professionally, I can't imagine him feeling comfortable coming in without permission. Whoever this was must have been caught off guard when Alejandro emerged from his studio and then made up a lie to explain his presence and another to get out of there quickly.

Not bothering with the cleaning supplies, I nervously grab my jacket from the hook by the door, stuff my arms into the sleeves, and slip the strap of my messenger bag over my head. After twisting the dead bolt, I ease the door open and peek out, but there's no one in sight. I open the door all the way and stick my head out into the corridor, which still appears empty. I quickly lock the door behind me, and then dash to the elevator. The wait for the car is interminable, and I jab the call button four or five times even though I know that won't make it come any faster. I don't exhale until I'm finally downstairs, pushing open the door to Second Avenue.

For a minute I stand on the crowded sidewalk, breathing in the crisp evening air and glancing all around me. Though many of the people around me are hurrying down the block, others are milling outside nearby buildings, and I let my gaze bounce from one person to the next. There's no one who stands out to me, especially fitting the description I've been given.

As I start for home, I wonder again if Alejandro misunderstood the man somehow. Maybe he hadn't mentioned the gallery. But regardless, why would someone be trying the door?

Oh god, what if the man who attempted to get into my studio is the same person who broke into my apartment? That would mean he's not a random creep but rather someone who's targeting me specifically and knows where both my home and studio are.

Deacon, I think, for the second time. He certainly fits the vague description Alejandro offered. And I realize now that after we'd had coffee near the New Museum on the day we met, he ended up walking me to my studio. Though my name's not on the buzzer, he could have figured out the floor and room number by asking a neighbor who emerged from the building.

So what do I do now? I can hardly call the police and throw him under the bus with so little to go on. Reaching my block, I glance nervously behind me, and as I do, I notice Mikoto striding in my direction.

"Skyler," she calls out. "I thought that might be you." She's wearing an oversized black peacoat over jeans and there's a backpack slung over her shoulder.

"Oh hi," I say, stopping and smiling. It's nice to see her again.

"Sorry I didn't answer your text earlier," she says, catching up with me. "I was going to get back to you after class."

"No worries. I hope I'm not being a nuisance. I just wanted to ask your advice on something."

"Of course. Are you up for a coffee now? We could go to Eighth Street Espresso."

"Sure . . . thanks." I'm certainly in no rush to get back to my apartment.

"Let me drop off my backpack first, though. Do you want to head over first and grab a table?"

"Will do."

I've passed the place a thousand times, but since I make my coffee at home to save money, I've never been inside. It's minimalist in style, with gray metal tables and chairs, but there's a welcoming vibe. Surprisingly, it's only half full, and I have no problem securing a table.

As soon as I'm settled, my mind goes straight back to the guy at my studio door, and so it's a relief when Mikoto arrives. We queue up together for decaf cappuccinos, which I insist on paying for, and when we return to the table, she finally slips out of her coat. She's wearing a burnt orange, boxy sweater with big gold hoop earrings, and her short hair is in that messy, spiky style that makes her look more like a supermodel than a law student. In my ancient flannel shirt, I feel like a schlub.

"How are you doing?" she asks. "I saw the locksmith out in the hall yesterday, so I know you took care of your lock."

"And I've upgraded to a better model."

"Good, you can try to put the whole thing behind you."

"I was hoping to do that," I say, shrugging a shoulder, "but I'm not so sure I can."

I describe what happened less than an hour ago.

"How scary," she says. "And it's also a pretty big coincidence, considering what happened the other night. Are you sure it's not someone you know?"

"That's exactly what I *am* starting to think."

She lifts a single eyebrow. "Does anyone come to mind?"

"Yeah, this guy I went out with a few times recently. I initially dismissed the idea, but now I'm beginning to wonder about him. When I told him I wasn't interested in pursuing things, he called me the *c* word."

"What a dick."

"Yeah. There's a big difference, though, between saying that and breaking and entering. Would he really go that far because I didn't want to go on a fourth date?"

Mikoto takes a sip of her cappuccino and licks the foam off her top lip. "Have you checked out his Instagram?" she says, setting the cup back down.

"You think he's *posting* stuff about me?"

"No, no. But I've always found you can tell a lot about a person from their posts, if you look beneath all the bullshit."

Because so many emerging artists are discovered on Instagram—I mean, that's how Josh first saw me—I had almost no choice but to set up an account, where recently I've posted updates on my work, details about the Meyer Gallery opening, and the occasional selfie of myself in the studio. The only time I scroll through on the app, though, is to check out and "like" something by either another artist or photos Nicky posts of her two rescue dogs.

"Good point," I say. "But I'm not sure that he even has an account."

"What's his name again?"

"Deacon Starr. Starr with two *r*'s."

She digs into her coat pocket and pulls out an oversize smart-phone and, after a couple of taps, starts scrolling. "There are a few people with that name. Red hair?"

"No, brown."

She keeps scrolling. "Young kids?"

"Not that he ever admitted to."

"Big hiker?"

"Yes, major."

"This might be him," she says, turning the phone around so the screen is facing me.

Yup, it is. I nod and use my pointer finger to scroll through his posts, almost all of which feature scenic photos of hiking trails, sometimes with him in the shot, sometimes not. There are no pictures with other people.

"Based on this," I say, returning the phone to Mikoto, "his only obsession seems to be with hiking trails."

She trains her gaze back on the screen, and because of the way her eyes flick back and forth, I can tell she's reading. Her expression suddenly clouds.

"What is it?" I ask her, feeling nervous.

"I'm looking at a post from late August. In between the hashtags #hikeNewHampshire and #hikemoreworryless, there's one that says #whinywomenshouldstayoffmountains."

I sigh. "He's obviously *proud* to be a dick."

She flicks her thumb down the screen a few times. "And god, his *captions*. 'Treadmills are for amateurs.' 'Don't tell me you can bushwhack. SHOW me.' 'If you haven't got the guts to scramble, don't hike with me.'"

"It's pretty clear he considers himself on a higher plane than people who don't hike," I say.

"But it's more than that," Mikoto says. "There's something vaguely hostile about the tone even if it's a caption about climbing Bear Mountain."

She passes me back the phone, which is open to one of the older posts, and it doesn't take long to see what she means. I end up back at the top, staring at the most recent photo, posted a week ago. The image features a trail almost overrun by tangled brush, with dark woods looming ahead. As I read the caption, my breath catches in my chest.

When the trail resists, refuse to take no for an answer.

17

Now

"OH WOW," I SAY, SWALLOWING HARD. "CHECK OUT *THIS* ONE."

She takes the phone from me, digests the caption, and shakes her head. "If he doesn't take no for an answer out in nature, where else is that word a problem for him? When you get home, why don't you do an internet search and see if anything turns up. If he's stalked other women, he might have even been arrested."

"Right," I say, already anxious about what I might find and kicking myself for not doing a thorough search when he first asked me to dinner. "Thanks for all your wisdom on this."

"I'm glad I could help a little," she says, and I realize she thinks this is the subject I wanted her advice on.

"Do you mind if I actually ask you something else, though?"

"Sure, go right ahead."

For a brief moment, I find myself hesitating. *Am I really going to share something so private with a near stranger?* I'm not in the habit of unloading stuff on other people, not even Nicky. And it feels like such an imposition, especially after all the advice Mikoto has given me in the two days I've known her. But I need to protect the money

and that means I need a lawyer, and she's the only person I can think
of who might have leads.

I give Mikoto the broad strokes: a guy named C.J. who I had a
one-night stand with over a decade ago has died and left me money
(I call it a "significant" amount rather than share the exact figure);
his wife is furious and is apparently going to claim I'm an extortionist; it's been suggested I consult with a lawyer, but I have no idea
where to find one.

"Wow," she says once I'm finished. "My life is starting to look
like twenty-four-hour C-SPAN compared to yours."

"Well, until last week, *my* life made C-SPAN look like a Jason
Bourne movie."

She laughs, then her expression turns serious. "When you say
you didn't speak to the guy again after that night, you mean *never*?
Not even one more time?"

"Right, never. No phone calls, emails, texts, anything. We didn't
even exchange contact info."

She nods softly, clearly accepting my answer at face value, which
is refreshing after Kane's dubious reaction.

"And he didn't leave any kind of letter with the estate lawyer
explaining his reason for making you the beneficiary?"

"No, nothing like that. And the lawyer claims to be in the dark
about the reason."

She cocks her head, clearly weighing what to say next.

"Here's my take—and keep in my mind I'm not an attorney yet,
okay?" she says, and I nod, eager for her to continue. "If you didn't
have any further contact with him, it's going to be impossible for his
wife to prove extortion. And that theory doesn't even make sense
anyway. If you were extorting him about a brief moment of infidelity, why would you accept terms that didn't give you the money until
he was dead?"

She's right. If I'd been desperate to get my hands on the cash, I would hardly have settled for a payday at some undetermined date in the future. I would have demanded it *immediately*. I feel a tiny swell of relief—until Mikoto flips her palms up, in a way that suggests she's about to deliver an "on the other hand" kind of comment.

"Of course, the wife might use other grounds to contest the gift, or she might try to hold it up in probate just for spite."

I prop my elbows on the table and let my face sink into my hands. "Oh god."

"A good estate lawyer will know more. The firm where I did my internship last summer doesn't have an estate practice, but my uncle's a lawyer here in the city, and he might have some names. I can give him a call."

"You wouldn't mind?"

"Not at all."

"Thank you," I say, incredibly grateful. "Thank you so much."

As she takes another sip of her coffee, her expression is pensive, and I sense she's still mulling over what I've told her.

"One more question," she says. "Do you have any idea yourself why this guy left you the money?"

I shake my head. "None. Zero. I've been racking my brain trying to figure it out, but I'm drawing a blank so far. My only guess is that it was a spur-of-the-moment thing after he found out he was dying. Maybe he'd always felt oddly nostalgic about our night together or it had happened during a difficult period in his life and for some reason that helped him get through it."

"And then when he found out he had only months to live, he decided to do something generous for you in return?"

"Right. Or maybe he just wanted to do one wild and crazy thing before he died."

Mikoto looks off briefly, pursing her lips together and then returns her gaze to me. I love how she manages to always seem engaged, concerned even, but at the same time unflappable. "Like I said before, I'm not qualified to give any legal advice yet, but if I were you, there's one step I'd take even before meeting with an attorney."

"Okay."

"You *have* to get to the bottom of why he made the bequest to you. One of the things they drive home in law school is the importance of understanding all the facts, and you need to do that now. Maybe the guy *was* nostalgic, or feeling a little reckless after his diagnosis, but are either of those really a reason to leave a chunk of money to someone you met only once in your life?"

Her tone has turned serious, and something about it scares me, like this is the scene in the movie where the female lead finds out a family of five was once murdered in the house she's just purchased or that patients from the hospital where she works are being put into comas so their organs can be harvested for transplant.

"Do you think that something weird is going on—or even illegal?"

"Illegal? You mean it's some of kind of hush money or something? No, it doesn't line up at all with the facts you have. But there's a reason he did what he did, and you have to do more than guess at it. Both for your peace of mind and to protect yourself legally."

I nod, grasping the soundness of her advice. Though I've been focused on the same question, I've been driven mostly by curiosity and a sense that if I can figure it out, this will all be easier to come to terms with. What Mikoto's saying, though, is that I *need* to know the answer. By uncovering C.J.'s motivation, it will help me defend myself if Jane Whaley attacks my credibility and reputation.

"You're right," I say. "I'm not sure how to go about it, but I'll try. Thank you, Mikoto."

"Any time, really." She drains the last of her cappuccino and smiles. "Let's do this again, okay?"

"Sure." An idea suddenly bubbles up in my mind. "By the way, an exhibit I'm in is opening at a gallery down on the Lower East Side next week. Can I text you the invite?"

She smiles. "I'd love that, Skyler."

I quickly finish my own beverage, though I was so caught up in sharing my plight, I don't recall taking a single sip. I assume Mikoto and I will walk back to our building together, but she announces she needs to swing by a shop she hopes is still open. Outside the café, I thank her again and watch as she dashes farther east on Eighth. Is she happy to be rid of me? I wonder, but then I reassure myself that she did seem genuine in her friendliness and willingness to help.

My agitation level creeps up again as I walk home. I think Mikoto's suggestion is a good one, but where do I even begin? This isn't a job for a Google search, and though I've got an inkling that Bradley Kane knows more than he let on, if he wasn't forthcoming that day in Scarsdale, why would he come clean now?

There's someone, however, who *might* be willing to share more: Caroline Whaley. Though she claimed to be clueless, there's a chance she was only being discreet and might be more revealing if urged. She'd given me her contact information, after all. I don't like the idea of calling her, but right now it's the only option I can think of.

As I'm closing in on my building, I check behind me a couple times to be certain there's no one following me. Once I'm through the vestibule, I bolt up the stairs, unlock my door as quickly as possible, and with a meowing Tuna trailing behind me, survey the apartment to check that no one's been inside again.

Finally reassured, I exhale, fish out the card Caroline Whaley gave me, and make the call. She answers on the third ring, a vague question in her "hello." She wouldn't have recognized my number, after all. I quickly identify myself and apologize for the interruption.

"That's not a problem," she says, her voice husky but her tone friendly. "I'm planning to sit down to dinner soon, but I have a few minutes now."

I relax a little. "I was hoping to ask you a question—if you feel up to it."

"If I feel up to it? I've lost one son to cancer, and the other has flown back to his home five thousand miles from here, so I don't feel up to very much these days. But I meant it when I told you I would be happy to be of assistance. Tell me how I can help."

I decide to get straight to the point but be careful how I phrase it. "I'm having difficulty understanding why Chris left the trust to me, and though he didn't share the reason with you, I thought you might be able to make a guess, or perhaps something occurred to you since we spoke,"

A short pause follows; I sense the question isn't one she was expecting.

"Not beyond what I said the other day, that you must have meant something to him—and he decided to express his gratitude."

"Uh, it's a lovely thought, but I'm not sure how much I could have meant to him when we knew each other so briefly."

She chuckles lightly. "I take it you don't want to accept this as one of life's wonderful, poetic mysteries that can't be understood."

"Maybe in time, I could. But I heard Jane is going to fight me for the money, and a friend with legal expertise said that I need to figure out Chris's reason for making me the beneficiary, so I have all the facts on my side."

"Ah, I see. Those sound like the words of a lawyer—as opposed to a poet."

"Please, is there anything at all you can tell me?"

Another pause, this one longer. Through my fourth-floor window I hear the wail of a siren, an ambulance or fire truck racing up First Avenue. Tuna lifts her head, curious.

"There *is* one additional thing I can tell you," Caroline says. "Something that might be worthwhile to share with a lawyer."

My stomach tightens as I wait for her to go on. It's so quiet on the other end that I check the screen to see if we're still connected.

"Chris and I weren't as close as I would have liked, as I mentioned last week," she finally says. "But I was privy to certain information about his life, and there's one development that I'm pretty sure played a large role in his decision. I should warn you, though. You're not going to like it."

18

Then

I DUG A CRUMPLED TISSUE FROM THE POCKET OF MY JEANS AND, still bent at the waist, wiped the rest of the vomit from my mouth. I pressed my other hard against the hood of my car to steady myself. It felt as if a sinkhole had opened beneath me, threatening to suck me into it.

I finally righted myself, and after wrenching open the door, I collapsed into the driver's seat. For a brief and crazy moment, I was overwhelmed with the urge to take off down the city street at eighty miles an hour, imagining that if I drove fast enough, I could leave the entire nightmare behind me.

Instead, I forced myself to breathe and tried to corral my frantic thoughts. As urgently as I needed to call my mother and stepfather and inform them of this new, terrifying development, I felt I should track down Jamie first. So much of what I'd believed to be true about Friday night was clearly wrong, and I needed to know exactly how wrong.

But Jamie didn't answer when I called her. Of course, it wasn't even eight o'clock and she was probably still asleep. I hung up and tried her number again, and again, and again, knowing that the more I called, the more likely she was to be roused by the ringtone. My heart was beating out of my chest, and I could feel rage building inside of me. I was livid at Jamie, I realized—for throwing that fucking party and letting it get so out of control that you couldn't find the person you came with or tell what was going on in that mammoth house. And I was livid, too, with her idiot friend Ryan, who swore he'd seen Chloe leave and cost me valuable time.

Finally on the fifth try, Jamie answered, muttering a groggy, muffled hello.

"Where are you?" I demanded, my voice shaking.

"What?"

"Jamie, it's Skyler. Are you back in Boston now?"

"Uh uh, I'm still at my parents' place. Why?"

"That guy Ryan was wrong. The girl he saw leaving wasn't my sister, and now I can't find her. Anywhere."

There were rustling noises on the other end, as if Jamie was throwing off her covers and sitting up. "Wait—you haven't seen her since the party?" she said, suddenly sounding more alert.

"*No.* The last time I set eyes on her was at your house, and no one I know has seen or spoken to her since."

"Oh god. What are you going to do?"

"I need to come back there. Is there anyone around I can talk to, anyone who was at the party and might have noticed what she was up to?"

"My brother's still here, too, helping with cleanup, so you could ask him, I guess. And you should talk to our friends from BU who came. They might have seen her."

"Why don't I start with your brother. Can you make sure he'll be up when I get there?"

"You're coming *now*?"

I was throwing any pretense at politeness out the window. "Yes, I'm coming now. I'll see you in half an hour."

I couldn't put off the call to my mother any longer, though the thought of breaking the news to her left me trying not to retch again. My hand shook as I tapped her name. I knew I probably wouldn't be waking her at this hour, but she'd go on high alert when she saw my name on the screen before noon on a Sunday.

"Hi, Sky," she said, quickly. Her voice sounded the tiniest bit froggy, as if she hadn't spoken yet today. "Is everything okay?"

"I'm not sure, Mom. Have you heard from Chloe this weekend?"

"No, we were going to talk later today. Why, what's the matter?"

Trying to keep my voice even, I blurted out a recap of events, ending with my discovery at the Carton Street house. There was a moment of silence and I suddenly wondered if my mother, the cool, collected optometrist, was going tell me that I was overreacting, that this was just "Chloe being Chloe," because no one knew my sister better than my mom did.

But that's not what happened.

"Good god," she exclaimed and then began firing questions at me: How many times had I called Chloe, had I texted her, too, had I spoken to her roommate, had anyone tried her friends, did I think she could be with her ex-boyfriend? Needless to say, none of my answers—a zillion, yes, yes, yes, not likely—were the least bit reassuring.

"But, Mom, I wouldn't worry too much yet," I said, trying to project a confidence I didn't feel. "Chloe isn't always good about checking in, and maybe she did get a ride back to the city with someone, just not that particular couple. And you know how bad she can be about her phone."

I sounded ridiculous, of course, like I was trying to make a case for the existence of leprechauns or the Easter bunny.

"If she had a problem with her phone," my mother snapped,

"she would have borrowed someone's and sent me a text, knowing I might be trying to reach her."

That made sense, of course. I started to explain what my plan was, but she yelled for David, and I heard snippets of her frantically relating the situation to him.

The next thing I knew, my stepfather was on the line.

"When was the last time you actually saw or spoke to Chloe?" he demanded. I could pick up the fear pulsing through him in his voice.

"Friday night."

He blew out a gust of air.

"And this couple you just went to see—are you sure she's not with them and they're telling you otherwise?"

"No, I'm sure. The girl I just spoke to looks a lot like Chloe, and it's clear the guy who sent me here made a mistake. But I'm going to drive to Dover right now, back to the house where the party was, and see what I can find out from my friend Jamie."

"Okay, good." I sensed him working hard to stay in control—because he was a guy who always took the bull by the horns. "Your mother said this is some girl you go to school with. It's her house?"

"No, her parents' place."

"Can you send me their number so I can speak with them?"

"They're out of the country."

"Jesus. Were there drugs involved in this shindig, Skyler?"

"Maybe some weed . . . but I didn't see anything else."

I couldn't be sure whether different stuff might also have been available. *Maybe Molly. And coke, too*, I thought, remembering those hotshot-looking older guys whose arrival shifted the mood and brought an edge to the night.

"Okay, let me know when you get there," he said. "I'm going to call college security and let them know. And . . . I'd better call 911 as well."

My mother let out a wail in the background as he mentioned "911." The situation seemed to be exploding in front of my eyes.

"Even if they say it's too soon to do anything," I said, remembering scenarios from television crime shows, "maybe they can at least check her phone data?"

David asked for the Dover address and Jamie's last name and then muttered a quick goodbye. I felt another surge of nausea threatening to barrel upward, but I managed to fight it off, taking deep ragged breaths. I dug the key fob from my jeans pocket and watched it bounce in my hand as I aimed it toward the slot. I started the car and pulled into the street, gripping the steering wheel as tightly as I could to keep my hands from shaking.

Though traffic had picked up since I'd started out that morning, it was still light, and I made it to Dover in thirty minutes. I parked at the top of the long driveway, which was now empty of cars, and bolted toward the house.

Jamie answered my knock right away. She'd gotten dressed in jeans and a T-shirt, but she looked like shit. Her usually clear skin was blotchy, and though she'd pulled her long raven hair into a top-knot, it didn't disguise how greasy it was.

"Anything yet?" she asked, ushering me into the front hall.

I shook my head. "No, like I told you, no one's seen or heard from Chloe." I noted the peevishness in my tone, and I told myself to shut it down. I needed her on my side right now. "The last time I saw her myself was here, at around ten, and we have to figure out where she went from here."

She nodded, biting her lip. "You think she left with someone? I mean, not the couple Ryan saw but someone else?"

That thought had crossed my mind, but *who*? "Maybe, but why hasn't she contacted me by now?"

"Oh god, you must be freaking out."

I nodded. "I'm trying not to. Do you remember seeing her at all, later on in the evening?"

She shook her head, her expression glum. "No, but maybe Rob did."

As if on cue, a male voice called out, "Yeah, I'm here," and I spotted him over Jamie's shoulder, standing barefoot on the landing of the large oak staircase. He raked a hand through his hair, which was the same dark shade as Jamie's, and took his sweet time descending the last flight. He had on skinny jeans and a dark red T-shirt with MIT stamped on the front in white.

"Did Jamie tell you?" I said, not bothering with any pleasantries. "About my sister?"

"Yeah, she filled me in," he said. "I think I met Chloe when you two first got here, but I don't really remember. There were a lot of people I needed to talk to that night."

Jamie shot him a withering look. "Great, we know you're popular, Rob. But Skyler thinks her sister might have left with someone, and we have to figure out who. Can you call some of the people who—"

"But first," I interrupted. "Since we have no evidence of her ever leaving, I think we need to search the house. It's possible she, like, passed out somewhere drunk and has been there all this time, too sick to even move."

I was trying to stay positive, thinking "too sick to move" instead of anything worse. If my mind went other places, I wouldn't be able to keep going. But even as I said it, I knew a hangover going into the second day was unlikely. I ran my gaze over the walls of the huge hall, as if clues awaited me, and when I glanced back at Jamie and Rob, I saw they were wide-eyed with alarm. This might all blow up in their faces.

"You think she's *here*?" Rob exclaimed. "We'd definitely know if she were. The house is big, but there aren't a ton of rooms."

Oh, come on, your parents have a fucking mansion, I thought, but then I remembered from my wanderings Friday night that, although the rooms were big, there wasn't actually an endless number of them. Still, there were plenty of places to tuck yourself away.

"We just have to look," I insisted. "Every single room."

Because it was seeming more and more possible that she'd never left the premises. *Unless someone had forced her into a car against her will*, I thought, and shuddered.

"Okay," Jamie said. "I've been through most of this floor cleaning, but do you want to see for yourself?"

I told her I did but took a minute to text my stepfather to let him know I was in Dover and about to search the house.

The three of us began a circular loop—moving through the living room, library, and dining room, all of which appeared clean and empty. I know it probably looked absurd to Jamie and Rob, but I peeked behind curtains and couches, too.

The kitchen was next, and it was still a major pigsty. In the center of the space sat a jumbo-sized gray trash can overflowing with garbage, and the granite countertops were littered with red plastic party cups, empty bottles, and wet tortilla chips. Despite the mess, it was easy to see Chloe hadn't passed out in one of the corners, somehow unnoticed until now. The adjoining breakfast/family room was also in need of a cleaning but didn't harbor any sign of Chloe.

"There's one more place to check downstairs," Jamie said. "The morning room."

We circled back to the living room, and then traveled down a short passageway to a small, pretty space whose two large windows overlooked the backyard. It was so removed from the rest of the house, I suspected that no one from the party had even ventured in here—I certainly hadn't.

As the three of us turned in unison to leave, something outside caught my eye.

"Wait," I called out. Past the border garden that lay just beyond the window, I could see the edge of the flagstone patio and one end of the swimming pool.

A terrifying image exploded in my mind. What if Chloe had gone out to the pool Friday night, had fallen in when no one was looking, and been too drunk to save herself?

19

Now

I'D BEEN STANDING IN THE MIDDLE OF MY LIVING ROOM WHEN I called Caroline Whaley, so anxious I couldn't sit down, but now I take a couple of steps backward and lower myself onto the couch.

"I can handle it," I say. "I-I just need to know."

"The one thing I insist is that you never reveal where this information came from," she says, her tone authoritative. It's not hard for me to imagine her running her own successful company. "Do I have your word?"

"Yes, you have my word."

She clears her throat. "Shortly before his diagnosis, Chris learned that Jane was having an affair with a very close friend of his. He confronted her, and she apparently called it off, but he felt horribly betrayed—not just by her infidelity but the fact that she'd chosen one of his oldest friends. Transferring the trust to you, I believe, was his way of delivering the reproach he felt his wife deserved."

Wow, pretty vindictive, especially for a man who hadn't seemed to think twice about hooking up with a grad student in Boston.

"If he was that angry, why did he stay married to her?" I ask.

"It's a good question. At first he did plan to divorce Jane, but once he received his death sentence, he changed his mind. His kids were devastated about the prospect of losing him, and he didn't want to make things any worse for them, especially during their last year of college. As far as Jane knew, he was trying to patch things up in their marriage, but that was never the case."

"So giving me the trust was his way of telling her that she hadn't been forgiven after all, huh?"

"Exactly. I know this makes Chris seem very bitter and vengeful, but consider what it would be like to live in that kind of marriage during the last months of your life."

I feel a sudden prick of sadness. What a dark, ugly family drama I've found myself swept up in. "I should let you go," I say. "Thank you for sharing this with me."

"I hope it wasn't too upsetting for you. It doesn't change the fact that you must have meant something to Chris. But other motives were driving his decision."

"Understood. Thanks again."

We sign off and I flop back against the couch, letting Caroline's revelation not only sink in but also shed light on everything I thought I knew—both about C.J.'s motives and the kind of man he was. It was clear to me as I sat in Kane's conference room that the assignment of the trust would be an affront to his wife, that she would be upset if she found out he'd left it to me, but I never guessed that was the whole point.

By this time, I'd almost convinced myself that I *had* meant something to him, but it's clear I was simply a means to an end. While he was dreaming up just deserts for his wife, a memory of me must have surfaced—perhaps because he was considering the enormity of her transgression compared to his one-night stand—and he decided to incorporate me into his plan. It's certainly not on a level with revenge porn, but it must be stinging for his Jane nonetheless.

The whole thing makes me feel nauseated—and sullied, too, like I've agreed to participate in a cruel practical joke on someone I don't know.

And what does this say about Christopher Whaley? He was certainly justified in his anger about his wife's transgression, but he'd strayed as well. And if the news about the trust leaked out, Jane could end up humiliated in their community. If C.J. was intent on sending her a fuck-you message, he could have easily left the money to a charity instead.

It's hard to reconcile his action—a middle finger from beyond the grave—with the seemingly nice guy I met in Boston.

I close my eyes, trying to send the world away. I feel a soft plop and sense a presence on the couch with me, a purring Tuna now by my side. I hear her start licking her fur in slow, even strokes. God, I wish I could be her right now—relaxed and content, not a care in the world.

But at least I finally have the answer.

"You ready to eat?" I ask Tuna, and she lets out a little meow in assent.

After pushing myself up off the couch, I fill her bowl and then peruse the cupboards and fridge for something to serve myself. Both are nearly empty, so I end up mixing a can of tuna fish with cannellini beans and tossing them with olive oil and vinegar. I take the bowl to my desk along with a piece of toast and a Diet Coke and boot up my computer. As if this business with the trust wasn't enough, I'm still unsettled by the break-in at my apartment and the mystery man at my studio, and I need to follow through on another of Mikoto's suggestions: that I investigate Deacon Starr.

An initial Google search of his name turns up his Instagram account, of course, as well as his professional website, which at least I'd checked out after our coffee date, and his LinkedIn account, which I *hadn't* bothered to skim beforehand. Though I don't expect to learn much from LinkedIn, I check out his page, anyway, first making certain that I've clicked the "anonymous search" setting—because the last thing I need is for Deacon Starr to realize *I'm* stalking *him*.

There's a friendly looking headshot of him in front of the background banner image, which, not surprisingly, features a hiking trail. The short bio mentions a couple of companies he worked for before going out on his own as a web designer, and he's included several testimonials from recent clients. During one of our two dinners, he'd claimed he had to turn away assignments left and right, that clients said his work was totally cutting-edge, but the most glowing terms used about him in the references are "professional," "timely," and "reliable." My only takeaway: if nothing else, he's a bullshit artist.

Next, I make a stab at finding out if he has an arrest record. I'm hardly a pro at Google searches, but I wade through the links offering free people searches and end up going down the rabbit hole on a few. Each insists they've found lots of info on a Deacon Starr, but indicate they need my email address before they can send it, and I don't want to provide that. Finally I find a legit-seeming site that lets me search for arrest records state by state, and if I'm to believe what they tell me, Deacon's never been accused or convicted of a crime in New York, New Jersey, Pennsylvania, Connecticut, or Massachusetts.

That doesn't mean he hasn't stalked women, though. He just might not have been caught. One way or the other, I'm going to feel uneasy in this apartment until I know who was inside here and at my studio door.

When I return to the kitchen to make a cup of herbal tea, I notice that my phone screen has blown up with texts. One is from a number I don't know, but it turns out to be James Tremlin, who's doing the piece about collage artists. He wonders if I'm free to meet tomorrow at either four or five and suggests a place called Hudson Clearwater on the far edge of the West Village. I tell him

that five works for me, and that the location is fine, and I've barely
hit send when he writes back to say he's got light brown hair and
he'll be wearing a dark leather jacket.

One of the other texts filling my screen is from Mikoto:

> My uncle will have some names for you by tomorrow. Talk
> to you then.

Thanks so much, I write back, amazed by how generous she's
been.

I briefly consider adding that I discovered the reason behind
C.J.'s actions but decide she's probably had enough of my drama for
one day.

I glance at the final message and my heart skips. It's from my
mother, who almost never texts me.

> David and I are concerned about parking Tuesday night.
> Do you have any suggestions?

I roll my eyes inwardly at how she can barely contain her excitement about the opening. But I immediately regret my annoyance, telling myself that she's right, parking can be a bitch in New
York, especially downtown. I text her back, promising to email her
a bunch of options.

I return to my desk, google parking garages close to the Meyer
Gallery's East Village location, and forward the links to her in an
email, but then, on the spur of the moment, I do something that
surprises me. I pick up the phone and call her. It's been a couple of
weeks since we last spoke and I'm hungry for the sound of her voice,
even though I know from experience that I won't get off the call
feeling sated.

"Hi," she says. She almost never says my name anymore, though

I'm not sure if this particular behavior started immediately after everything that happened with Chloe, and I didn't notice, or it's been a more recent development. "I guess you got my text?"

"Right, and I just emailed you some suggestions."

"Good, thank you. I'll pass them on to David."

It's easy to picture her on the other end of the line, probably sitting on one of the white wooden kitchen stools. She's tall like me and very slim, a by-product of speed walking around the local high school track three or four times a week, which she's done for years. When I was growing up, I often heard people exclaim how pretty she was, and though her features are mostly the same, you wouldn't use "pretty" to describe her these days. There's a near bottomless-looking crevice between her brows, and her eyes droop, sadly, at the ends. For years she dyed her shoulder-length hair an arresting shade of ash-blond, but she stopped just over a decade ago and let it go gray, and she chopped it much shorter as well.

"I'm so glad you can come," I say. "I guess it means taking a day off from work, right?"

"Just the afternoon. It's not a problem, though. I've got a lot of vacation time stockpiled."

"Well, I really appreciate it, Mom." And I do. "Here's a thought, and I'm not sure why I didn't bring it up earlier, but should the five of us grab a bite after the show? There are a couple of restaurants right near the gallery."

For a few seconds she doesn't respond, and I hold my breath.

"Let me talk to Nicky, okay?" she says finally.

"Sure, of course. It won't be hard to get a reservation at one of these places, so just let me know whenever you can."

"How's the cat?"

"Oh, she's good. She seems to have taken a sudden shine to me. . . . Are you and David ever going to get another pet, do you think?"

"Maybe after we're settled at the town house. We'll see."

The conversation seems so stilted, but I have no clue how to make it better.

"By the way, let me know if you need any help with the move. I could lend a hand with some packing next week, after the show."

"I think it's all under control. In fact, I should go. I've got a potential buyer coming for the snowblower. But I'll see you Tuesday."

"Yup, see you then. Bye-bye."

I set the phone down and drain the last of my Diet Coke. Okay, maybe she's not bursting with excitement about the show, but at least she's coming all the way from West Hartford, and taking off early from work, too.

As much as I've thought about what next Tuesday night could mean for me as an artist, in the back of my mind I've also held on to a vague hope that it could be a turning point in my relationship with my mother. She's aware I've been doing art again, but as far as I know, she thinks I'm only dabbling, engaged in a kind of lark. I'm praying that once she sees my collages hanging at the gallery and hears what Josh says about me in the opening remarks, she'll discover that I'm *not* dabbling, and that I might have a future as an artist.

And maybe that will be the moment she sees I'm not the total screwup she thinks I am. Maybe she'll even put her hand on my shoulder and tell me how proud she is, something she hasn't done in a dozen years.

20

Now

SKIP THE STUDIO THE NEXT MORNING, SOMETHING I PROBABLY would have done, anyway, because the specs came in for my next graphic design job. It's the kind of work I have to do at home on my desktop Mac. But beyond that, the thought of being in the studio freaks me out. What if the mystery guy comes back? It's even more clear to me now that something shady was going on. If the person was an acquaintance paying a surprise visit, and Alejandro had simply misunderstood, why wouldn't he have followed up with a call or text saying he'd been looking for me?

After spending the morning at my computer and then wolfing down a mug of chicken noodle soup, I set out with my tote bag for the Zara on lower Broadway—because I can no longer put off buying an outfit for the gallery opening, as much as I wish I could. I need to look the part, and at the same time I want clothing that will provide armor and help my anxiety from spiking out of control.

But my heart sinks as soon as I enter the store. It's bursting with cropped tops, ruched tops, cutout tops, vest tops, lace tops, and camisole tops, as well as racks of miniskirts and Post-it-size dresses, none of which are what I need. Yeah, they might work on the right woman, but I'd feel totally exposed in a skimpy outfit, and if someone asked me a question, nothing more than a squeak would emerge from my mouth.

Finally, after almost two hours of searching, trying things on, and endlessly kicking my own clothes out of the way on the floor of the dressing room, I settle on a dark green ribbed turtleneck—which I can top with an unconstructed blazer I own—and a camel-colored skirt that hits midcalf. It's not very glamorous or fun, but with chunky boots and the right earrings, I'm hoping it will be okay. And the turtleneck will hide the red splotches that are guaranteed to surge up my chest and neck that night like a toxic red tide. Of course, I'll just have to pray the weather next Tuesday is cooler than it is today, or I'll faint from heat exhaustion.

Though I'd planned to stop off at home after Zara, I've run out of time, and so I head straight to my five o'clock appointment with the *ArtToday* reporter. I walk north and west, arriving outside the café just a few minutes ahead of schedule. I wish I didn't feel nervous, but I do. This is the only validation I've had in years that I'm actually an artist—besides Josh inviting me to be part of the show, of course. And I need to sound like one. I tell myself to do my best to be authentic and not put on any artsy-fartsy pretentious airs, not that I have any.

Entering the café, I glance around for a nerdy freelancer type, though I assume I'm the first to arrive. I don't see anyone who looks like it could be James Tremlin on the ground floor, so I take a short set of wooden stairs to the second level, and as I reach the top step, a guy at a rear table, probably in his early to midforties, lifts his hand in a tentative wave. He's wearing a black leather jacket, as he told me he'd be, so I snake my way through several empty tables toward him. He rises from his chair with a polite half smile, waiting for me to close the gap.

His appearance is a definite surprise. He's nice-looking, with deep blue eyes, a couple days' worth of scruff, and light brown hair that's thinning just a little. Besides the expensive jacket, he's wearing a white dress shirt and a pair of well-cut jeans.

"James Tremlin," he says, offering his hand. For a second I'd wondered—because of both his clothes and his manner—if he might be British or European, but there's no trace of an accent.

"Skyler Moore." I say back, hoping I don't seem as awkward as I feel.

"Thanks for agreeing to meet," he says, waiting for me to take a seat. "What would you like to drink?"

His tone is polite but reserved, telegraphing that he's not interested in chitchat. That's fine with me. When my social anxiety first began to develop, I was able to handle one-on-one and one-on-two situations decently enough, but I'm out of practice, and my comfort level with them has diminished in the past couple of years. The section of my brain that handles small talk feels, for the most part, as vestigial as my appendix.

"A cappuccino would be great."

Effortlessly, he flags the waitress, another skill I'm next to useless at. After ordering two cappuccinos, he reaches into a messenger bag on the floor to fish out a pristine notebook and rollerball pen. He's not wasting a minute.

"As Josh Meyer probably told you, the piece I'm working on will be a roundup," James says, returning his attention to me. "So there's not a lot of space for each artist. But there'll be enough room to cover some key points."

I nod. "Sounds good, and thanks for including me. Just curious, who are the other artists in the story?"

A look of mild disapproval passes over his face. "I'm sorry, but I'm not at liberty to say yet."

How is it possible that I've been here sixty seconds and I've already said something stupid?

"Got it, okay."

He flicks open the notebook to a blank first page and pops the cap off his pen. "What got you interested in collage?" he asks. "And is it a medium you've worked in for a while?"

"Actually, I only started concentrating on collages a few years ago. Early on I worked mostly in oil and acrylics, though I tried a couple of collages here and there. But a while back I saw the big Matisse Cut-Outs exhibit at MOMA, and I fell in love. I couldn't get the idea out of my head, and eventually I began experimenting."

Our coffees arrive, and he takes a small sip of his before moving on.

"Besides Matisse, then, who have been your biggest influences?"

"Good question. I've studied the collages of Picasso and Dubuffet, which I guess everyone does if they're interested in the medium, but I especially admire some of the collage artists who came after them, like Eileen Agar and the German artist Hannah Höch, who did these amazing photo montages in the 1930s. Some of my favorite collages these days, though, are by the Kenyan artist Wangechi Mutu. Her work is just so bold and imaginative. I'd love to have my pieces awe people the same way."

"Interesting," he says as he scribbles in his notebook, though he doesn't look all that impressed with the answer. "Why do you think you like doing collage so much?"

I figured that would be one of his questions, and, over the past day, I've fashioned a response in my mind that sounds halfway decent to me. I have to leave out one big fat detail, though: the fact that when I finally summoned the nerve to make art again, I knew I couldn't return to oil painting, which I loved so much in grad school. I decided I'd have to explore a new medium so that there was no danger of being sucked back into the past.

"Collage feels to me like such a unique creative process, very different from painting," I say. "When I'm making one, it's like I'm in the process of telling a story I don't yet know the ending to. I guess it's kind of like reading a mystery novel and wondering the whole time who did it and how the story will turn out."

As soon as the words are out of my mouth, I groan inwardly. It all sounds so corny and unserious, like next I'll be telling him I keep crystals on my worktable and burn sage before starting a new piece. James Tremlin's face betrays no reaction, though.

He thumbs back a page or two, appears to read over some notes, and then returns his gaze to me.

"You did your MFA at BU, right?"

"Uh, I only completed one year of the program," I say, caught off guard. I wasn't expecting him to travel that far back in order to write a few hundred words about me.

"Didn't like it?"

I lift my shoulders in an awkward shrug, buying myself a moment. "No, I did. But I couldn't swing the second year financially," I lie.

He offers another polite nod, though something in his gaze makes me wonder if he knows I'm bullshitting.

"There's one thing I'm especially curious about," he says, glancing quickly back down at his notebook. "The pieces you display on your website are all dated within the last couple of years, and when I searched online, I couldn't find any references to work you'd done in the twenty-tens or earlier. What kinds of pieces were you creating between grad school and when you began experimenting with collage?"

I stare at him, hopelessly tongue-tied. Why has he felt the need to dig this far into my history? I thought we lived in a world where no one is interested in anything that happened even five minutes ago.

"I just think people will be curious about what you were doing previously," he adds, clearly noticing my reluctance. "And how and why your work evolved."

"I actually didn't do art for a few years," I manage to say, stumbling over the words. "There were some things that, um, prevented it. Things in my personal life."

"Right. Well, life can certainly be disruptive." Fortunately, he seems to have no interest in pursuing the topic.

"I think that about does it, Skyler," he says. "Thank you again for agreeing to do this."

"Thank *you*," I say, though I'm surprised that he's already wrapping it up. We've only been speaking for twenty minutes or so, and I haven't even finished my drink. Did he pick up on my panic over the last question and thus wants to bring the whole thing to a merciful end?

He signals for the bill, and we sit in awkward silence until it arrives. Though I offer to contribute, he tells me that *ArtToday* will be covering it and lays a few bills on the table. On the spur of the moment, I explain that I'm going to stay for another cappuccino. I don't actually plan to order a second, I just want to finish the one in front of me.

He rises and wishes me goodbye, his tone still polite and a bit removed. As I watch him descend the stairs to the lower level, I feel deflated. Has he chalked me up as a total amateur, someone who dropped out of grad school and couldn't get her act together but has now limped her way into a show at a small gallery?

I drain the lukewarm cappuccino while drawing circles on the wooden table with my finger. Why did he have to bring up grad school? It's been hard enough to have to think about my time in Boston as I revisit the night with C.J.

Time to go home, I think finally. Maybe Tuna will let me practice my conversational skills with her—because I damn well need to improve them by Tuesday night.

I'm just about to rise from the table when my eyes wander to the room on the lower level, which has gotten busier while I've been in the café. My breath catches. At a table against the far brick wall, his face in profile, is Deacon Starr. Did he *follow* me here?

But no, it doesn't seem that way. He's with someone, a woman with dark red hair, and they each have a beer in front of them. I watch as he reaches across the table, takes the woman's hand, and runs his thumb back and forth over her skin in a clearly romantic way. She says something to him—I can see her lips move even in profile—and Deacon pulls her hand to his mouth, kissing her palm.

In that moment, my gut tells me everything I need to know. He's not the intruder. I'm hardly an expert on the behavior of fucked-up men, but it seems clear that a guy who's obsessed enough with a woman to break into her apartment wouldn't be nearly slobbering over someone else a few days later. Deacon obviously got his venom toward me out of his system and probably hasn't thought of me since.

It's a relief in some way, until I realize this doesn't change the bottom line. Some guy broke into my apartment, then tried to get into my studio. And I haven't a single clue who he is—or why he's after me.

21

Then

"WE HAVE TO CHECK THE POOL," I SHOUTED AT JAMIE AND ROB, feeling my panic swell even more. "Chloe might have fallen in."

Rob shook his head emphatically. "No, I was out there yesterday, and I would have noticed."

I exhaled a long, ragged breath, but my relief didn't last. "Let's look around the second floor now," I said. I was thinking of the girl descending the main staircase and that toad of a guy surprising me in the corridor outside the bedrooms. People had definitely been roaming around up there Friday night.

"We should probably check the basement first," Jamie said.

My heart skipped. "What's there?"

"Well, for one thing, a game room. We didn't want anyone using it the other night, but given how the party turned out, people might have ended up down there."

As she led the way, dread seeped through my pores, making my legs heavy. Once we reached the kitchen, Jamie swung open a dark wooden door in one corner and flipped on a light to reveal a set of descending stairs. We were still traveling as a pack, and I was about to suggest that we split up and search the house separately to save time, but I quickly nixed the thought. It just seemed better to stick together so that I made sure no space was overlooked.

Jamie's instinct turned out to be right. As soon as we stepped into the game room, I picked up the scent of stale beer and spotted several red cups on the rim of the pool table, a few half full and one with a cigarette butt floating in the middle of it. The floor was sticky as we walked, suggesting beer had spilled in spots. When I pushed open a door into a half bathroom, I saw a couple of red cups resting on the small sink, as well. But there was no specific sign that Chloe had been one of the guests who had set foot in this part of the house.

"Shit, Jamie, we're gonna have to get out the mop down here, too," Rob said, surveying the scene with disgust.

That's what you're worried about?? I wanted to scream but ignored him and asked Jamie what else was on this level.

"The wine cellar," she said. "And the laundry room."

She took the lead again, down a long, narrow corridor. My trepidation built with each step, but each of the other rooms we checked was empty, and it looked like partygoers hadn't ventured this far. Finally, we encountered a door to what Jamie called "the utility room." When Jamie swung open the door and I saw that there was nothing in the space but a furnace, I let out a small moan of relief.

"I understand you're worried," I heard Rob say from behind me. "But I just don't think she's here. We've been in the house the whole weekend and we would have known."

"Can we look in the bedrooms now?" I asked Jamie, ignoring him again.

"Okay," she said, but she was starting to look somewhat dubious, too, as if she was running out of patience with me, just as her brother seemed to be doing. "Rob and I have been in *our* rooms, so we know she's not there, and I had to go in my parents' bedroom Saturday morning. But there are a couple of guest rooms."

We ascended to the kitchen and, after making our way back to the front of the house, climbed the wide staircase to the second-floor hallway, which was covered in white-and-gold-striped wallpaper. There was only one window at the very end, and none of the sconces had been turned on, so the space was eerily dim and quiet.

What were my mother and David doing right now? I wondered, gazing down the hall. Had they spoken to the police? They were waiting desperately to hear from me, I knew, but it seemed better not to contact them again until I'd completed the search of the house.

Jamie pointed to the second door on the left. "This is the first of the guest rooms," she said. "We never come in here."

She tugged open the door, and I followed her inside. It was empty, but the pale yellow spread on the bed was badly rumpled, as if someone had been rolling around on it.

"God, what asshole would do that?" Jamie asked. While she pulled the bedspread back, obviously checking to see if the sheets had been dirtied, I glanced into the en suite bathroom, even behind the door to the tub. Empty. We returned to the hall.

"The other guest room is down there," Jamie said, cocking her chin toward the end of the corridor. I started in that direction, moving at a clip.

"Hey, hold on," Rob shouted from behind me.

Maybe his impatience was snowballing, and he wanted to call the whole search off, but there was no way I was stopping. I reached the last door on the right, and as I pushed it open, I heard Rob call out again in protest.

This bed was rumpled, too, but the duvet had been kicked onto the floor and the sheets were in a tangle. A beer bottle sat on each of the bedside tables. Had someone spent Friday night in this guest room? Did this have something to do with Chloe?

And then, as I stood there surveying the space and feeling overwhelmed with despair, a tall young guy stepped out from the en suite bathroom. He was Asian American and wearing only jeans, without a shirt or shoes. I gasped in shock. At the same moment, I felt a presence behind me and spun around to find Rob inches away, his face pinched in displeasure.

"This is *my* room," he announced, exasperated. "The guest room is across the hall."

"But who's that?" I said, jabbing my finger at the stranger.

"This is my boyfriend, Dan. *Jeez.*"

"Oh, sorry, sorry," I said, now seeing my mistake. I apologized to his boyfriend, too, and as Jamie joined us, to her as well. And then without any warning, I started to sob, unable to contain my panic any longer.

"Skyler, don't worry," Jamie said, touching my shoulder. "As you can see, she's not here, but I'm sure she's okay."

How could she be so stupid? Chloe *wasn't* okay, and nothing could be more obvious.

"What's going on?" Dan asked, moving toward us. His dark eyes registered concern.

Rob briefly explained the situation, and, as Dan nodded sympathetically, I remembered seeing him at the party. He'd been in the kitchen as I'd passed through on my search for Chloe, supervising the beer and wine table. I wiped my eyes with the sleeve of my sweater and took a couple of desperate breaths, forcing myself to calm down.

"You were tending bar the other night, right?" I asked Dan.

"Sort of. The party was supposed to be only for college friends, but all of a sudden these dudes we didn't know crashed it and started guzzling down all the booze. I don't drink, myself, so I told Rob I'd hang in the kitchen and keep an eye on things."

"Do you remember seeing my sister?" I asked desperately. "She's a blonde, super pretty, about five three."

"I remember someone who looked like that."

"Not the blonde with really long hair," I clarified. He might have been thinking of the one Ryan saw jumping into the car. "My sister's is shoulder-length."

"Yeah, I know who you mean. In a tight blue top."

"Yup, that's her. What was she doing when you saw her? Was there someone with her?"

He shook his head and grabbed a T-shirt from the end of the bed. "When I saw her, she was by herself, but it seemed like she had a date—because the second or third time she came through the kitchen, she had a sweater around her waist. Big, like it probably belonged to a guy."

"Right, right," I said. So he had noticed it, too—the hunter-green sweater. A crewneck, I vaguely remembered.

"I think she might have gone somewhere with him after that," he added, pulling the T-shirt over his head.

"In a car?" I exclaimed.

He shook his head again. "I don't think so. She grabbed a bottle of wine from the cooler, and when I suggested she put it back and pour a glass instead, she just gave me this flirty smile and kept going."

"Going *where*?" I pleaded.

"She went out the kitchen door to the backyard. I'm pretty sure I didn't see her again after that."

My knees buckled. Chloe, I realized, might still be here on the property, but not inside the house. I'd been looking in all the wrong places.

22

Now

AFTER GRABBING MY TOTE BAG FROM BENEATH THE TABLE, I slowly head down the stairs of the restaurant, doing my best not to snag Deacon's attention, which isn't hard. He looks too enamored of his date to notice anything else in the room.

I hurry outside and dash across Hudson Street with a pit in my stomach. As much as it sickened me to picture Deacon in my apartment, at least he was the devil I knew, which gave me the tiniest sense of control. Now I'm dealing with the complete unknown.

I walk for about five blocks without even paying attention to where I'm going and finally realize that I'm headed down Bedford Street when I should be traveling north and east. As I do some zigzagging to get back on track, my phone rings. It's Nicky.

"Am I speaking to Skyler Moore, the famous collage artist?" she asks when I pick up, her voice full of her typical joie de vivre.

I smile. "In my dreams."

"Well, dreams *do* come true when you want them badly enough."

Oh, Nicky, is that what you really believe? I wish I could ask her. "What's up?" I say instead.

"Just checking in. You must be getting excited, right? Matt and I can't wait for the opening."

"Yeah, and I'm so glad you're both coming."

"Are you going to be speaking to the crowd? I mean, about your artwork?"

"No, that won't be necessary. Josh, the gallery owner, will make a few remarks and I basically only have to say thank you after that."

"Oh."

I can almost picture her mouth in a little moue of disappointment. Nicky has no idea how much being in a gathering of five or more people petrifies me, let alone *speaking* in that kind of situation. I used to wonder if opening up to her about how bad my anxiety has become might actually help ease it, like lancing a fetid wound, but eventually decided that wouldn't do any good and might even add to my angst. Despite how empathetic and caring Nicky is, she doesn't always let your truth win over hers. If I confessed right now that nothing would make me want to say more than a few words at the opening, that if I was forced to do it my heart might explode in my chest, she'd try to convince me that I'd be brilliant on my feet if I only gave it a chance.

"What's up with you these days?" I ask, switching subjects. "You and Matt going to do anything for Halloween this year?"

"Yeah, we've got a party to go to. How 'bout you? Are you going to be dressing up?"

"No, Tuna nixed the costume idea. She just wants to do a quiet night at home." I realize suddenly that Nicky must have barely gotten in the door from work, so it seems a little odd that she's calling me now. "Was there anything specific you wanted to talk about?"

"Nope, just saying hello. Oh, there is one thing, though. Mom said you'd suggested that we all go to dinner after the reception. That would be so nice, but I think she and Dad are worried that by the time the event is over, it will be close to eight o'clock and if we eat after that, we won't get home until super late."

Ahh, the *real* reason for the call. Nicky had better never cheat on Matt or spy for the United States of America, because she's the world's worst liar.

"Would they want to do it before the show?" I ask. I'd been planning to arrive at the gallery even before six, but I could probably pull off an early dinner.

She pauses. "I don't think that's going to work, either. Dad is nervous about driving into the city during rush hour, and he wants to make this particular trip a quick one."

This particular trip, huh? It's not as if there have been any others. David and my mother never come into the city, either to see me or do anything else.

"Right. Maybe it would be better if you all took the train?"

"I know they considered that, but you know how long it takes, and Penn Station is so far from the gallery."

She seems to have an answer for everything. Picking up my pace a little, I can tell that my cheeks have started to flush with shame. It's clear that my mother has no interest in celebrating my accomplishment on Tuesday night, and Nicky has been recruited to be the messenger, as usual. And as usual, she's trying her hardest to cushion the blow.

"Got it," I say. "I should let you get on with the evening."

"Thanks, Sky. And see you Tuesday, okay?"

"Yup, see you then."

I end the call and drop the phone in my purse, still feeling the heat in my cheeks. Am I just being defensive, too quick to see anything my mother does as a sign that she hasn't forgiven me, or even worse, has ceased *loving* me? I try to view the situation from her perspective. Driving into New York at rush hour is certainly not something I'd enjoy doing, and Nicky was right about the train. Station to station, the trip can take over three hours, and the cab or Uber downtown would add a minimum of thirty minutes, and that's just one way.

Let it go, I tell myself. At least my mother is coming. And I'm still hoping she'll be impressed by what she sees.

After a quick stop at the deli, I finally reach my building. The street is bustling with the usual mix of hipsters, students, tourists, and weirdos, but I still check behind me at the base of the steps, and then again as I unlock the front door. Of course, I don't even know who or what I'm looking for.

There's no one in the stairwell or corridors, and the building feels deserted, though on the second-floor landing I pick up muted bickering from behind a closed door. Reaching my floor, I pull back with a start to see something taped to my door: a handwritten note. After glancing around, I move close enough to read it.

To my relief I see Mikoto's name at the bottom and the message, "Can you drop by?" above it.

Without stopping at home, I make my way to her apartment and knock a few times. Seconds later she eases the door open an inch, and then, seeing it's me, removes the chain and swings the door all the way open, greeting me with a smile. She's wearing a white sweatshirt and yoga pants..

"I have some names for you from my uncle," she announces. "Want to come in?"

"Sure," I say, stepping inside.

This is the first time I've had more than a glimpse of another apartment in the building, and I can't help but be curious. Not surprisingly, her living room is small like mine, but she's done a great job of fixing it up in the short time she's lived here. Almost everything in the room is white—the walls, curtains, slipcovers on the couch and armchair, even the small pieces of wooden furniture. On the wall opposite the door, there's a single shelf of blond wood, almost like the top of a mantelpiece, and it's lined with sun-bleached shells and conchs. The air smells of fir trees, thanks to a scented candle burning on top of the bookcase, and the whole vibe is incredibly serene and calming.

Except for a few textbooks piled on the coffee table, it looks like a magazine shoot.

"Wow," I say after taking it all in. "This feels like a beautiful spa retreat. Ha, not that I've been to one, but I've seen pictures."

"Thank you," Mikoto says. "My mom is Japanese and one of many things I've gotten from her, besides my name, is an appreciation for Zen-like interiors."

"You mentioned you were in a doorman building before this. Was it nearby?"

"No, uptown. I worked for a tech company before law school, which meant I could afford a pretty nice place. Once I had to quit work for school, I brought in a roommate to cover costs, but she turned out to be a nightmare, so I gave up the apartment and managed to get a much cheaper one down here."

I smile. "And now, whenever you need a tattoo, a vintage dress, or a dumpling, you're only steps away from it."

"Exactly," she says, laughing. "Though I'll take life on Seventh Street over having a roommate any day. . . . How are you doing, by the way? Has the guy's wife made any more trouble?"

"Not yet, but I still definitely want to talk to an attorney."

"Okay, well, I've got a couple of names, and I thought I'd explain what my uncle says are the pros and cons of each one. You want a drink while we go over it? I was about to have a glass of white wine."

"I'd love one," I say, touched by her hospitality. "If you sure it's not too much trouble?"

"None at all."

The layout of her apartment is almost identical to mine, just in reverse, and as Mikoto slips into the kitchen, I lower myself onto the couch. I can't remember the last time I had a friendly drink with someone else or even sat in another person's apartment. When I moved to New York from Boston, I worked at a magazine website for two years, designing pages, and then for a small marketing agency, and at each place I had a couple of colleagues that I sometimes socialized with. We'd meet for drinks at a bar or occasionally do a potluck dinner at someone's apartment.

But over time it became too much of a strain to fake it around other people, to contain my grief and fury at the world and plaster on an insipid if-I-can-make-it-here-I-can-make-it-anywhere smile. Once I left the agency to go freelance, I let those people fade from my life, and though a few persisted with calls for a while, most gave up without a fight.

"Here you go," Mikoto says, returning with two long-stemmed glasses, frosted a little on the sides. I wait until she takes a seat and then indulge in my first sip. The wine has a buttery taste and is refreshingly cold, as if she's had it chilling in the refrigerator for hours. Does being so together come naturally to her, I wonder, or is it a skill she honed over time?

"I hope I'm not interrupting your studying," I say, nodding with my chin to the textbooks on the coffee table.

"No, I'm done for the night. After you leave, I'll make an omelet and go to bed. Though I often have to study at night, I'm really a morning person and get more done early."

"Are you glad you did it? I mean, law school."

"Yeah, I think so." She wrinkles her nose a little. "Though if you'll excuse the expression, the jury's still out. My uncle says being happy as a lawyer all comes down to picking the right area of expertise for yourself and the right firm, so I'll have to see what the future holds. . . . And speaking of my uncle, let me give you those names."

Still holding her glass, she uses her free hand to tug a sheet of paper from beneath one of the textbooks and holds it out in front of us so we can study it simultaneously. There are three names typed on the page—one woman and two men—and beneath each one is a short description of their education and expertise. All three have degrees from fancy colleges and specialize in estate law. She gives me a minute to digest it all, but I have no idea where to start.

"My uncle says they're all good," Mikoto says, as if sensing my confusion, "but from what he told me, I think Rebecca Rosenbaum would be the best fit. Her practice is newer, so she might not charge as much, and since she's a woman, you have less of a chance of getting attitude about the one-night stand."

"What do you think her hourly rate might be?"

"My best guess? About seven hundred, maybe eight."

"Holy cow. And how long do you think it might take to get in to see her?"

"Lawyers are generally hungry for work, so it might only take a couple of days."

I nod. I wish it were tomorrow, but I have no immediate sense of Jane breathing down my neck, so the timing should be okay. "I took your advice, by the way, about trying to figure out why the guy left me money. It turns out you were right—it had nothing to do with nostalgia or warm, fuzzy feelings. He was apparently furious with his wife for sleeping with a close friend of his and I was part of his revenge on her."

"Ouch," Mikoto says. "Well, at least you know now. And what about the other situation, with that guy you dated?"

"Oh, I forgot, there's a bit of news on that front, too." I tell her about getting a look at the clearly besotted Deacon and the doubts I now have about him as the culprit. "Which means I'm back to square one, without any clues," I add.

"You can't think of anyone else? Maybe someone who seemed weirdly interested in you at a party, for instance? Or at a gallery show of yours?"

I shake my head. "This is my first show, and socially, I-I mostly keep a low profile."

Mikoto sets her glass on the coffee table and furrows her brow.

She stares at a spot on the far wall while tapping her hands lightly together a few times. It's not hard to picture her doing that one day as an attorney, thinking through a strategy.

"Hmm," she says finally. "Here's a crazy thought. Could the break-in have something to do with the inheritance?"

The hairs on the back of my neck stand up as I try the idea on for size. God, maybe Mikoto is right. If Jane Whaley really intends to prove I extorted her husband, she'll want to find out anything she possibly can about me, and what better way to do that than searching my home and studio. Would she really dare to cross that kind of line, though?

If the answer is yes, I'm up against someone more dangerous than I ever imagined.

23

Now

BRING MY HANDS TO MY TEMPLES, PRESSING WITH MY FINGERTIPS as if that will help me think faster.

"How could I have been so dense?" I say to Mikoto as things start to fall into place. "That idea never even crossed my mind."

"Why would it?" she says with a shrug. "If you're having an issue with someone, you don't automatically assume their next move is to break into your apartment."

I take another long sip of wine, still trying to puzzle it out. "Okay, she has a motive, but I've met the woman, and it's hard to imagine her dashing down from the suburbs and sneaking into our building in her Jimmy Choos."

Mikoto lifts an eyebrow. "She could have hired someone to do her dirty work. A classmate of mine worked as a paralegal at this sketchy law firm and she told me they'd sometimes use private investigators who weren't afraid to break the law, if it meant getting their hands on the right information."

I consider her suggestion for a moment. "The wife in this

situation could certainly afford to hire someone like that . . . but it seems so extreme."

"I don't mean to sound all woo-woo," Mikoto tells me, smiling wryly, "but there's a law in the cosmos saying that when a lot of money moves from point A to point B, it's bound to unsettle the natural order. Which can lead to extremes."

I grimace. "If it *was* her, she was probably hoping to find evidence I was in touch with her husband before he died, since she certainly wouldn't have turned up anything like that on his phone or computer."

"Right. And that would explain why the person went through your belongings but didn't take anything."

"Wait, though . . ." I say, suddenly seeing a hitch. "The break-in happened the same day I ran into her in Westchester. I think that's part of why it hadn't occurred to me that she could be involved. How would she have set things in motion so quickly?"

"Hmm," Mikoto says. "Good question. But when you told me about the wife confronting you, you said she seemed to know you'd be in the building. So . . . maybe she'd already hired someone to go through your things, knowing you'd be away from your apartment that day."

A chill runs down my spine. "Jeez, yeah, maybe. This is starting to sound like some series on Netflix that I don't have the nerve to watch all the way to the end."

"I know. . . . When you meet with the attorney, be sure to fill her in. Would you like me to top off your wine?"

I glance down at my glass and discover that I've completely drained it. I've surely overstayed my welcome.

"No, no, I should get going," I say, folding the list and tucking it into the pocket of my jeans. "Thank you for everything. The wine, the names, all your advice and wisdom."

"My pleasure. And keep me posted, will you?"

"Will do."

I say good night to Mikoto and let myself into my apartment. After giving Tuna a distracted back scratch, I inspect each room even more closely than I have before. If the intruder was an unscrupulous private eye, he might be able to gain entry even with my new sturdier lock in place, but nothing appears disturbed. And why would he come back, anyway, if his first search showed that there was nothing here to connect me to the late Christopher Whaley?

Do I have Kane to thank for some of this? I wonder. If he tipped off Jane Whaley that I was the benefactor of the trust and that I'd be meeting with him on Monday, he could have also provided her with my address. Though a private eye could have found it easily enough, too.

Back in the kitchen, my mind spinning, I grab a sad-looking peach from the crisper drawer and collapse on the couch. Tuna hops onto my cushion, arches her back, and curls up next to me. It's nice to know that she actually seems to like me now, but her presence offers little solace at the moment. Just a few days ago I seemed to be so close to what I wanted the most—the chance to live life as an artist, the chance to be a *mother*—but now someone's trying to yank those things from my grip, and perhaps smear me publicly in the process.

And though it's been helpful to get to know Mikoto a little bit and take comfort in her unflappability, I'm embarrassed by how much I've imposed on her over the past few days, and the way I've been extracting information from her. Though she's seemed willing to help, she must think I'm the neediest person alive. I've got to stop pestering her.

Which means I'm on my own.

I take a bite of the peach. It's tasteless and mealy, and I imagine it was harvested hundreds, maybe thousands of miles away and transported here in refrigerated trucks and maybe even first by ship. If only I could be there right now, in the warm, sunny place where the peach was grown, or anywhere warm and inviting for that matter, but I can't afford a mini-vacation, not until this all gets sorted out.

With my free hand I stroke Tuna's head, feeling the vibrations as she purrs. Though the urge to flee the city is strong, it would be tough—and expensive—to leave her in a kennel.

A thought occurs to me. What if I went to West Hartford, taking Tuna with me, and spent a few nights in my old room? Though it was turned into a home office/man cave for David a decade ago, it's got a pull-out couch where I sleep when I'm there. But years have passed since I showed up at my mother's house just to hang, and it hurts even to imagine the strained tone of her voice if I were to request an impromptu visit.

As I take another bite from the peach—only because I'm famished—my gaze rests on the lidded wicker basket next to my desk, which is the other place I store objects that might work for a collage.

Though I'd planned to give my brain a few days to decompress before starting to create again, I see now that I can't wait. I'm going to use tomorrow afternoon, I decide, to scavenge for more components to use in the next collage. I need a diversion, something to keep me from dwelling on what might be coming next, and even more than that, I want to lose myself in that strange, intoxicating place I go to when I work on a piece of art.

I WAKE EARLY THE NEXT DAY AFTER ANOTHER RESTLESS NIGHT WITH the table against the front door as an extra safeguard. At exactly 9:01, I call Rebecca Rosenbaum's office, giving a short explanation to the assistant who answers the phone. She explains that Ms. Rosenbaum isn't available, but she'll pass along the message to her.

Less than two hours later, I'm working on my newest graphic design job when the lawyer phones me back.

"How can I be of help?" she asks, friendly and self-assured.

I quickly run through a short spiel I've rehearsed and explain I'm hoping for a consultation so she can review my situation and offer me legal advice.

A fairly long pause follows, and I wonder if she's going to say something like *Lady, I wouldn't touch this mess with a ten-foot pole.*

Instead, she offers a few details about her firm, asks some smart-sounding questions for clarification about my issue—which I answer as succinctly as possible—and then announces she'd be happy to meet.

"But unfortunately," she adds, "I'm going to be on the West Coast for a bit and won't be able to do a consultation with you until next Friday. I have two o'clock free if that works for you."

I could try the other two lawyers on the list but since Rosenbaum was Mikoto's first choice, I want to stick with her. Plus, there's something reassuring about her voice that makes me think she's the right match for me.

"I'm totally free then," I tell her.

"In the meantime, have you heard from opposing counsel?"

"No, nothing yet."

"Good. I think we should be okay in the meantime, but if you do hear from anyone, call my assistant at this number." She provides the address for her office and politely signs off.

I'm glad I took action, but wish I felt better than I do. The consultation, she'd said, will be free, but after that, it's seven hundred dollars an hour, which will add up nauseatingly quickly, and I have no idea if this woman can really help.

Still in my pajamas, I finish up the design work, and then, after a quick lunch, I slip into jeans, a turtleneck sweater, and a jacket. I won't end up using everything I buy or find today, or perhaps not any of it, but this will get the process started. In some ways this is always the most enjoyable stage of a collage for me because it's all about discovering and imagining and letting my mind off the leash and there's no pressure to create, or to fix, or to finish.

At some point, though, I'm going to have to go back to my studio, where most of my supplies are as well the worktable where I compose my collages.

I can't tell if I'm being overly paranoid. I know someone broke into my apartment, but how would Jane Whaley know about my studio, which is only a rental? It's still possible that it's all a misunderstanding.

On the spur of the moment, I rummage through my desk drawer until I locate the business card Alejandro offered me once, saying that he'd like me to have his number in case there was any kind of emergency with the building when he was traveling back to Mexico. To be polite, I'd offered him my contact info in return. I hardly want to drag him into the nightmare the way I've done with Mikoto, but maybe if I speak to him, I can clarify a few details and put my mind at ease.

"Skyler, hi," he says instead of hello, which means he must have programmed my number into his phone. "What a surprise. . . . Is everything okay?"

"Yeah, and sorry to bother you—but I had a couple of questions."

"Of course."

"You know that guy you saw outside my studio? Did he definitely use my name when he spoke to you?

He doesn't hesitate. "Yes. He said he was looking for Skyler Moore."

"And he definitely said he worked at the gallery? Is there a chance you could have heard him wrong?"

"I'm sure he said it. He told me he needed to drop something off for you, though it must have been small because he didn't have any packages with him."

So there clearly hasn't been a misunderstanding on Alejandro's part. The guy outside my door was up to no good, and more than likely, he's the same guy who searched my apartment. What if Alejandro hadn't scared him off and I'd come back from the bathroom to find him in the studio?

"Was that the only time you saw him?"

"Yes, though I rarely go in and out during the day. Is there a problem?"

"I'm not sure. I'm just concerned because the gallery said it wasn't anyone who worked there. If you notice him around again, would you mind texting me and letting me know?"

"Yes, yes, for sure. Are you planning to come in at all?"

"No, not this week at least."

He sighs. "It's probably not the best time anyway."

"What do you mean?"

"You didn't hear? We lost power at around five yesterday. We had to use our phones to get down the stairs, and I heard a woman from another floor tripped and sprained her ankle."

"Was it a Con Ed thing?" In the past five minutes, I've said about a hundred times more words to Alejandro than ever before, but I need to know exactly what happened.

"Apparently not. I didn't stick around, but another tenant called me later and said the super thought the problem originated in the building."

"But they fixed it?"

He lets out another sigh, louder this time. "They did—but it's worrisome. The super felt maybe some kids had been in the basement and had messed with the circuit breaker."

What if it wasn't kids, though? What if it was the same guy who tried my studio door, and this time he wanted the building all to himself?

24

Now

THAT'S SO SCARY," I BLURT OUT. "COULD YOU LET ME KNOW IF IT happens again?"

"Yes, of course," Alejandro says. "Please don't worry. And I'll keep an eye on your door."

My heart's racing as I hang up. I grab my tote bag, wish Tuna goodbye, and head out. All I want right now is to lose myself in my search for materials.

I've made it only a few blocks west when my phone rings and Josh's name is on the screen.

"So tell me," he says after we've greeted each other. "How did the interview with James Tremlin go?"

"Okay, I think." I cringe a little, recalling how awkward my coffee with the writer actually was. "Did you hear anything about it?"

"Not yet, but I'm sure you were great. Listen, I also wanted to arrange a time for the two of us to go over the installation before the opening. We're hanging the pieces Monday when the gallery is closed, so what about eleven Tuesday morning, right when we open?"

Wow, this is all really happening. My art is about to hang on the wall for the world to see, or at least the little world of downtown Manhattan gallery browsers.

"That sounds fine," I say.

"Good. This way it will give me time to make adjustments if there's anything you hate about the positioning—but I promise, you're going to love what I have in mind. Anyone who comes into the gallery that day can place an order, but the official opening isn't until that night, of course."

The idea of the party still terrifies me, but I can't deny how excited I am about the actual show.

"I know you mentioned that your family was coming to the opening," Josh adds. "Are you planning to celebrate with them later?"

"Unfortunately, no. They have to get back to Connecticut."

I hope my voice doesn't betray that I've been throwing myself a little pity party about this detail.

"That's a shame. But why don't you come out to dinner with me and some friends I've invited to the opening? You need to be toasted."

The invitation catches me completely off guard, and I feel my cheeks instantly redden.

"That's so nice of you, Josh. Um . . . ." The idea of going straight home to Tuna after the opening depresses me, and it would be great to mark the occasion in some way, but it would be even worse for me to sit around a restaurant table with a whole bunch of strangers.

"It will just be four of us," Josh says to my relief.

"Thank you. I'd love that."

After we sign off, it occurs to me again that Josh might have an interest in me beyond the professional. He's an attractive guy, for sure, and though at times he's seemed overly smooth, he's smart and well-spoken, and the fact that he's so savvy about art makes him even more appealing. But it's hard to fathom that I could be his type. No, I remind myself, this is just him being thoughtful—and remembering that when he asked me for a list of people to add to the guest list, I had only nine.

I continue west and then south to SoHo, where I meander through several pricey home stores, just to look around. After that, I stop at two stationery shops I love and end up buying several sheets of vintage-looking wrapping paper, one featuring elephants, the other ancient Egyptian hieroglyphs.

Done with SoHo, I walk up Broadway and stop at Evolution, a store specializing in science and natural history artifacts that's pure heaven for me. After wandering the aisles for over half an hour, I buy a small bunch of African porcupine quills for a mere three dollars. From there I head to Greenwich Village, only browsing at a few places and making purchases at a couple of others. I end up with remnants of fabric, a packet of old postmarked stamps, a couple of travel books from a remainder bin, and a set of amazing vintage postcards from Rome, Istanbul, Niagara Falls, and the Thousand Islands, the archipelago that straddles northern New York State and Canada.

Are there really a thousand islands in the St. Lawrence River, I wonder, or is it simply marketing hyperbole? What would it be like to travel along that river, seeing those islands one by one? And what would it be like to fly to Rome or Istanbul finally, to climb the Spanish Steps and sail across the Bosporus? I worry that I'll never know.

By the time I finish up in the Village, I'm starving. Chelsea Market, the huge food hall, isn't far, so I walk up there, my tote bag loading me down, and order a caprese sandwich on an enormous roll from a shop called Cappone's. Though it's Friday afternoon and things are bustling, I score one of the metal tables along the passageway outside the shops.

Halfway through my sandwich, I can't help but notice how serene I feel. Maybe I haven't traveled anyplace exotic, but miraculously, all the browsing and shopping accomplished exactly what I hoped they would. I've released much of my anxiety in the process.

And I'm starting to see a few things from a different angle. Maybe the loss of power in my studio building *was* due to a prank by kids or just a random power outage. It certainly seems likelier than someone going after me on purpose. And if whoever intruded into my apartment actually was a private eye looking for proof I extorted a fortune from C.J., he came up empty-handed and would have no reason to return. So I should stop worrying about being in my apartment or the studio.

And I should stop agonizing about Jane Whaley, too. Since I know for sure that I didn't blackmail C.J., she won't be able to wrench the money from my hands.

And at that moment, just as I've given the words *three and a half million dollars* permission to bounce around my head, my gaze falls on a baby inside a stroller next to a nearby table. Facing me, he looks to be about six or seven months, with round eyes the same shade of blue as the little cap on his head. I capture his attention and he studies me with that knowing look certain babies have, the kind that makes you wonder if there is actually a thirty-five-year-old person inside, someone who's totally aware of what's what but has no way of conveying it to you yet.

In the past, the sight of a baby might have left me heartsick with longing. Not today, though—because now I have a plan in place. My next appointment at the clinic is booked, and I'll soon have money in the bank to pay for the IUI. There may not be any boats across the Bosporus for me this year, or anytime soon, but perhaps creating my next collage will help ease my pining for that. And besides, I want a baby more than I want to roam the world right now.

Done with the sandwich finally, I wipe the grease from my hands on the paper napkin so that I can take another look at the porcupine quills I bought and mull over how I might use them. I reach behind me to unhook my tote bag from the back of the chair and start to reach in.

I notice the sheet of white paper right away, folded in half and lying on top of everything I bought today. I squint, trying to recall what it could be, as I pluck it out and unfold it.

The paper is totally blank—except for a word in the middle of the page, made, it seems, by a rubber stamp.

Whore.

25

Now

MY BREATH HITCHES AT THE SIGHT OF THE WORD. BEFORE I CAN spin around in my chair, I catch myself, worried about being too obvious. Instead, I shift my position the tiniest bit and, with my heart pounding, slowly turn my head to look behind me.

The concourse seems even busier than when I sat down fifteen minutes ago: a continuous stream of tourists and foodies moving in both directions. It would have been easy enough for anyone to stuff the vile note in my bag, which I'd stupidly left dangling behind me on the chair. There's no one who looks furtive or otherwise suspicious in the throng, and yet the person who left the note could be close by, waiting to see my reaction.

Was it just some run-of-the-mill woman hater? New York City has more than its share. But it feels like too much of a coincidence. I know how strongly Jane Whaley considers me a tramp, maybe equivalent in her mind to being a whore, and she must have had her sick helper drop it in my bag—the same guy who broke into my apartment and possibly showed up at my studio door. Which means that he's followed me ever since I set out from my apartment building this morning. The note might have actually been left before I even arrived at Chelsea Market, when I was stopped at a street corner on my way from the last shop I visited.

Holding the note in my other hand, I force my eyes back to the word in middle of the page. Someone's clearly used a black ink pad and a rubber stamp, the kind some small businesses still employ to mark something with the phrase "paid in full" or "do not bend."

I wonder how often the company that made this one gets a request for a stamp that says "whore"?

I refuse to let the word get to me. I'd never felt so much as a twinge of guilt about spending the night with C.J. and I still don't. He wasn't wearing a ring, and if he actually *did* have a wife, I reasoned at the time, then he was the one responsible for the adultery, not me.

No, it's not the word itself that's throwing me. It's that Jane Whaley has graduated from searching my apartment without an obvious trace to trying to spook me. Is she hoping I'll get so worn down from a combination of legal maneuvering and harassment that I'll throw up my hands and refuse the trust?

I quickly gather my things, eager to leave. At a trash bin by the door I chuck the sandwich wrapping and start to rid myself of the note as well, but then something tells me I should hold on to it. I end up stuffing it in my jacket pocket.

Though I'd planned to return to the East Village on foot or by bus, there's no way I'm doing it now, since I don't know if I'm still being followed. Miraculously I spot a free cab barreling down Ninth Avenue, so I raise my hand, flag it down, and hurl myself inside. As the driver takes off, I glance back, but don't see anyone leap into a car behind us. I can't believe I'm being forced to worry if someone is tailing me.

Twisting back around, I sink into the seat. It's good to be in the safe cocoon of the cab, weaving our way first through Chelsea and then the crazy, narrow streets of the Village, but I know the relief will be fleeting. Because as soon as I get home, I'll be holed up with a table against the door, wondering what other nastiness Jane Whaley has up her sleeve. If only I could see Rosenbaum sooner. For a minute I toy with the idea of reporting the harassment to the police before dismissing the idea. What crime would I be reporting? It's hardly against the law to call a woman a whore. Guys do it all the time.

Finally, we cross Broadway into the East Village. Though the driver seems to be using GPS, he pulls up by mistake to the building just before mine. I don't have the mental energy to explain the error, so I unbuckle my seat belt and bolt from the cab.

Hoisting my tote bag over my shoulder, I take a few steps toward my building before coming to a sudden stop. There's a young guy in a preppy-looking tweed blazer standing to the left of the stoop. He's about six feet tall, with reddish-brown hair, and he's swaying a little from one side to the next, as if he's waiting for someone.

With a start, I realize it's C.J.'s son.

He must notice my movements out of the corner of his eye because he quickly glances over in my direction. It seems to take him a second to put two and two together, but then I see his body jerk a little in recognition.

"What are you doing here?" I call out from a few yards away on the sidewalk. And then it dawns on me: If he's in the city, he could be the person who followed me today and dropped the note in my bag. If he knows where I live, he could have been the one who searched my apartment, having driven into the city that day after seeing me in the lobby. The timing would have been tight, but he could have pulled it off.

"My name's Mark Whaley and I need to talk to you," he says. He makes a slight move in my direction, and I stretch out an arm, signaling for him to stay where he is.

"How did you know where I live?" I demand.

"It wasn't hard to find out."

Right. Jane Whaley clearly had my address all along.

"Please, I just need to talk to you," he adds, taking a step in my direction this time.

"No, get away from me."

I shift backward, stumbling slightly. There's a scattering of people on the block—a man walking a bulldog, two girls, arm in arm, talking animatedly—but they all seem to be receding, absorbed into the dusk. I don't know yet how scared I should be.

"It's really important," he insists. "I promise it won't take long."

"You followed me around the city today?"

He looks confused. "*What?* No."

"Did you stuff that note in my bag? Did you break into my apartment?"

He lets out an exasperated sigh. "God, no. I didn't follow you or leave you a note or break into your apartment. I got here thirty minutes ago and when you didn't answer your bell, I decided to stick around and see if you showed up."

"So you just took a wild guess that I'd be coming home now?"

"Well, it *is* the time of day when a lot of people get back from work," he says. "Please, all I want is a few minutes of your time. And then I'll go. I'm supposed to be in school in Philly now, anyway."

There's nothing especially menacing in his tone, just arrogance and the diction of someone who grew up with every need catered to.

I should hear him out, I decide. Maybe he'll accidentally reveal something about his mother that will be useful to me. "All right."

His shoulders sag a little, seemingly in relief. "Is there someplace around here we could grab a beer?"

"I don't want a beer," I tell him. I cock my chin toward the white brick Catholic church squeezed into the center of the block. "Let's talk over there, in front of Saint Stanislaus."

I don't like the idea of him right in front of my building, but at the same time, I want to stick fairly close. Though he might not look threatening, I can't be sure.

"Okay," he says tersely, and I let him get a start ahead of me. Though I'd had a brief glimpse in Scarsdale, I finally have the chance to absorb his appearance once we're by the front of the church. He has a strong nose, full lips, and his mother's brown eyes, set in a slightly round, soft face. He's attractive in his own way, but not nearly as handsome as C.J., in my memory. The dress shirt he's wearing under the blazer is wrinkled, in the way you sometimes see privileged, private-school guys trying to telegraph: *I'm certainly not going to iron it myself.*

"So what do you want with me?" I ask.

He blows out a gust of air. "First, let me say I don't have anything against you. And I'm not passing judgment, either. What went on between you and my father has nothing directly to do with me."

How very sweet of him. "Can you please get to the point?"

"Okay, okay. Losing my father has been devastating for me and for my sister."

As he says *father*, his voice catches, and his face creases briefly in what looks like grief. Unless he's a great actor, he's sincerely hurting.

"I'm really sorry for your loss," I say.

"Thank you. I don't know all the details about you and my father, and frankly I don't want to. But this whole business with you and my mother is making everything even worse. I came here to ask you to do the right thing."

"And what do you think the right thing is?" I ask, though I have a pretty good idea where he's going.

"Find a way to assign the trust to my mother."

I can't believe what just came out of his mouth, and with real conviction in his voice, as if he not only thinks his request is reasonable, but that I might actually entertain it.

"We really shouldn't be having this conversation," I tell him. "Because it's not going to end up anywhere you like."

He furrows his brow. "What do you mean?"

"Your father clearly wanted the trust to go to me, so by keeping it, I'm already *doing* the right thing."

He holds up a hand, palm forward. "Maybe he *thought* that's what he wanted, but because of the illness, he really wasn't thinking straight."

This must be his mother's plan B. If she can't show that I extorted C.J., she'll try to demonstrate he was unable to make the decision.

"His lawyer didn't seem to think that was the case."

Mark shakes his head. "Not out of his mind, but extremely morose. And tormented."

"That sounds pretty normal for someone who'd been given only months to live."

"If he'd really been himself, he wouldn't have wanted to cause us any extra anguish as a family. He was a good father to me and my sister, and though he and my mother had their issues, it's not like him to have boxed her out this way."

A stiff fall breeze fights its way down the street, sending a strand of hair across my eyes, and I swipe it away with one hand. I should leave right this second and not be dragged into a back-and-forth with this kid, but I can't resist the urge to set the record straight.

"Mark, I heard he had every intention of boxing her out, actually. And if you want to know why, you'll have to ask her."

"You've been speaking to my grandmother, haven't you?"

"I can't say, but you can trust that the information came from a valid source."

He shakes his head, his lips pressed tight, as if I've clearly missed the point. "Well, it's bullshit. My father would never have purposely humiliated my mother, no matter how furious he might have been."

"Even if she'd humiliated him first?"

"No, he wasn't that kind of guy. He didn't *do* revenge."

A couple walks past us, and I see them look discreetly in our direction, obviously noting the contentiousness in Mark's tone. It's time to extricate myself. Mark Whaley isn't going to change my mind on the matter, and I'm certainly not going to change his.

"Again, I'm really sorry for your loss," I say, "but according to your father's lawyer, he knew exactly what he was doing, and I'm going to honor his wishes. Good night."

I watch indignation begin to boil inside him and contort his features into an ugly pout. He looks like a spoiled little kid who's just had his water gun taken away.

"Well, *fuck* you then," he says. "Fuck you to hell."

He spins on his heel and strides off down Seventh Street, the tails of his blazer flapping with each stride he takes.

Shaken, I grab a breath and hurry back to my building. As soon as I cross the threshold of my apartment, Tuna runs toward me and snakes back and forth between my legs a few times. It's comforting to feel her warm body against mine, but it's not enough to keep Mark Whaley's *fuck you* out of my head. He's no better than Deacon, trying to take me down to size.

With my pulse still racing, I drop my tote bag on the couch and do a quick check around the apartment, making sure there are no other land mines waiting for me. Next, I feed Tuna and pop open a can Diet Coke from the fridge. As I chug down half the contents, leaning wearily against the counter in the kitchen, the face-off continues to play on a loop in my mind

I don't doubt Mark Whaley's grief, but I'm sure his plea tonight had more to do with his mother's money grab—money that will go to him and his sister when Jane dies. She might have even sent him here, one more twist of the screw to add to the pressure she's already exerting on me.

And though it's hard to picture him picking my lock in that preppy sports jacket, he could be the one who slipped me the nasty note today.

As my heart rate finally normalizes again, my mind finds its way to a comment of Mark's that didn't snag much of my attention at the time.

He didn't do revenge.

So Mark was never a witness to a vengeful streak in his father; it doesn't mean C.J. lacked one, that he didn't have a dormant nerve deep down, triggered when his wife stepped out on him with his friend.

There's one thing that's beginning to seem like an irrefutable fact, though—that C.J. had been a good father.

I push off from the counter, soda can in hand, as thoughts line up in my head, demanding to be reexamined. Ever since I spoke to Caroline the other night, I've bought into her theory that my financial windfall is a form of retribution. But even if C.J. *was* furious at his wife, why would a loving father have exacted the kind of retribution that would impact his kids as well?

Whether or not Jane sent Mark Whaley tonight, he's clearly in a tailspin about what's transpired, and I bet his sister is, too. In the midst of their loss, they've had to watch a family trust be transferred to a complete stranger, manage their mother's fury, and confront the knowledge that their father had a one-night stand with a college student.

Things suddenly aren't adding up to me. Surely C.J. had other payback options that didn't make his kids collateral damage. He could have simply transferred the trust to them instead of Jane, for instance, or donated it to charity, sparing them the sordid details about me. Maybe Caroline hates Jane so much that she's read her son's actions all wrong.

Though alone except for Tuna, I find myself shaking my head vigorously. No, this wasn't revenge on C.J.'s part, which means there has to be another reason for what he did. He must have made the decision *despite* the fact it would rattle his family, not because of it.

I'm back to square one, having not the faintest clue why Chris Whaley did what he did.

26

Then

I REACHED OUT TO A NEARBY DRESSER AND PRESSED AGAINST IT TO steady myself as I digested what Rob's boyfriend just said. I felt light-headed, like I might faint any second if I let myself.

Forcing myself to focus, I turned from Dan to Rob.

"H-How big is it?" I stammered.

"The house?" Rob asked, a crease forming between his eyes.

"No, the property—including the wooded area in the back." I'd noticed the woods the night of the party, bleeding out from the lawn beyond the pool patio.

"Uh, we've got about twelve acres," Rob said. "There are paths through some of the woods, but a lot of it is too dense and steep to go through."

I was about to tell him I didn't care how fucking dense and steep parts were, that we had to search everywhere, but I was interrupted by the ring of my phone. It was David.

"Are you still at the house?" he asked, his voice fraught.

"Yes, nothing so far, but we're going out to search the grounds now." I maneuvered around Rob and Jamie to exit the bedroom and retreated down the hallway. "Rob's boyfriend is here, and he just told me he saw Chloe go outside with a bottle of wine Friday night." Without meaning to, I let out a low moan on the last words. "He thinks she might have gone out there with a guy."

"*Jesus.*" I heard David choke back a sob. "Okay, I'm glad you're still on-site. The police said they should be there shortly."

"They agreed to help already? I thought—"

"Campus security kicked things into gear with the Boston cops. They checked her cell phone. It's off or out of juice, but they can tell the last time it was on was Friday night, at the house in Dover."

Oh god. She had to be here then, maybe not even far from where I stood now.

"And the Boston police are on their way?"

"No, they reached out to the local cops, who agreed to swing by the house. The property seems huge on Google Maps. Is it?"

I sighed. "Yes. It's around twelve acres, and a big part of it is woods."

"The people who are helping you search, Skyler . . . Are they standing right there now?" There was an edge in his voice, so I moved even farther down the hall. "No, they're in another room."

"Do you think they know more than they're saying? Are they covering their asses?"

"I don't think so," I said, keeping my own voice low. "I mean, they're nervous, but because they don't want anything to be wrong."

"You need to keep an eye on them anyway."

"I will," I promised. "Can I talk to Mom for a minute?"

"She's too upset to even get on the phone. Did you hear what I just said?" he asked. There's a sternness in his voice that wasn't there before. "You need to watch these people you're with and make sure no one leaves the premises without talking to the police, okay?"

"I heard you. We're all going outside now."

"No, you need to sit tight for now. But text me the minute the cops arrive."

He disconnected without a goodbye. As I stumbled back toward the bedroom, I heard Rob talking to Jamie between clenched teeth. "The next time you want to throw a party while Mom and Dad are off traipsing around Europe, don't include *me* in your little plan."

"Fuck you, Rob. You can—"

Stepping into the room, I saw the three of them huddled in a circle by the bed, and their heads instantly swiveled in my direction. They looked alarmed, and possibly guilty. Were they actually hiding something or simply worried about what might rain down on them?

"Any news?" Jamie asked.

I shook my head. "Not about Chloe. But my stepfather said the Dover police are coming."

"Coming *here*?" Rob exclaimed. "We can't let them trample all over the house without a warrant."

"For god's sake, Rob," Jamie said. "Her sister is *missing*. Can't you think of anyone but yourself for a second?"

"And what are you afraid they'll find, Rob?" I demanded, glaring at him. I felt a sudden urge to rip his eyes out of their sockets. "*Drugs? What?*"

"Look, I don't mean to sound like a dick, and I'm sorry about your sister, but I also don't want to start a shitstorm for my family." He swept a hand nervously through his hair. "It's not like there was a kilo of something lying around the other night, but people were smoking weed, and some of those dudes who came with my cousin brought coke. There could be stuff still around the house that Jamie and I didn't notice during the cleanup."

Instinctively I pressed both hands to my ears because I couldn't bear hearing another word out of his mouth. "Just shut up, okay? It's not the house that needs to be searched anymore, it's the grounds.

And we can't wait for the police anyway. We all have to start looking out there, right this minute."

Though David had insisted I sit tight, I knew I had to be in motion right now, or I would go out of my mind.

Jamie nodded in agreement, and Dan surprisingly stuck his feet into a pair of slip-on loafers and grabbed a jacket from the back of a chair. I spun around and hurried from the bedroom, hearing the others behind me. Jamie stopped in her room for her phone and a jacket but joined us only seconds later in the front hall.

"Actually, Rob, I think you should wait behind," I said. I was ignoring David's advice again, but it seemed crucial for a family member to greet the cops. And if I had only one search partner, I wanted it to be Jamie. "Let us know as soon as the police arrive."

"Yeah, okay," he said, but I saw him flash Jamie a look.

"You better call Dad," she told him. "Let him know what's going on."

"Shouldn't you—"

"Just do it, Rob."

Turning her back on him, she led Dan and me to the family room and opened a French door to the patio, which ran across much of the back of the house. Beyond it lay a huge lawn, interrupted by the rectangular black-bottom pool. At the farther end of the pool was a small stone building I hadn't noticed from the morning room but now recalled seeing the other night when I'd come outside to look for Chloe.

"What about there?" I said, jabbing my finger in that direction. I'd been stupid not to remember it until now.

"The pool house?" Jamie asked. "I think Rob checked yesterday to make sure there was nothing to clean up, but we can look."

She sounded a little frayed around the edges now, but I didn't care. I rushed toward the building with Jamie and Dan trailing behind me and twisted the handle of the door as soon as I reached it.

"It's locked," I said. "Do you have a key?"

Instead of answering, she squatted down by a heavy planter next to the door, tipped it to the side with one hand, and used the other hand to fish out a key from underneath. I held my breath as she unlocked the door and pushed it open to reveal a single room.

But I could immediately tell no one had recently been inside. The place smelled musty, and the cream-colored armchairs and matching couch looked untouched. I noticed two doors at the end of the room opposite the wooden bar, and just to be sure, I swung them open, one at a time. Inside the first was a toilet and sink, and in the second, a shower and wooden bench. Neither appeared to have been used since last summer.

"Is this everything?" I asked Jamie. "I mean, there's no basement, is there?"

She shook her head. "This is it," she said.

Dan had come in while I was opening the far doors, and when I turned to leave, I spotted the worry in his eyes. It should have made me feel worse, but it was actually comforting to know that he was on the same page as me, and not, like Jamie and Rob, concerned his ass might be on the line.

"You definitely think Chloe went outside Friday night?" I asked him, even though I knew the answer.

"I'm positive. I saw her open the kitchen door and leave with the wine—though I have no idea what direction she went in." He paused for a moment. "This might not be worth anything, but the way most people were getting out to the pool was through the door in the family room. Since she went out through the kitchen, maybe she was headed someplace else instead."

But *where*? The three of us shuffled out of the building, and Dan glanced back at the house, seeming to focus on the door from the kitchen. Then he swiveled his head and looked out across the lawn. There were clusters of dogwood trees at the end, already blooming with white and pink flowers, and the thick wooded area rose behind them.

"Rob mentioned there were paths in the woods," I said. "Where do they go?"

"The main one goes to a gazebo," Jamie said wearily. "It's about a ten-minute walk from here, in a little clearing."

My heart seemed to kick the wall of my chest. Is that where Chloe had gone—to the gazebo?

"Show me how to get there."

I was aware that I was barking orders at them, but I had to keep moving—because the constant motion was the only thing making me feel there was still a reason to hope.

Jamie ended up in the lead, and Dan and I trekked behind her across the lawn. The sun had been shining when I'd left the hotel this morning, but now huge cumulus clouds muscled their way across the sky. We reached the dogwoods, snaked through them, and found ourselves at the start of the real woods—a mix, it appeared, of firs, maples, and oaks. I spotted the mouth of the trail right away. It hadn't been visible from the house, or even the pool, but if someone had been wandering around out here, using the flashlight on a phone, they could have easily come upon it.

With Jamie still in the lead, we entered the woods, where my nostrils instantly filled with the scent of fir trees and decaying leaves left over from last fall. The path was pretty wide at the start, and easy to follow, but within a couple of minutes it narrowed, and the woods grew denser and dimmer.

Would Chloe have really come here the night of the party? There was something so ominous about the path and the woods and all the twisted branches, like a scene from a scary fairy tale. But Chloe was impetuous, a risk-taker, someone usually game for adventure. So, yeah, it was easy to see her sneaking off here with a guy from the party, on a mission to reach the gazebo.

A fresh wave of fear gripped me, but I forced myself to put one foot in front of the other, trying to keep pace with Jamie. Though the path was still fairly well defined, we were suddenly going uphill, and a ravine plastered with rotting leaves was taking shape on our left.

A ringtone sounded ahead, freezing the breath in my chest. It was from Jamie's phone, I realized, and she stuffed a hand into the back pocket of her jeans to pull it free.

"It's Rob," she called back to us.

Had he found something?

She brought the phone to her ear, spoke to someone briefly, and then glanced back at me.

"He said the cops are at the house and they need to speak with Skyler."

"Okay," I muttered, instinctively clenching my hands. Someone else was in charge now, which I wished could have calmed me, but it didn't. If I let go, how could I be sure they took every possible step to find Chloe?

"We'll go with you," Jamie said, jogging back toward me. I turned on the path and began to reverse course toward the house. Dan, who had been last in line, now passed us to head farther into the woods, his loafers crunching the ground beneath.

"I should keep going, right?" he called out. "So we don't lose time?"

Should he? I asked myself, my heart beating hard. Maybe the police were only here to interview me at this stage, and it would be better to have Dan out here looking for evidence of Chloe's presence. But, I realized, the cops would want to speak to everyone, including him.

I spun around to tell him to stay with us, but he was already a few yards away, about to round a bend in the path.

"Wait," I yelled to him. "You need to come with us. . . . *Wait.*"

He didn't answer me, but instead stopped dead in his tracks and craned his neck to the left. Then he took a few steps in that direction, toward the ravine we'd been following, and leaned over a little from the waist.

"Oh god," he screamed suddenly. "Jamie, get *over* here."

My knees buckled. *Please*, I thought, *please, please, please*, no. I regained control of my legs and propelled myself in Dan's direction, stumbling along the path and dizzy with panic. I could hear Jamie coming up behind me, panting, until she suddenly overtook me, running toward Dan.

"Oh fuck," she exclaimed as soon as she reached him, her attention trained on the same place as his.

"Skyler, don't look," Dan called out as I closed in on them. "I beg you—don't look."

But I did look. I twisted my head to the left and stared through the tree branches, already thick with leaves, and down the steep, scraggly side of the ravine.

She was there, at the bottom. My beautiful sister Chloe. Lying faceup and wearing only her jeans and a single boot, her pale white breasts pointed toward the sky and her blond hair fanned out around her head. Her eyes appeared to be closed, and her head was tilted at a weird angle. For a few brief seconds I let myself wonder if she'd been horribly injured and was lying there waiting for help, but that was stupid of me. It was clear that Chloe was dead.

27

Now

LIFT THE HALF-FULL CAN OF DIET COKE TO MY LIPS AND THEN think better of it. The last thing I need is more caffeine and fake sugar to add to my jitters. Instead, I pour myself a glass of water and wander into the living room. Part of me yearns to call Mikoto, to ask for her help. But I decide I've already wasted too much of her time.

What would she say, I wonder, if I laid out Mark Whaley's visit for her? If I explained that the most recent theory I had about C.J.'s gift to me (revenge) now seems as flawed as my earlier ones (goodwill toward struggling artists/nostalgia/lingering lust). She'd surely remind me that if I don't get all the facts, I'll be at a disadvantage, and that I need to keep digging.

But where to look?

Absentmindedly I pick up my tote bag from the couch and set it in a corner. Earlier I couldn't wait to spread out all my purchases and begin imagining how I might use them, but right now the thought of working on that specific collage holds zero appeal.

At the same time, I feel an urge to keep myself busy, to shake off the ugliness of the late afternoon. I open the narrow closet by my front door and take down a sheaf of eighteen-by-twenty-five-inch construction paper from the top shelf. After removing a sheet, I lay it on my small dining table. The whiteness is almost blinding, but at the same time it beckons to me.

I *do* want to make a collage, I decide, just not the one I had planned on when I set off this afternoon.

I stare at the paper for another minute, and then, almost without thinking, I pick up my phone and scroll to an album from twelve years ago. Eventually I find what I'm looking for: a picture of me taken one early April afternoon in the Boston Public Garden by my long-lost friend Tess. I'm wearing a short, flippy skirt and a jean jacket and holding a double-scoop chocolate ice cream cone. Though the sun is making me squint, I've managed a big grin. Tess and I had been playing tourist that day, meandering around the park, devouring our cones, and coming up with funny names for the ducks in the pond.

Though I could have described the photo generally, it's still a shock to behold some of the details after all this time. My hair's much longer than I remember it being back then, and despite the grad school pressures I was under, I look thrilled to be alive and in Boston. I seem confident, if not cocksure, that I'd be able to bend the world to my will.

So much for that.

I email the picture to myself, open it on my computer, and print it out in color. Then I crudely cut around the outline of my head and body with a pair of big scissors. For a brief moment I consider crinkling up the image and flicking it into the trash basket under my desk—because there's no way to look at the picture without summoning up everything horrible that transpired within a few days of when it was taken. But instead, I rub a glue stick along the back and press the picture down in the middle of the blank construction paper.

What I'm about to do, what I *need* to do, is make a collage about the night I spent with Christopher Whaley. Perhaps bringing it to life on paper will help me better understand what he took away from our encounter and the real motivation behind his befuddling choice.

And the collage has to have my picture smack in the center, doesn't it? C.J.'s decision to leave me an obscene amount of money might not reflect nostalgia or lingering lust on his part, but it had something to do with me, directly or indirectly.

My phone rings just as I'm pressing hard on the photo to adhere it. Nicky, I think, probably calling to feel out whether I'm stewing about the absence of a celebratory dinner next week—because she'd never come right out and ask me—but when I grab my phone, I spot Alejandro's name on the screen. *Oh, no*, I think. Maybe the skulker has struck again.

"Hey," I blurt out. "Has something happened?"

"What? No, sorry to alarm you." He chuckles, the sound deep and warm. "No more difficulties with the power or mad dashes down the stairs in the dark."

I sigh inwardly, grateful for that at least. "Good, thank you for letting me know."

"But I could tell on the phone that you were worried about the man who came by, not knowing who he was. I thought it would be helpful if I made a sketch of him for you."

Alejandro's artwork, which I've caught glimpses of when his studio door has been open, seems to be mainly abstract expressionism, very vivid and arresting, but that doesn't mean he can't draw a decent figure.

"Could you really do that without seeing him again?"

"Yes. I have an eye for faces and a memory for them, too. I realized I got a good enough look at the man that I could do a sketch of him."

I can't believe it. I might actually find out what the guy looked like.

"Thank you so much, Alejandro. How long do you think it will take you to do it?"

He laughs. "Oh, it's already done, so I'll send it right now. I just wanted to alert you before texting it."

"Okay, standing by."

Holding my breath, I put my phone on speaker and lock my gaze on the screen. A few seconds pass. Will it be Deacon, after all?

The sketch arrives a couple of seconds later, and I pull back a little in surprise. It's definitely not Deacon. It's not Mark Whaley, either, or anyone else I know. The guy's hair is dark, like Alejandro described the other day, but wavy, not at all what I pictured when I thought Josh might have been the guy who'd come by. And though Alejandro's sketch only includes the shoulders and upper torso of the man, it's clear from his build that he's heavyset.

And I see there's something else Alejandro didn't mention the other day.

"He had a mustache?" I ask.

"Yes. Did I forget to say that? I guess because you seemed to know who it was right away, I didn't elaborate. This isn't someone you're familiar with?"

"No, I've never seen him before."

"Maybe I should have been more suspicious at the time, but when he said he was with your gallery, I assumed everything was okay."

"That's okay. Truly, it's so helpful to have the sketch. Thank you again, Alejandro."

"Please, it's my pleasure. Have a good night. And don't worry, I'll let you know if I see him again."

After I sign off, I study the sketch further. It's very well done, and my sense is that I'm staring at a close likeness. I can't tell if I'm projecting, but it strikes me that there's something definitely sleazy-looking about the guy's face. Is he an unscrupulous private eye, as Mikoto suggested, or some other kind of henchman?

Though I'm bone-tired and want nothing more than to crawl under the covers, I set the phone down and return my attention to the construction paper. After a minute of staring at my twenty-five-year-old face, I use my computer to pull up the website for the Kensington and click on the tab for "rooms and suites."

My breath quickens as soon as the main gallery photo comes into view. Surely the rooms have been refurbished or redecorated in the intervening years, but at first glance the overall look seems very much the same. The room's luxe curtains, armchair, and thick pile rug are all in muted shades of taupe, and though the bed is a four-poster, it's very modern in design.

And there's a sleek gas fireplace along one of the walls, something I'd forgotten about. I remember suddenly that C.J. had turned it on while we ate our room service meal, and we'd had sex the second time in the glow from the flames.

There aren't many rooms in the hotel, and as I click through photos of the various sizes and styles, I realize that the photo I first looked at might be the exact room we stayed in.

I print that out, too, as well as pictures of the bar on the ground floor, then cut off the accompanying type and glue the photos on the paper near my image. I also add a photo I find online of Boston rooftops, because I could see a cluster of them from my own room, and another of the Public Garden and a sign for the Freedom Trail, both of which were only a few minutes from the Kensington by foot.

I briefly consider adding Chris Whaley's photo from the obit, but he looks too different from what I remember. Instead, I scrawl out the initials C.J. with a magic marker on a piece of note paper, tear it off, and add it to what I've done so far. I also add a scrap of paper with the words *Two Truths and a Lie*.

Is this insane? I wonder. It's taken me over a decade to leave Boston behind, mentally and emotionally, and yet here I am, trying to time travel back there. And now that I've started, I don't think I can stop.

My phone rings again, making me jump. It's after nine, not a time when Nicky ever calls. I pick up the phone from the far end of the table, and to my surprise, Bradley Kane's name is on the screen.

"Ms. Moore, good evening," he says after I answer. "Am I catching you at a bad time?"

"Define *bad*."

"Well, it's not an hour when people are eager for calls. But I was hoping you had a minute. I wanted to set up a time to meet with you in person again. Tomorrow if possible."

"You want me to come to Scarsdale again?" I don't mind if he can hear the exasperation in my voice. I'd been planning never to set foot in that town again for as long as I live.

"No, my club in the city is a lot closer to you. I'm going to be playing squash there tomorrow morning, and we could meet afterward in the lounge."

"And you think I should trust you enough to speak to you again?"

"Why do you say that?"

"You led me to believe our meeting the other day was confidential, but then Jane Whaley ambushed me in the lobby of your building. How do I know it wasn't you who told her I'd be there?"

He clears his throat. "I assure you it wasn't and that we've been investigating the situation. As I mentioned to you, I alerted Mrs. Whaley to the fact that the trust was being transferred to someone other than her, but I never revealed your name. That would have been unethical. And besides, Mr. Whaley was adamant that she not know who the beneficiary was."

Hmm. That's another interesting morsel. Could it also indicate that C.J. wasn't trying to humiliate her?

"Then how did she find out?"

"We're not sure yet, but it's emerged that one of our paralegals has a sister who was at school with the Whaley children. We think she might have alerted them to what was happening. If that turns out to be the case, she'll be terminated, of course."

"Am I supposed to believe that the paralegal also got her hands on my address and turned that over to them as well?"

"I'm not following," he says, and he sounds sincere.

"Jane Whaley knows where I live, and she and her family have been harassing me here in New York, practically since the minute I left your office."

I hear an intake of breath. "What do you mean?"

"My apartment was broken into and searched the day we met, and I'm almost positive she was behind it. She's clearly trying to find evidence that I had an ongoing relationship with her husband. She also had someone leave a note in my bag calling me a whore—and then if that wasn't enough, Mark Whaley showed up outside my building tonight to try to get me to renounce the trust. And he hurled a few expletives at me in the process."

A pause follows, and I wonder if I've managed to rattle the seemingly imperturbable Mr. Kane.

"It makes sense that the Whaleys are upset," he says. "I think you can understand what this must be like for them. But if your apartment was broken into and people are leaving you nasty notes, I'd be shocked if Jane Whaley were responsible. She's a shrewd lady. Why would she complicate her standing in a potential suit by breaking the law?"

"You think it's all a coincidence?" I ask, not bothering to keep the skepticism out of my voice.

"I'd say yes—when you consider that New Yorkers have their apartments broken into all the time and often have disturbing things happen to them."

I sigh in frustration. It's pretty clear I don't have a shot at convincing him of what the Whaleys are up to, and even if I did, he probably wouldn't acknowledge it anyway. I bet fancy firm attorneys like him have to keep every response a hundred percent neutral.

I decide to go for broke on another front.

"I'd be in a much better position to evaluate all this if you would just explain why C.J. assigned the trust to me," I say. "Something tells me you know more than what you've told me."

There's another pregnant pause, and I sense him making a calculation, deciding how much to divulge.

"I can understand your frustration, Ms. Moore. This can't be easy for you. But if you'd be willing to meet me tomorrow, I have information that may help put some of your concerns to rest. And then you can get on with your life."

Finally, I think. Finally, I might know.

"All right," I say.

"I'll see you at the University Club on West Fifty-Fourth Street. Eleven o'clock."

28

Now

'VE NEVER BEEN TO THE UNIVERSITY CLUB, NEVER EVEN HEARD OF it for that matter, but when I arrive at the corner of Fifty-Fourth Street and Fifth Avenue on Saturday morning, I realize I've passed it without knowing what was inside. It's an intimidating Renaissance Revival building, made of sand-colored granite. The metal and glass awning above the entrance doesn't have a name or even a symbol on it, because clearly there's no need for the place to advertise its presence. If you're a member, you're aware where it is, and the rest of us peons have no business knowing.

Miraculously, I'd woken up this morning with a little voice in my head urging me to look up the dress code, maybe because my mother and stepfather are members of a country club where you can be turned away if you show up in jeans. The rules at the University Club turned out to be absurd. According to what I found online, women—known as "lady members"—are required to wear suits, dresses, or skirts and dress shirts. Pants are only allowed if paired with dress shirts or "elegant" sweaters or scarves. A whole host of items are strictly forbidden, including capris, cargo pants, rompers, leggings, bare midriff tops, and anything at all made of denim.

There are no capris, cargo pants, or miniskirts in my closet, and certainly no rompers, but my go-to going-out outfit, on the rare occasions when I need it, almost always includes leggings. I ended up deciding to go with the black silk shirt I'd worn to the meeting in Scarsdale and the mid-length skirt I'd bought for the gallery opening, praying it won't attract a giant stain today.

A doorman ushers me into a small foyer, where I'm greeted by another man in uniform. Standing at a podium in the grand lobby and wearing the expression of someone about to dispatch cars for a funeral procession, he asks for my name and directs me to the entrance of an old-fashioned yet luxurious lounge.

Though the room, with butter-colored walls and silk drapes, is nearly empty, Kane is parked at one of the tables against the far wall. He spots me as soon as I cross the threshold onto the thick, patterned carpet.

Bradley Kane tries to be subtle, but I spot him running his gaze over my outfit as I approach. Is he worried I'm going to be booted out because it doesn't meet the club's definition of "elegance"? I notice that he's wearing a jacket and dress shirt but no tie. I guess the club dropped the tie requirement for males once most of the businessmen in the country stopped wearing them.

"Thanks for coming," he says, rising. "I know it was short notice."

"That's okay, " I say, taking a seat in the cushioned chair across from him. If he's finally going to give me the information I need, no notice is too short.

"Let me get you something to drink. A coffee? A cappuccino?"

I haven't come for refreshments, but I request a cappuccino just to play along. Kane scribbles our beverage order on the page of a small pad on the table, signals for a waiter, and passes the order to him.

"I'm sorry to hear you've been going through a difficult time lately," he says as the waiter moves off.

"It doesn't sound like you believe me about what's been happening."

"It's not that I don't believe you. It's just hard for me to accept that the Whaleys would stoop to harassing you or breaking into your apartment."

I want to note that, at the very least, Mark Whaley tracked down my address and confronted me outside my home, but I let it go. I'm not going to convince Kane, and besides, it's not the reason I showed up at this club, a relic from another century. Instead, I simply fold my hands on the table, waiting for him to get to the point.

"Have you been able to find an attorney to advise you on the trust?" Kane asks.

"Yes," I say, not adding that I haven't met with her yet.

"Good, I'm happy to hear that. It's important to have someone looking out for your interests."

Our drinks arrive. Giving the waiter time to retreat again, Kane flicks a packet of Splenda a couple of times, tears it open, and empties it into his coffee.

"You said you had something to tell me, something that would be helpful," I say, trying not to sound as desperate as I feel.

"Yes, I do. It's actually a proposal, which ideally will make the entire situation much better for you."

I'm confused. "A proposal from *you*?"

He takes a sip of coffee and sets the cup back in the porcelain saucer with a clink. "Not from me. From Jane Whaley."

As soon as he sees me startle in my seat, he raises one hand. "Just so you know, neither I nor anyone in my firm represents Mrs. Whaley. But since she's aware that I worked with her husband on the trust assignment, she approached me to assist in this matter."

"Oh, so now you're acting as her intermediary?" I say, shaking my head.

"Actually," he says, then clears his throat. "She'd like to present the proposal to you herself. She knows you two got off on the wrong foot, and she wants to correct that by meeting with you."

"Meeting in *person*?" The last thing I want to do is encounter her again.

He nods. "She's actually waiting in the reading room here. If you're willing, I'll ask her to join us at the table."

I feel totally conned, and a rage begins to build in me, just like the one I saw come to a boil in Mark Whaley last night. I wonder how Kane would react if I stood up in the middle of his snobby club and shouted, *Fuck you then. Fuck you to hell.*

But I have to suck it up and do as he asks—because by talking to Jane Whaley, I might be able to extract some of the facts I need. I breathe in slowly, trying to calm myself.

"All right," I say, finally, meeting his gaze.

He flicks his eyes around the room, then he discreetly slides a phone from the pocket of his pants and begins typing, never lifting the device above the table. The club probably forbids the use of mobile phones.

He nods to let me know she's received the text, and we sit in silence. Holding my breath, I prepare for the experience. *Let her do all the talking*, I tell myself. *Betray no emotion. Observe her carefully.*

Within seconds Jane appears in the doorway and strides confidently toward us. She's wearing high heels, black crepe pants, and a chic black-and-white blazer with three big bows where the buttons should be. A small lock of her raven-colored hair has fallen over her eye again, which means the look must definitely be intentional. How does a stylist convince a woman to go that route? *You won't be able to see as well, but you'll be making a real statement.*

"Thank you for agreeing to meet," she says once she reaches the table and slides into the chair to my right. Though she might be trying, she hasn't managed to hide the snootiness from either her tone or the expression on her face.

Kane extends a hand for the pad, obviously to order her a drink, but she dismisses him with a brisk wave and turns her attention back to me. Caroline Whaley had told me that C.J. was besotted with Jane in part because of her self-possession, but in the intervening years, it's clearly morphed into a brittle arrogance.

"As you can imagine, Ms. Moore," she says, widening her large brown eyes, "this has been an extremely trying time for me—losing my husband, seeing my children lose their father—and then this difficult matter with the trust. But I also appreciate it's been a confusing time for you, too."

She pauses, as if expecting me to thank her, but I say nothing.

"And I'm sure you're concerned," she adds, "that things will become even more difficult."

That sounds like a threat.

I force myself to look her right in the eye. "What is it you wanted to discuss, specifically?"

The shadow of a smile crosses her face. Maybe I've impressed her by cutting to the chase.

"All right. As I believe you've heard, I've been working with a team of highly skilled attorneys to contest the assignment of the trust. But I'd be willing to cease those efforts if you agree to split the trust in half with me. And if you do so, I'll also write you a check now for twenty-five thousand dollars—on top of your half—as a show of good faith."

I stare at her, too stunned to speak. Does she really think I'll give back half the money to end the harassment and whatever legal threat she presents? Who's the extortionist now?

My lack of response seems to fluster both her and Kane. Jane straightens her back, looking tense, and Kane rubs his fingers back and forth on the wooden table, as if he's trying to remove a mark.

I gather a breath, preparing to tell her just what I think of her pathetic proposition, but then I catch myself. If I create a scene, I'll have no chance of getting what I need from Kane today.

"Hmm, that's very interesting," I say, staring into the cappuccino I have yet to touch. From the corner of my eye I see her hands uncurl ever so slightly. She must be buying the idea that I'm open to her little plan.

"But I need some time to think about it," I continue. "I'll follow up with Mr. Kane, if that suits you?"

"Of course," she says, smiling tightly. "I'll wait to hear from Bradley."

Seconds later she's striding purposefully back across the room and out the door, and I could almost believe she wasn't here at all.

"Thank you," Kane says softly. "And I'm glad you took the time to listen. I know the attorneys Mrs. Whaley has hired, and they can be real barracudas. If you accept her offer, it will guarantee that you'd have half the funds—which is still a great deal of money."

I nod, continuing with my charade. I need to play along for now so I can get what I came for.

"Why couldn't you have told me this on the phone last night instead of putting me on the spot?"

"I wanted to give you the chance to hear her out."

I finally take a sip of my drink, gathering my words, then set the cup down. "Since I came all this way, maybe you could at least tell me what I thought you were going to share."

He looks confused. "And what was that?"

"I thought you were finally going to explain why Chris Whaley left the trust to me."

Kane's brow knits further. "As I told you the other day,

Ms. Moore, I don't know why he chose you as the beneficiary. He refused to go into it."

"You can't wager a guess?" I say. "You said you'd been friends."

Kane shifts in his seat, looking uncomfortable again. "We went to the same high school, and by chance to the same college, but we'd drifted apart over the years. Plus, C.J. tended to be a very private person. I can assure you he didn't offer me a clue. He simply said he owed you."

My heart skips. This is new.

"*Owed* me? Why didn't you tell me that before?"

"I thought it was implied. After all, why would he leave you such a huge bequest if he didn't feel indebted to you? But it seems to me that the only person who can determine the reason is you."

"Well, I haven't yet," I say. "But I'm going to."

He studies me intently for a couple of beats. "Let's get back to the other matter. When you do you think you'll have an answer for Mrs. Whaley?"

"Actually, I'm happy to give you the answer now," I say, feeling my anger spike again. "Tell her I have no intention of splitting the trust with her."

Kane flinches, but he looks resigned. "As you wish."

I tell him I need to leave, and we exchange polite enough good-byes, though I feel the urge to toss a handful of Splenda packets at his head before I walk out the door.

BACK HOME, AFTER AN HOUR'S WORTH OF TRAVEL BY SUBWAY AND foot, I take a minute to refresh Tuna's water before starting to pace my living room, massaging my brow as I go. The more I think about Jane's so-called proposal, the more furious I feel. She's saying that unless I'm willing to "go halfsies" with her, she'll sic her high-priced lawyers on me, which could possibly result in me losing the trust and having my name smeared in the process.

But as disgusted as I am by the offer, I can't help wondering if I've made a mistake by not at least entertaining it. Because one million seven hundred fifty thousand dollars is a hell of a lot better than zero.

She probably won't have any luck with the "sextortion" angle—as I've repeatedly assured myself, there's not a shred of proof on that front or even anything that could be ginned up to resemble it—but if she moves on to questioning C.J.'s state of mind when he made me the beneficiary, it's possible she could recruit enough friends and family to testify that her husband's illness compromised his ability to think rationally. I've been taking comfort in Caroline's assertion that C.J. was clear in his thinking, but Jane's lawyers could work with the obvious: Who in his right mind leaves so much money to a one-night stand from a dozen years ago? Especially one like me. The women who end up with jackpots from rich dudes tend to be the buxom bombshell type, not lanky, small-breasted women with short brown hair and a wardrobe from Zara.

I feel even more eager to meet with the lawyer. Maybe she'll be able to predict Jane's odds of winning. She might even advise me to accept the offer, guaranteeing myself money in the bank rather than nothing to show for my troubles but a big old pile of legal bills.

I finally cease pacing and drift over to the table, where my collage is still sitting. The girl in the center of the paper, the long-gone girl in a flippy skirt and jean jacket, stares back at me, her lips the tiniest bit parted as if she's about to speak. *What are you trying to say?* I think. Does my twenty-five-year-old self know something about that night that she's not telling me, something that will make me understand?

I think back to the only thing I got out of Kane today, which I've almost forgotten in my fury. C.J. told him he *owed* me. Owed me for what, though? Something I said or did without knowing how significant it was?

There's a term Mikoto used at the café the other day that's been lingering at the back of my mind: "hush money."

She'd been dismissive of the idea, but what if that *is* the explanation? Did C.J. leave me the trust in gratitude for my never exposing a secret he shared that night? It's not like he'd rolled over in bed at some point and announced he'd embezzled from his company or held up a 7-Eleven as a troubled teen. Or was it for keeping the actual fact of his infidelity secret? But that doesn't make sense—because he ended up revealing its existence himself, by leaving me the money.

I pick up my scissors and spend the next few minutes adding items to the collage, images I rip from magazines and pictures I find online: a glass of rosé, like the one I ordered at the hotel bar; lobster rolls; a cotton fisherman's sweater, because I had a favorite one that I think I wore to the hotel that night; and a black crocodile luggage tag. I don't recall what C.J.'s suitcase looked like, but I remember noticing the expensive-looking tag on it.

Finally, I drop the glue stick on the table, ready to call it quits for now, but then catch myself. As frayed around the edges as I feel, there's one more thing I need to add. From a small pad of paper, I tear off a sheet and scrawl the word *owed* on it with black marker. I swipe the glue stick along the back of the paper and press it onto the collage, right next to the photo of myself.

This is what I need to focus on now, isn't it? If Christopher Whaley thought he was in my debt, I need to know why.

29

Now

Late Saturday afternoon, I get a text from an art direc-tor I regularly work with, pleading for me to take on an eleventh-hour job due Monday. I say yes. Not only is the money good, but it will keep my mind off Jane Whaley. I need to stop dwelling on her, wondering what her barracuda-like lawyers are up to or what act of intimidation she might be planning now that she knows I'm not waving a white flag of surrender. I end up working like a maniac most of the day Sunday, dressed in flannel pajamas and with Tuna curled on my lap.

I've told myself I need to keep my head clear by avoiding the collage until after the opening, but the table in my tiny living room is only three feet from my desk so it's hard to do. I eat dinner Sunday night on the couch and later, as I'm returning from the kitchen with a mug of herbal tea, I end up wandering to the table, where my gaze is drawn immediately to the last word I pasted there: *owed*. Why in the world did C.J. think he owed me?

I drop onto one of the two rickety dining chairs. Most of what I learned about him came from our rounds of Two Truths and a Lie.

He'd been fun to play with, I recall, clever with the statements he made, so that differentiating fact from fiction wasn't easy for me. When I'd played the game with new college friends, the fabrications they cooked up were often either ridiculously far-fetched, like *I grew up on an island*, or boring, like *I hate milk in my cereal*, but C.J.'s lies were intriguing and plausible enough to be true. In one round, he told me that he'd broken off an engagement with a college sweetheart and had regretted it for years—a lie.

As I'm standing by the table with my mug in hand, I suddenly remember another one. He told me he'd taken the LSAT—the law school admission test—for a friend who'd been ill and hadn't been able to study. I'd immediately guessed that one as a lie because he seemed like someone with a stronger code of ethics—ironic, I know, since he was cheating.

But what if he *had* been the kind of guy to take the test for someone else? What if some or all of the "lies" he'd told me were actually true? Maybe he was voicing transgressions so that he could finally get them off his chest while simultaneously seeing what type of reaction they prompted. And then later, he might have wondered if I'd guessed what he was up to.

This could be why he thought he'd owed me, because I'd never done anything with the lies that might have really been truths. But how could I begin to know what was actually true and what wasn't, without him being here to tell me?

ON MONDAY MORNING I FINISH UP MY FREELANCE DESIGN PROJECT, shoot it off to the art director, and spend the next hour speed walking around Tompkins Square Park because the only recent cardio I've had is the spikes in my heart rate from anxiety. After returning to the apartment with a take-out salad, I eat at my desk and then buckle down to prepare for the opening. First, I try on the new sweater and skirt I bought with my brown unconstructed blazer and short brown boots I'm planning to wear with them. Once everything is on, I examine the results in the full-length mirror on the back of the bathroom door. To my horror I discover I look like a greeter in a college admissions office, not an emerging downtown artist.

Maybe accessories will help, I think, and I spend fifteen minutes picking through my Ziploc bag of costume jewelry and trying on the five pairs of dangly earrings I own. None are perfect, but the ones with the fake amber stones at least go with the outfit and make it seem a tiny bit hipper. Next, I tidy up my boots, using one of those little kits that comes with polish, a brush, and piece of white buffing cloth and lets you pretend you shine shoes for a living. Finally, I wash out a pair of dark brown tights from the back of my drawer, which I'm relieved to see are free of runs.

I'd thought that getting my outfit together would give me a sense of control, but by the time I swing the wet tights over the shower rod, my panic is mushrooming. In college, I'd dreamed of having a gallery show in New York, where people would gaze at my work on the walls and then some of them would buy it for *their* walls. But now that it's upon me, I'm terrified, and not just because of the party tomorrow night. What if none of my collages ends up selling?

Like many galleries, Josh explained to me once, his no longer signals that a piece of art has been sold by sticking a red dot beneath or to the side of it on the wall. So if no one purchases a collage, I'll be spared public humiliation during the reception, at least. But still, *I'll* know at the end of the night if nothing sold, as Josh will, too, of course. And though my mother will be in the dark initially, she'll probably find a way to worm the information out of me at some point.

In an attempt to assuage my unease, I curl up with Tuna and watch a couple of hours of TV, but it doesn't help much. Before changing for bed, I rifle through the back of my medicine chest for the plastic container of clonazepam that my last therapist prescribed me for social gatherings. There are a few pills left, which thankfully means I'll have enough for tomorrow, but I also take one before crawling into bed. Still, it takes me forever to fall asleep, and it doesn't help that Tuna, perhaps sensing my disquiet, jumps on and off the mattress repeatedly.

I WAKE THE NEXT DAY RAGGED FROM LACK OF SLEEP AND WITH MY nerves on fire.

Staggering out of bed, I decide to drink tea instead of my usual morning coffee and eat only dry toast for breakfast. I feel vaguely like a hospital patient recovering from an appendectomy or an exploded gallbladder, but I get it down.

After dressing in jeans and a black turtleneck—I'm saving my opening outfit for later—I lock up the apartment to head off for my preview of the exhibit. As I step outside onto the stoop of my building, a guy jumps out of a delivery van that's double-parked right in front of me. He's carrying some kind of floral arrangement wrapped in paper, with colorful flower heads poking out at the top. He peers at the number on the building and bolts up the steps.

"Morning," he says distractedly and moves past me.

Are they for Mikoto? I wonder. She seems like the type of woman people send flowers to. I turn and watch as the delivery guy scans the buzzers, and then to my surprise, I see him press the one next to my name.

"Wait," I ask. "You're looking for Skyler Moore? That's me."

"Yup, Skyler Moore," he says, looking back at me. "You got ID with you?"

I fish through my messenger bag for my wallet and then flash my driver's license at him.

After I scrawl my signature on his device, he passes me the bouquet and scurries back down the steps. I tear off half the paper, and though the flowers are even lovelier than I realized—a fall-color-themed mix of mums, roses, and sunflowers in an antiqued black ceramic vase—it's the name on the card I'm interested in. Who could possibly be sending me a bouquet?

Congratulations, Sky! We are so excited for you. Love, Mom, David, Nicky and Matt.

My eyes prick with tears. The last time my mother sent me flowers was when I was bedridden with bronchitis my first semester in grad school. I've been thinking that tonight could be a turning point of sorts with her, that she'll be impressed with the art I've done and begin to view me in a fresh light, as someone capable of success. The flowers seem to be proof that I'm right.

I make a quick dash back to my apartment, where I set the vase of flowers on the kitchen counter, and then return to the street. I'm running a little behind now, but I stick to my plan to walk to the gallery because I need to try to burn off at least some of my jitters. I make reasonably good time, but the sidewalks on the Lower East Side are clogged with pedestrians and I have to hustle for the last few blocks. I reach the gallery at exactly eleven and, glancing through the window, I spot Nell at the desk. I try the door, and when it opens, I step inside the gallery's front room.

"Ah, right on time," she says.

She calls out Josh's name and he yells, "Be right out," from the back. As I wait for him to appear, I run my gaze over the stunning black-and-white photographs that line the walls in the front room. It's not hard to picture every one of them selling tonight.

A minute later, Josh strides into the front room.

"Morning, Skyler." He's carrying two mugs of what seems to be coffee and offers one to me.

"Oh, thank you," I say, taking it. I'm still planning to avoid coffee today, but I don't want to seem rude.

"You ready to take a look?"

"Yes, all set."

I inhale deeply and follow him into the rear of the gallery, keeping my eyes trained on the floor and praying it will all look okay.

"Ta-da," I hear him say.

I raise my eyes, and as I take in the collages, my lips part in . . . awe. Yes, awe. The ten collages, all mounted rather than framed, have been hung in perfect relation to one another. The surprising juxtapositions of images in each one, along with the vivid colors, are attention-grabbing, beckoning the viewer to come closer. And though the collages aren't really a series, they play off each other perfectly. I want to cry, I'm so happy.

"The look on your face tells me we got it right," he says.

"Josh, thank you," I say. "I'm blown away."

"Excellent. And I've got some great news for you."

Please, I think, *don't tell me that there are now two hundred people coming to the reception tonight.*

"Is it about the interview?" Maybe he'll tell me that James Tremlin didn't think I was full of shit.

"The *ArtToday* one? No, but I'm sure that went great. The news is that I've already sold one of your pieces."

"*What?*" This revelation both stuns and thrills me.

"Yup. A collector I work with, who's also a friend, dropped by yesterday when we were hanging the show. He not only loved what he saw, he bought one of your pieces on the spot—the one titled *Daydream*. When I told him it was three grand, he didn't bat an eye."

"Gosh, th-that's amazing," I say, glancing over at that particular collage. It's one of my favorites.

"It's a testament to your talent, Skyler. And trust me, there's more to come."

I sense he's got plenty to do before tonight, so I thank Josh again and head out, promising to return at least fifteen minutes before the show begins. On the walk north back to the East Village, my feet barely touch the ground, and as soon as I reach my neighborhood, I decide to do something I haven't done in ages: take myself out to lunch.

I stop at a small bistro only a couple of blocks from my apartment, one I used to go to with Lucas—in those early days, before he grew frustrated with my gloomy moods and my failure to keep the past from torturing me. Though it's not even noon, the place is open for business, and a waitress shows me to a wooden table tucked in a corner in the back. As I take my seat, I hear Tracy Chapman's "Fast Car," one of my favorite songs, playing softly in the background. I take that as a positive omen for the day and, after perusing the menu, order the chicken schnitzel and a celebratory glass of pinot grigio.

Without any warning, I'm overcome with the same rush of elation I experienced after leaving the gallery last week. Maybe standing in a room whose walls are covered with my work tonight will be so rewarding that my panic will be diffused, and I'll be game to answer any question that I'm asked. And perhaps more of my pieces will sell, kicking off my art career, and it won't even matter if I ever see a dime of the trust.

And maybe tonight is the moment when, after a long, sad slump, I emerge into the world as a new person, someone who'll once again spend sunny afternoons wandering through parks while eating double-dip chocolate cones, someone my mother will feel reconnected to, and someone with a child of her own.

After topping off my lunch with a cup of herbal tea, I head home to take care of a few household chores I've ignored all week. I also carry the flowers my family sent out to the living room and set the vase down next to the collage in progress. My eye is drawn once again to the word *owed* and I'm tempted to pull out a chair and ponder for a while, but I force myself away. I want to stay as positive as I can today.

At four, I take my second shower of the day and change into my outfit. My tights are still the tiniest bit damp, but I look okay, I decide, and I thank God it's only sixty degrees out—at the very least, I won't be sweating profusely during the party. Not wanting to scuff my newly polished boots, I treat myself to a cab to the gallery.

I arrive outside at exactly five thirty, earlier than necessary, but being here seems less nerve-racking than puttering around my apartment. As I reach for the door handle, I can see through the glass that the front room is empty of people, but a long, narrow table has been set up with plastic glasses, along with bottles of Perrier and white wine. The second I open the door, Nell strides in from the back, carrying a large ice bucket.

"Hi," I say. "Is it okay that I'm a little early?"

"Sure—as long as you don't mind hanging out by yourself. I've got to finish setting up and Josh is on the phone in his office."

"Of course, no problem." I give a little wave and start toward the rear room. "I-I guess I'll just wander back and look at the installation again."

"Go right ahead," she says, smiling, as if newly impressed with me. "A bunch of people who were in today told us how much they liked it."

Thrilled by the news, I thank her and disappear into the back room. Though I can hear the drone of Josh's voice from his office, I've got the space to myself, and the rush I feel is even more intense than before. And because I'm alone this time, I don't feel a need to disguise my glee.

Even the last piece I did, which I was in such a rush to finish, looks good to me. As I study it from across the room, though, my heart suddenly skitters. There seems to be a stain on the lower right-hand corner, a smudge mark of some kind.

I take a tentative step closer, then another. And finally it comes into focus. Stamped in the lower-right corner, on an old photograph I'd used as part of the collage, is the word *whore*.

I reel back, horrified. It's the same stamp mark as the one on the note I was left. Before I can think, I wheel around, letting my eyes go from piece to piece.

The word *whore* has been stamped on every single one of them.

30

Now

CLAMP MY HANDS OVER MY EYES AND LET OUT A WAIL OF DISTRESS. This can't be happening. *It can't be happening.* I'm going to release my hands and find out I've imagined the whole thing.

I hear footsteps—from two different directions. Someone touches my shoulder. As I lower my hands, I see that it's Josh. Nell is on the other side of me, and they're both asking if I'm okay. I open my mouth, but I can't catch a breath long enough to speak.

"Nell, get her some water," Josh orders, and she scurries away. He puts a comforting arm around me.

"Skyler, what is it?" he urges.

"I-I . . ." Nothing else comes out. I feel swamped by both panic and despair, like I'm on the top of a fog-covered mountain and have no idea how to find my way down. I slip out of Josh's hold and point to the stamp mark on the nearest collage. He shifts his attention to the spot.

"What the fuck?" he exclaims.

Still unable to summon the words, I jab my finger at the other collages. Josh begins to circle the room, running his gaze over each piece as his eyes widen with alarm.

Nell returns with a cup of water and I attempt a few sips, but my hands are so shaky half the liquid splashes onto the front of my sweater. She brushes at the wool with one hand, flicking off the water, and then joins Josh by the wall, clearly confused as to what's going on.

"Oh my god," she blurts out, then looks back at me. "This isn't something you added, is it?"

"No, it's not something she fucking *added*," Josh snaps. "Someone obviously came into the gallery and defaced them. Was there anyone acting weird or out of the ordinary today?"

Nell clasps her long thin arms to her chest, as if she's suddenly cold, and shakes her head. "Not that I noticed. But of course I can't see people what people are doing back here."

"Was anyone in here by themselves?" he asks.

As I try not to hyperventilate, she stares at the floor, clearly searching her memory. "Uh, a few people. A woman with a little dog. And a couple of different guys on their own. But no one for a very long, or I would have come back to check it out."

"Shouldn't we call the police?" I ask Josh. Though I'm finally able to speak, it comes out as a pathetic squeak.

"Uh, I guess. I don't think we should have them come *now*, at the start of the show, but I'll call the precinct first thing tomorrow." He looks back at Nell. "Give us a few minutes, okay?" he says bluntly. "And lock the front door. If anyone comes early for the party, don't let them in."

As soon as she rounds the partition, Josh steps closer to me again.

He's visibly shaken. "Skyler, I know this is horrible, but we're going to work this out, okay?"

Sure, my collages are ruined and everything I've hoped for has turned to shit, but we'll work it out, right?

I shake my head. "But how?"

"We're insured, needless to say, and I'll help you get the collages repaired. But first we have to talk about how we're going to handle this tonight."

There can't be a show, of course—at least of my pieces.

"I-I have to call my family," I say, suddenly picturing them walking over from the parking garage at this very minute. "I have to let them know not to come."

Josh lifts his hand in a *hold on* gesture. He taps a fist against his lips a couple of times and strides around the room, quickly examining each piece again. At the last one, he pauses and rocks back on his heels. "Wild card idea," he says. "It's really far out there, but I want to salvage the show if we can, and we've got twenty minutes." He glances back at me. "What if you took a black marker and just blotted out each of the stamp marks? It could seem like part of each collage and—and even unify them as series."

I gulp for air, trying to fight off the panic, which is coming now in waves.

"I want to fix this, too," I say, "but it wouldn't make any sense to have an ugly black rectangle on each piece. What point would it be trying to make? Besides, even with a marker, the letters might bleed through."

"Okay, but bear with me a minute," Josh says. "Remember the Andy Warhol *Marilyn* paintings, the ones the performance artist shot at? The damage became part of the art."

"But I'm not *Andy Warhol*," I tell him, raising my voice without meaning to. "And even if I covered up the word successfully, *I'd* know what was underneath."

"Okay, okay, I hear you," he says, scratching hard at an eyebrow. "So-so we're going to have to come up with an excuse. That maybe there was, uh, some kind of damage. Water damage, let's say, and we're postponing your part of the show until you can make repairs."

I nod, unable to think of any other excuse.

"Nell," Josh yells toward the front part of the gallery. "Come back in and help us take these down."

He steps into action before she returns, lifting a collage off the wall, carrying it into his office, and then returning for the next. His moves are slightly frantic, like he's expecting an invading army. I fumble through my bag for my phone and text Nicky, my fingers trembling so much that I have to backspace and correct my words a couple of times.

Sorry. There's a problem. Meet me outside gallery. Do not come in.

Nell returns and reaches for one of the collages.

"Hold on," I say before she can remove it from the wall. With my hand still shaking, I scroll through my photos until I locate the sketch Alejandro drew for me and hold it up for her. "Did you see anyone who looked like this today?"

She steps closer and examines the screen.

"Maybe," she says. "Yeah, it could be one of the guys who came in alone. He had a baseball cap and sunglasses, but I could see he had a big face and a skinny mustache."

"Wait, what are you saying?" Josh asks, as he returns from the office.

"Someone's been stalking me," I tell him. "He broke into my place, and also left me a note with the same stamp mark on it."

He stops in his tracks, and a deep crease forms between his brows, marring that handsome face of his. "You think it's the same guy?"

"It must be."

"And you *know* him? Is it someone you were involved with?"

I swear his shoulders relax a little; perhaps he's relieved to discover this has nothing to do with the gallery.

"No, I don't know him at all. But someone seems to be after me, because of some money that was left to me."

Josh shakes his head. "I'm really sorry and we can talk later, but for now we need to get the stuff down." He glances at his watch. "Shit, it's ten till. Can you help me—because I need Nell back out front?"

"Yup." Though I can't bear the thought of touching the pieces, I don't have any choice.

Josh grabs another collage, and I follow suit, and before long all ten are leaning against a wall in his office. I stare at them, my stomach roiling. I'd taken such care to wrap and pack each piece before transporting them to the gallery, and now they look like castoffs, which I guess they are. There's a good chance no one will ever set eyes on them.

"Can you keep your office locked?" I ask, turning back to Josh. "In case the guy comes back?"

"Just a sec," he says. He's got his phone out, typing at the speed of light. "Okay, I've let our PR person know. And I'm thinking now that we probably shouldn't claim there was water damage because, well, for one thing, it might make the gallery look negligent. Let's just be vague, okay? We can say that a couple of the pieces were lightly damaged en route and since the collages are meant to be a series, we're holding off until we can present everything together down the road. How does that sound?"

How does it sound? It sounds like his first priority is covering his ass.

"Sure . . . I'd better go now."

"You don't want to stick around for the party?" he asks, finally making eye contact again. "There'll be collectors here, you'd at least get to meet them."

"No, I need to find my family."

"Gotcha. I'm sorry again. Let's talk tomorrow," he says, looking over my shoulder. I turn to see Nell in the entranceway.

"Harry is here," she says. "And I think Skyler's family might be out on the sidewalk." She glances at me. "Four people, including a girl who looks kind of like you. I told them that they need to wait outside for a bit."

I nod, mutter a goodbye, and stumble from the office into the front room of the gallery. There's a guy pouring himself a glass of wine, and I recognize him as the photographer whose work is hanging in the front room. Instead of complimenting him, though, I rush right by and step out into the night.

It *is* my family who Nell saw: my mother, David, Nicky, and Matt. They look slightly bewildered, like tourists who've been out sightseeing all day and now can't find their way back to the hotel. After offering what must be the most pathetic smile in the world, I get quick hellos and hugs from everyone. The one from my mother feels clunky, like we're old acquaintances who are stumped by exactly how to greet each other.

"They're not letting people in yet?" Nicky asks. She's in a bright red coat I've never seen before, with her butter-blond hair piled on top of her head in a messy bun. "Is that why you wanted us to wait out here?"

She's no sooner finished speaking when two men approach the gallery, swing open the door, and step inside.

"No, it's not that," I say. I indicate with a few awkward hand gestures that we should move down the street, away from the door. "They had to cancel my part of the show tonight. It-It's not happening."

"It's not *happening*?" my mother exclaims, rearing back a little. She's wearing a nondescript dark brown coat, and the only effort she appears to have made in terms of makeup is a swipe of mauve lipstick. "Why in the world not?"

"Some of my pieces got damaged." I can feel a sob fighting its way up my throat. "And there's no way they can be displayed to-night."

"Oh my god, Skyler, that's awful," Nicky exclaims, pulling me into another hug.

"And the gallery just noticed the problem now?" my mother asks. She's always had an internal alert system for bullshit, and it's clearly going off.

"Yes, because it happened only a little while ago. The collages were put up last night and someone came in this afternoon and van-dalized them when no one was looking."

"Jesus Christ," David says, sweeping a hand through his thick gray hair. "Is the gallery going to take responsibility?"

"Yes, of course. They're really upset, too."

"But why would someone *do* that?" my mother asks. "Is your stuff hugely controversial?"

"No, it's not controversial, Mom," I say. I have to fight to stop my jaw from quivering. "Someone did it just to be mean and horrible."

"Nicky's right, this is *awful*," my brother-in-law says. For the first time, I focus a little on him. He's wearing a trench coat over his shirt and chinos, and he looks like a solid wall of khaki. "Can we do anything?"

"There's really nothing to do tonight," I tell them. "They have to go ahead with the reception for the other artist—the photographer—but the gallery owner and I are going to talk tomorrow."

"Can your work be repaired?" Nicky asks.

"I don't really know. I haven't thought that far ahead yet."

My mother sighs. "I feel bad for you, but why have I got the feeling there's more to this than you're letting on?"

"You think I'm making this up?"

"Not making it up, no, but it doesn't seem like we're getting the full story. Why do we always have to pry information out of you?"

"Mom," I say, nearly pleading, "I *am* being straight. I only found out about this a few minutes ago, and all I know is that my collages are ruined."

"Look," David says. He's using a soothing tone, as if trying to keep things from unraveling even more. "Why don't we all go someplace and get a drink?"

"Yes, please," Nicky says. "Is there a café around here, Sky? Or a little restaurant?"

I'm about to suggest a place I've noticed nearby, until I catch sight of my mother's face and see her staring blankly across the street. I wait a moment for her to add something, to announce, *Yes, we all need to sit down and deal with this as a family*, but her lips stay pinched together.

"Thanks, but I think I better go home," I tell them. "I'm so sorry you had to drive all this way for nothing."

I turn to leave, to flee, really.

"Sky, wait," Nicky calls out. "Are you going to be okay?"

"Yes, I just need to get over the shock. Thanks for coming." I glance at my mother again, whose arms are now folded across her chest. "And thanks for the flowers, Mom."

Her expression suddenly shifts to perplexed as she processes my words. She doesn't know what I mean, I realize. It was Nicky who sent the flowers, not her.

I turn on my heel and take off without another word, moving north, walking fast. It's only after I see a few passersby glance in my direction that I realize there are tears streaming down my cheeks. Someone is trying to ruin my life, and there's not a soul in the world who can help me.

31

Then

"CHLOE," I SCREAMED, STARING DOWN THE RAVINE AT HER BODY. *"Chloe."*

I took one step closer to the edge and then crumpled onto a clump of wet, dead leaves, as if someone had whacked me hard in the backs of my knees. *"No,"* I wailed. *"No, no, no."*

An arm was suddenly around my shoulders, and I realized Dan was crouched beside me.

"Skyler, I'm so sorry . . . Please, let me help you up."

"We have to get down there," I begged. I couldn't see how, though. The far side of the ravine sloped gradually in places, but this side had a nearly sheer drop to the bottom, and there was no apparent way to descend. With Dan holding my hand, I scrambled back up to a standing position.

"There's nothing we can do now," Dan said. "We need to wait for the police." He grasped my elbow harder and pulled me away from the edge. "Don't look down there again, okay?"

But I did look, and this time I retched, so hard it felt like my insides were trying to free themselves.

"Jamie, why don't I stay with Skyler," he said. "You go get the police."

I glanced at Jamie. She looked wild-eyed, like she'd heard the rumbling of an avalanche above us.

"Okay," she said, and after a backward glance at the ravine, she took off down the path, her arms flailing as she ran.

As soon as we were alone, I felt a sob building in me, making my body shake. "Oh god," I said to Dan. "Are you *sure*? Are you sure there's nothing we can do?"

"Yeah, I'm sure," he said. "It looks like her neck might have been broken."

I looked at him questioningly, my eyes blinded by tears.

"I'm in my second year of med school," he said by way of explanation, and I nearly howled with laughter. He thought that made him some kind of expert? But when he wrapped his arm around my shoulder again, I leaned into it, grateful for his kindness.

"I need to call my parents," I said. "God, they're going to *die*. This will ruin their entire lives."

"Let me know if there's anything I can do, okay? Anything at all."

I closed my eyes, overwhelmed, barely able to catch a breath. How had Chloe ended up at the bottom of a ravine with only half her clothes on? She'd clearly come down the path with someone. Chloe might be a risk-taker but she didn't like being in the dark alone. Had it been the guy who loaned her the sweater—the sweater that was now nowhere in sight?

I retched again as the story finished in my mind. He must have assaulted her, ripping off her top, and when she'd tried to fight him off, he'd killed her and shoved her body over the side of the ledge.

If only Jamie's friend hadn't told me she left with a couple, if only I'd ended up talking to Dan that night and found out she'd gone outside. Then I would never have left the premises. I would have kept searching for Chloe, eventually learned about the gazebo in the woods, called 911. Maybe she was still alive at that time. Maybe I could have saved her life.

I was crying even harder now, with snot bubbling from my nose. I knew I needed to get control because I couldn't call my mother in that state. Nothing I said or did would make anything better for her, but at least I could break the news without sounding hysterical and making it all about me.

Voices suddenly came from down the path. Footfalls, too, and the sound of twigs snapping. In unison, Dan and I turned our heads in that direction. Jamie was walking toward us, along with two cops in uniform. A few yards away, she came to a full stop and indicated the ravine with one hand. The cops halted, and I watched as their eyes found Chloe and they each winced at the sight. As the younger cop pulled a flashlight from his belt and trained it down the ravine, obviously for a better look, the older one closed the gap to me and Dan and introduced himself. He seemed to know already that I was the sister, but he asked me to confirm my name, and he wanted Dan's, too. He told us that we needed to return with him to the house immediately. His partner would remain and protect the scene until additional police arrived.

"What about an *ambulance*?" I pleaded. Maybe Dan had it all wrong? "What if she's only unconscious?"

"Yes, we've called one," he said. "But I'm very sorry to tell you. It doesn't appear that your sister's alive."

His words seemed to fly over my head, like they were meant for someone else, and I felt myself go strangely numb. Jamie threw her arms around me and squeezed tight.

"Oh, Skyler," she said. I could feel her tears on my face. "I'm so sorry."

"Please, everyone," the cop said. "You need to leave now so we can clear and secure the scene." He walked back to his partner, said a few words under his breath, and then rejoined us.

The next minutes were a blur. The four of us headed back to the yard, Dan holding my hand, and my legs moving only thanks to some unknown force. At one point on the path, the cop hung back a little, speaking into a walkie-talkie, but his voice was too low to be overheard.

Once we reached the yard, the cop told Dan and Jamie to take seats by the pool with Rob, who was now sitting there looking shell-shocked, but the officer ushered me into the pool house.

"I think you'll be more comfortable in here," he said, directing me to one of the chairs. "A detective will arrive shortly to take your statement, and there'll also be someone from victims' services."

Victims' services. The numb sensation that had spread through me as we'd been walking began to melt, and I could feel panic and desperation building in me again. If I was going to call home, it had to be now, when I still had control. *Leave,* I wished I could say to the cop. *Please, fucking leave me alone.*

And then just like that he did. I dug out my phone, fell onto the chair, and, trying not to sob, practiced the words a few times. "Mom, I'm so sorry, Chloe's dead. We found her body here on the property." I had to get it out in one go, not make her wait for the truth.

With frantic fingers, I finally pressed the numbers for my mother's cell phone. Two rings and a half ring. David answered, though, not my mother. I had no choice but to tell him first.

"David, I'm so sorry. Chloe's—"

"We know," he said, his voice breaking. "The police just called us."

"Can I talk to Mom?"

A howl came from the background, like a wounded animal.

"I don't think she can speak right now," he said. "She's too distraught."

"Please, just for a second."

I needed to hear my mother's voice, needed to comfort her, to have her comfort *me*.

The next thing I knew David was directing his voice away from the phone, saying something I couldn't hear.

Then another howl, the sound a little closer.

"How could she *leave* her like that?" I heard my mother wail. "How *could* she?"

I knew who she meant. She thought this was all my fault.

"Skyler, I'm sorry," David said, speaking into the phone again. He sounded beyond anguished, but I could tell he was fighting to keep it together. "I need to speak to the police again. Stay where you are, and I'll get back to you."

He ended the call, and I realized that somehow I'd risen without noticing it and had been pacing the room while I spoke to him. I collapsed back into the chair.

And then, as I sat in that musty pool house, I saw my future in front of me, spelled out with perfect clarity.

There would be no Chloe ever again. She'd never be an intern at a television station or date another hockey player or become a TV star or get married and have kids. She'd never hitch another ride with me, or rub my feet on the couch in the den, or flash one of her megawatt smiles in my direction. Her death would be a huge, awful, gaping hole in my family.

And there would be a ripple effect, I realized. Because how, after this, could I ever stay in Boston or at BU, with my grad school friends and crushes? No, nothing in my life would ever unfold as I'd planned.

32

Now

WITHIN A FEW MINUTES OF WALKING NORTH ALONG ALLEN
Street, I'm winded, so I slow my pace enough to catch a
breath. A few more people glance in my direction, slightly curious
in that city way, and I realize it must look like I had a spat with a
romantic partner and have stormed off in a snit. Using the sleeve of
my blazer, I swipe at the tears smeared on my face.

After another half a block, I glance behind me, wondering if
there's any chance that my family is trying to catch up with me.
But the only people I see are strangers, probably heading home from
work or out for their nights on the town.

I turn back around and almost collide with a pedestrian walk-
ing toward me—a tall, striking woman with short, spiky dark hair.
I pull back, muttering, "I'm sorry," and to my shock discover it's
Mikoto.

"Skyler," she exclaims. "Where are you going?"

"Uh, home. You?"

"I'm going to your *opening*. Do I have the night wrong?"

Oh god, I'd completely forgotten I'd invited her. "No, um, it's the right night, but my part isn't happening. I should have called you—but I just found out. My pieces got damaged, and they can't be shown now."

"That's horrible," she says, her shoulders sinking. "Can I do anything?"

To my dismay, my eyes well up again. "There's nothing anyone can do."

"At least let me take you out for a drink—so we can talk about it."

"Thanks, but talking isn't going to help." It comes out more snidely than I'd intended, but I'm not in the mood to care about my manners. Besides, I can't become too reliant on Mikoto, crying on her shoulder at the drop of a hat. "I'm sorry, I have to go."

I brush past her and keep moving north, until Allen morphs into First Avenue, and then finally turn right on Seventh Street. The thought of being in my apartment alone suddenly fills me with dread and I end up continuing east past my building. At Avenue A, I cross the street and hurry along the southern end of Tompkins Square Park to a divey bar on the corner of Avenue B, a spot I'd been to with friends from the website where I once worked. Thankfully it's only a quarter full. In the back, I settle down at a beat-up wooden table by a door that says "Employees Only. Do Not Enter" in huge, bold letters, as if anyone else who steps through will burst into flames. Actually, bursting into flames doesn't sound half bad right now.

The waitress moseys over, her hair a mix of pink, purple, and blue strands. I order a white wine, only fitting, it seems, since that's what people at the gallery are drinking in those little plastic cups right now. The front room is probably already packed with hip, downtown types, none of them—other than Josh and Nell—aware that my collages are resting against a wall in the back office in desperate need of repair.

Are they repairable? I finally ask myself. With the help of adhesive remover, I can certainly scrape or peel off the damaged image on each collage, but then what? These aren't paintings that simply can be touched up. For one of the collages, unfortunately not the one with a buyer, I know I can find an exact replica of the image that was damaged, but there's little chance of that with the other nine. I'll have to find new images for the empty spots, images I not only find compelling on their own but make the collage as a whole come together again. Of course, no matter what I come up with, the pieces will never be the way I first envisioned them.

And even if I do manage to repair each and every one and Josh confirms another show, what guarantee do I have that Jane Whaley's minion won't return and try to wreck the new ones as well? For that matter, what *else* does she have in store for me?

The wine arrives and as soon as I take a sip, I'm seeing the party again in my mind's eye, and Josh offering up the lame "damaged en route" excuse to anyone who even remembers there was a second artist listed on the invitation. *Josh*, the guy I actually thought might be interested in me. Though I'd always known he was slick, I'd found that appealing in its own way. He knew what he wanted and didn't hesitate to go after it, wielding his charm when it could pay off for him. But I'd glimpsed him tonight in a whole new light. Frenzied, the opposite of smooth, more worried about the fate of the party and his potential liability than what the damage meant for me—and then relieved-looking when he found out I'd probably brought the nightmare on myself.

My phone pings from inside my purse, startling me. I dig it out and see that there's a text from Nicky.

Hey, are you okay?

Can she really think I *might* be?
Instead, I type, Just having a drink, trying to process everything.

> I wish there was something we could do. We all feel dev-
> astated.

For the first time I can recall, I feel livid with my younger sister. She's trying to be helpful, of course, trying to ease the sting of our mother's veiled disdain tonight by encouraging me to think it's all in my head. But by covering for our mother over the years it's only made matters worse, I realize. She's allowed me to hold out hope, to pretend I might simply be misinterpreting the situation when that isn't the case at all. Now, I finally get it.

I'm tempted to order another glass of wine just so I don't have to go home yet, but it has a cheap, weird aftertaste. And I'd only be delaying the inevitable: sitting in my apartment with just Tuna for company. I signal for the check, pay without swallowing the last inch in the glass, and step into the night again.

Though I've been in the bar less than an hour, it feels much cooler outside now. The wind has kicked up, too, blowing plastic bags and scraps of paper down Avenue B. I glance to my right, into the park. It's open until midnight, but from this angle, there seems to be no one in there.

Seventh Street, at least the block I'm trudging along now, seems deserted, too. I pick up my pace, unsettled by how desolate it feels. A dog barks from somewhere inside the park, and a second later I hear the muffled command of its owner. As I glance instinctively toward the sounds, I catch sight of something out of the corner of my eye and twist my neck to see behind me. There's a man back there walk-ing in the same direction as I am. He's tall and stocky, and wears a long black coat, but I can't quite make out his face in the darkness.

I quickly face forward again. Avenue A isn't that far, and I can see cars shooting by on it, trying to catch the green light. Just to play things safe, I increase my pace even more.

But so does he. With my stomach dropping, I hear the scuff of his shoes on the sidewalk and a few seconds later, the muted pant of his breath.

It's nothing, I tell myself. *He's probably in a hurry, too.* But a second later, a primitive part of my brain orders me to sprint, and I'm running as fast as I can in my chunky heels, praying that I won't end up splayed on the sidewalk.

The crosswalk light on Avenue A changes from Walk to Don't Walk just as I approach the corner, and I skid to a stop, nearly colliding with another man.

"Whoa, look out," he exclaims. He's out walking a small brown and white dog and looks annoyed.

"Sorry, someone was following me," I say, gasping for breath. As I spin around, he follows my gaze. No one's there. Not the man in the overcoat, not anyone. He must have ducked into the park from a Seventh Street entrance point. The dogwalker, a guy of about sixty with a bristly beard, shrugs and resumes walking.

Once the traffic light changes, I dash across the avenue, and though my lungs are still tight from exertion, I jog the half block to my building and race up the three flights of stairs. It takes a few seconds to slide the key into the lock, but I finally manage to open the door and stumble into the apartment.

Tuna's on the back of the couch, licking a paw, and she eyes me intently, as if she senses something isn't right. Stripping off my blazer while I move, I do a quick check of the apartment and then drop onto the couch. My heart's beating so hard I can feel it in my fingertips. After catching a few more breaths, I peel off my boots, which already look like crap. That's the problem with cheap, trendy boots you order online. You're not really supposed to walk in the fucking things.

I flop my head back against the lumpy cushion. Was that guy behind me just in a hurry, headed into the park for drugs or a hookup or simply to burn off steam? Or was he sent by Jane Whaley? Every one of her ambushes has seemed to come out of nowhere, and I won't have a clue when the next one will happen or what it might entail. She defaced my art and ruined my opening, and it's hard to imagine what could be worse.

That's wrong, actually. Dying could be worse. For the first time, it occurs to be that my life could be in danger. Whaley bragged yesterday about her team of lawyers, but it's possible they've told her that she doesn't have much of a case against me, and she's been toying with other options. If I die, the trust will bypass her and go to her kids, but that might provide all the satisfaction she needs.

Behind me I feel Tuna shift position, and I twist around to make sure she's okay. As I run a hand down her silky back, I notice her eyes suddenly dart to the right, and I spin back around, thinking she might have seen a mouse, but there's nothing there.

Just thinking *mouse*, though, triggers a memory of a comment Jane Whaley made the first time we met. "Go ahead, scurry away like a little mouse," she'd said. That's exactly what I did. And it's what I've been doing tonight as well. Scurrying out of the gallery, scurrying away from my family, scurrying home down Seventh Street. In fact, it's what I've been doing ever since I met her—running scared. I'm afraid every time I enter my apartment, afraid to even venture into my own studio to work on my art.

I can't let her win. I can't allow her to destroy my chance of living life as an artist . . . and realizing my dream of parenthood. I have to find a way to stop her.

I struggle up from the couch and wander over to the table, staring down at my collage. The scrap of paper with "owed" scrawled on it seems to stand out from everything else that's been glued to the page. I think back to the idea of hush money. What if one of the so-called lies C.J. told me—like taking the law school admission test for a sick friend—was, as I suspected the other day, actually true?

On my phone, I pull up his obit again and double-check the

name of the college he attended: Bowdoin. If he'd been hoping to go to law school the fall after graduating, he would have taken the LSAT during his senior year, which means that if he did pose as a friend of his, that person might have been at Bowdoin with him.

A memory blooms, making my breath catch. At our first meeting, Bradley Kane said he'd gone to the same college as C.J., and the two shared mutual friends. Had the two been closer than he admitted? Is it possible that C.J. took the LSATs for him? I think back to the photo Kane had showed me of him, C.J., and three other guys on the day of a regatta. Though the two men would hardly have been considered dead ringers, they were both tall, clean-cut, sandy-haired white guys. It's possible C.J. could've impersonated him.

I've been suspicious of Bradley Kane on and off from the moment he called me, and now it seems that there could be a reason. Perhaps it's not Jane Whaley who's been wreaking havoc in my life.

33

Now

WAKE THE NEXT MORNING WITH WHAT FEELS LIKE A MASSIVE hangover—a pounding headache, queasy stomach, and jittery limbs. Raising myself onto one elbow, I snap on the bedside lamp. In the light that it casts I see that the top sheet is coiled like a rope from the thrashing I did in my sleep.

What I want more than anything is to flop back onto the bed, return to unconsciousness, and escape from the dumpster fire that my life has become. But I've promised myself I'm going to take control, and I have too much to do. I swing my legs gingerly over the edge of the mattress and drop my feet to the floor.

As soon as I've fed Tuna and made coffee, I send a text to James Tremlin. I need to give him an update before I even begin to tackle the Whaley situation,

> Hi James, it's Skyler Moore, the collage artist you interviewed. Would you mind giving me a call? I need to talk to you as soon as possible.

It's possible Josh will remember to contact him, but I've got no guarantee. I have to tell him myself that the pieces aren't being displayed at the gallery and there's no reason for him to drop by. I have photos of all the collages, so maybe he'd be willing to look at those—and still include me in the story.

Next I text Mikoto.

> Sorry to be rude last night. I was just so upset. But I really appreciate your interest in the show and hope I can make it up to you. In the meantime, any chance I could ask your advice again?

I hear back from her as I'm toweling off from a shower. She tells me she understands and adds that though she's got class all morning, she'll be back for lunch and suggests bringing over Chinese takeout. I tell her yes, to just order me whatever she's having; I'm eager to run my LSAT theory by her, but I'm also craving the comfort her company always seems to bring.

Midmorning, I'm in the middle of cleaning my bedroom, just to stay busy, when Josh calls me.

"Hey, how are you feeling?" he asks. He's back to smooth, sales-y Josh, with all the frantic energy purged from his voice.

"Pretty awful still."

"I would have called you first thing, but I wanted to touch base with the police first."

"You spoke to them already?"

"Yeah, but it's not good news. The guy at the nearest precinct said I can drop by later and fill out a report, but he doubts there's much they can do. Welcome to New York City."

"They can't take fingerprints or anything like that?"

"Based on the amount of damage and the moderate value of the art, he doesn't see that happening. He did ask if we had cameras and I explained that we'd never felt the need, but that reminded me of the sketch you have. Once I've filed the report, maybe you should go to the precinct yourself and explain the situation more fully."

"I will, that's a good idea," I tell him. "H-How did the event turn out?"

"We had a good turnout, and we ended up selling almost all the photographs. Some people did ask where the second exhibit was, but they seemed to take the explanation in stride. A friend of yours was looking for you, by the way, and he seemed really sorry your stuff wasn't on display."

My skin prickles. "What did he look like?"

"Midforties, tall guy, dark-haired. With a fairly thick accent. Maybe Spanish?"

Sounds like it could have been Alejandro, though I never mentioned the show to him. "Thanks for letting me know."

"I have to jump on another call, but let's talk later and figure out next steps."

He's sounding a little more sympathetic than he did last night, but I still sense he's relieved that this appears to be a matter I've brought on myself.

"One more thing: Are you around tomorrow? I thought I could have Nell drop off the collages in the morning so you could . . . well, take another look and decide what you want to do."

"Okay, but have her come to my apartment. Not the studio."

The thought of all the wounded collages inside my home, piled against the wall, fills me with fresh despair, but I'm not planning to go to the studio anytime soon, not after what happened last night.

As promised, Mikoto arrives at noon, dressed in black jeans and a maroon crewneck sweater and lugging a plastic bag from a nearby Chinese restaurant.

"Sesame noodles, chicken and broccoli, spring rolls," she says with a smile.

"Perfect," I say, then gesture to the coffee table. "I've got work on the dining table, so we'll have to eat here if that's okay."

"No problem."

As she goes about arranging the food, I grab plates, glasses, a couple of serving spoons, and a liter bottle of fizzy water from the kitchen and return with it all to the living room. I plop down on the couch next to her, and we take turns loading up our plates as the smell of soy sauce and ginger fills the room.

"I feel so terrible about what happened last night," Mikoto says, tearing the wrapper from her chopsticks. "You must be devastated."

"Yeah, I guess that's the right word for it."

"Can your collages be fixed?"

"Maybe, but it's going to take a lot of time and effort, and there's no way to be sure the same thing won't happen again."

"Wait, what do you mean?"

Famished, I take a bite of a spring roll and then describe the stamp mark on each of the collages and how I'm sure it has to do with the trust. I also catch her up on the other events of the past few days: the note stuffed inside my tote bag, the surprise visit from C.J.'s son, the proposal from Jane Whaley that I turned down flat, and the man behind me last night.

Mikoto's eyes widen in astonishment. "This is getting really scary. Have you called the police?"

"The gallery owner did, but they told him there's not much they can do."

"Skyler, you have to watch your back. This woman is escalating the situation every day."

I nod. "It is scary, but I'm not so sure anymore that she's behind it."

"Don't tell me you're suddenly giving her the benefit of the doubt?"

"Sort of. I'm actually starting to wonder if someone else is responsible, and I wanted to get your input." I pause. "What would happen if a practicing lawyer was found to have arranged for someone else to take the LSATs for him?"

Mikoto cocks her head and finishes chewing a mouthful of food. "Well, for starters, there'd be sheer amazement that the person pulled it off. I mean, security is incredibly tight with these kinds of tests."

"This would have been around twenty-five years ago."

"Okay, things probably weren't nearly as stringent back then, so somebody might have managed it. As for the repercussions, as far as I know there's no statute of limitations on cheating, which means his law school would strip him of his law degree. You said he's a practicing attorney? Then his firm would give him the boot, and he'd be disbarred."

"Wow. So, there's a whole lot at stake." But that's not all I want to know. "What about the guy who took the test for him? Would he be in trouble, too?"

"Oh, for sure. But where are you going with this?"

I fill her in on what C.J. said during a round of Two Truths and a Lie and take her through my idea that the trust might be an act of gratitude for me keeping his secret all this time. Mikoto listens intently as I speak, her expression pensive, and I have an even stronger feeling that I might be onto something.

"So?" I ask when I'm done.

Mikoto shakes her head in a slow, measured way, then looks at me. "I think it's way too much of a stretch," she says at last.

"*Really?*"

"Yes. Even if he did take the test for someone else and confessed it to you as a quote-unquote lie, it's hard to imagine him worrying that you'd guessed the truth, let alone that you'd try to use it to your advantage. That just seems far-fetched."

"Yeah, I agree, it is far-fetched. But so is everything else about the situation."

"But it's also ass-backward. Hush money is usually paid on the front end—because you want to *prevent* a person from revealing damaging information about you. You don't offer it twelve years later as a thank-you, especially if you'll be dead soon anyway."

I flop back on the couch, exhaling loudly. She's right, it sounds absurd in the cold light of day.

"I know this must all be making you crazy," Mikoto says, "but you'll probably have more clarity once you speak to an attorney. Did you have any luck getting an appointment?"

I nod and help myself to another piece of broccoli from my plate. "Yeah, she's out of town, but I'm seeing her on Friday. I know it will help, but it's not like she'll have the answer to the most important question: Why me?"

Mikoto reaches out and taps my hand. "Don't give up. The answer might become clear over time."

We're both full by that point, but there's still food left over and Mikoto urges me to keep it, saying she'll be out tonight and won't have any use for it.

"Hot date?" I ask.

She smiles and rolls her eyes. "It's really just a study date with a guy in my criminal procedure class, but I'm praying he's going to look up at some point and realize he's totally smitten with me. What about you? You should be with friends at such a crazy time."

"Yeah, I'm all set," I lie.

Against my protests, she packs up the leftovers herself and puts them in the fridge. "I wish I could do something for *you* for a change," I say. "It feels like a one-way street, me coming to you for help on everything from a lost cat to an avenging widow."

"Please, not at all. This has been a pretty big switch for me—

giving up work, going back to school—and it's great to have a pal next door. We should grab dinner out sometime."

"Yeah, I'd like that. Oh, speaking of eating, let me give you some cash for my half."

As I fish through my purse for my wallet, Mikoto gathers her things behind me.

"Oh, wow, is that your next collage?" she asks. I turn around and she lifts her chin toward the table. "Mind if I take a peek?"

"Sure, but it's not 'artwork' really, just something I've been messing around with—to help me get more of a handle on that night we've been talking about."

She takes a few steps toward the table, and I watch her eyes drift across the paper.

"Boston, right?"

My heart skips a beat hearing the word. "Yeah. . . . Have you spent much time there?"

"A little bit. I went to Dartmouth undergrad, and we'd spend the occasional weekend down there—when we needed a break from Bumfuck, New Hampshire." She turns her attention back to the collage. "So you met the guy there?"

"Yeah, I did. I'm hoping the collage will help jog my memory, though it's been tough for me to revisit all those images. M-My sister died there. Actually, nearby. And it was the same weekend I had the one-night stand."

"Oh my god, Skyler, I'm so sorry," she exclaims. Her concern sounds heartfelt and genuine, though her expression is perplexed. "Is that why you were at the hotel? Because your sister had just died in the area?"

"No, I was going to grad school in Boston then, and my sister was there, too—as an undergrad. One Saturday night a friend comped me a room at the hotel she was working at, and the very next morning, I learned Chloe was dead."

Mikoto nods. "Do you mind my asking how it happened?"

"She died from a broken neck—in a ravine behind a house where a big party was going on. Though we were never sure exactly how it happened, it seemed she must have been shoved over the edge during a sexual assault. There were no obvious signs of a struggle, but her blouse was missing. Maybe she was up for fooling around with some guy and then changed her mind, and that infuriated him so much he pushed her, or he attacked her without warning, got the blouse off, and then pushed her when he saw that she would be too much of a challenge. It's possible she even fell getting away from him."

She shakes her head, looking bewildered. "That must have been so horrible for you. . . . And what a bizarre coincidence."

I glance away, weighing her words.

"You mean that it happened the same weekend I met this guy C.J.?" I say. "Yeah, I guess. Though at the time I had no idea that I'd ever hear another word either from or about him."

"Well, life is pretty strange, isn't it? . . . If you ever want to talk about your sister, let me know. I'd be happy to listen."

"Thanks, Mikoto."

After she's gone, and it's just me and Tuna and the muted sounds of car horns and people calling out to each other on Seventh Street, I return to the couch and drain the rest of my fizzy water. Exhausted even though it's only the early afternoon, I lean back against the cushion, closing my eyes.

In the past decade, I've told no one except Lucas about losing my sister, and I wait for a wave of regret to hit me, but it never materializes. In fact, I feel calmed by having shared this with Mikoto. Maybe I should have continued with grief counseling back then, at the very least unloaded to the friends I had, but for me the sorrow was *more* intense when I gave it words, not less. So I mostly kept my mouth shut and, over many years, learned to chase most thoughts about Chloe away.

Of course, it's certainly hard to keep them at bay now. This whole nightmare around the trust has dredged up the past, forced me to remember not only the night with C.J. but also what it was like to wake the next morning and realize with a surge of panic that Chloe might not be okay.

I think about what Mikoto said, about life being strange, about the bizarreness of the coincidence. I met the man who would eventually leave me three and half million dollars the same weekend my sister died. It's as if I can trace everything significant about who I am right now to a single weekend in Boston.

My eyelids shoot open, and a chill races through me. After struggling to rise, I cross the small room to the table and stare at the collage.

What if there's nothing coincidental about it after all? What if the two most momentous experiences of my life didn't simply overlap in terms of timing? What if, in some horrible way, C.J. was connected to Chloe's death? Is it at all possible that he'd been at the party in Dover that night, but I never knew it?

34

Now

FOR THE LONGEST TIME I JUST LIE ON THE COUCH NEXT TO TUNA, overwhelmed by the thought I've had. I keep telling myself that it's improbable that there's a connection between Chloe and C.J., that he couldn't have been at the party, let alone have killed her. The only common denominator between the two of them—at least the only apparent one—was me.

And yet it's just as improbable, I'm finally beginning to see, that the two events that have altered my life indelibly, the death of my sister and a hookup that might end up making me rich, occurred within a single day of each other but are completely unrelated.

From the moment Kane broke the news to me about the trust, I've been drumming up all sorts of possible explanations for C.J.'s choosing me as his beneficiary—he'd fancied himself as a patron of the arts; he'd never been able to get me out of his head; he was exacting revenge on his unfaithful wife; he was grateful I'd been a good secret keeper. But at the end of the day, none of those reasons have added up to three and a half million dollars. When you start talking about life and death, however, a big payout suddenly makes sense.

And yet C.J. wasn't even in Boston the night Chloe died, I don't think. He arrived in town late Saturday afternoon, the day after the party. Because when I first set eyes on him, he was checking into the Kensington.

My old friend Tess's face floats ghostlike across my mind again. I can see her wavy, bright red hair and olive-colored eyes, and even the subtle but mischievous grin she flashed as she handed me the key card to my room at the hotel. She'd tried so hard to comfort me about Chloe's death—calling every day, delivering muffins and milkshakes to my apartment, urging me not to drop out of BU, but I'd rebuffed all her efforts. The last time we spoke was twelve years ago, the day I packed my car to leave Boston, and though she tried to keep in touch, I'd let her calls go to voice mail and never even listened to the messages.

Should I call her now? I wonder. Is there something of value she could tell me? Because of the nightmare that unfolded that weekend, I'd never gotten around to sharing what had transpired at the hotel, the way I would have under other circumstances. But even if I had, it feels so unlikely she'd remember anything about C.J. from that day at reception.

Another question asserts itself, raising the hair on the back of my neck. What if he *hadn't* been checking in when I first spotted him? What if he'd actually been staying at the hotel for a few days and was only at reception with a question about his bill or to change rooms? But no: though my memory may be faint in places, I can still see him with his roller bag in the lobby, pulling it behind him as he advanced to the desk.

Of course, just because it was C.J.'s first night at the Kensington doesn't mean it was his first night in *Boston*. He could have been staying elsewhere and then decided to relocate, which would make sense if he'd done something horrible and wanted to reduce his exposure by switching hotels.

It's still not making any sense, though. Even if he'd been in Boston earlier in the week, it's highly unlikely he was at Jamie's on Friday night. Yes, the house was overflowing with party crashers as well as invited guests, but because of his age and his debonair vibe, C.J. would have stuck out like a sore thumb, and I would have recognized him the very next night.

And beyond that, it's impossible for me to believe he pushed Chloe over the edge of the ravine twenty-four hours before going to bed with me. He'd seemed fairly relaxed Saturday night, at ease in his own skin. Though I've read that psychopaths can be emotionless and unremorseful, nothing I've learned about C.J.—so far at least—suggests he was one.

I finally summon the psychic energy to make myself a cup of tea before returning with my mug to Tuna and the couch. I try to abandon the idea of a connection between C.J. and Chloe—but my racing pulse and roiling stomach won't let me. So what do I do?

Another long-ago name flutters into my mind: Dan Lui, the boyfriend of Jamie's brother, Rob. Dan had helped in the search of the property and had comforted me when we found Chloe at the base of the ravine. I'd been a little wary of him that day, and even more so of Jamie and Rob, wondering if one or all of them was harboring a secret. But the police soon determined that all three had been at the party the whole time, and I realized that their awkwardness on Sunday reflected their fears over how Jamie and Rob's parents would react.

Jamie and I had quickly drifted apart, but oddly Dan and I became close for a bit. He regularly called and texted me, checking in to see how I was. He shared that when he was only eleven, he'd lost an older sibling in a car crash, and he knew a little about what I was going through, which gave me hope that one day, like him, I'd be okay. I cried my eyes out to him over the phone, able to let go with him in a way I hadn't been able to do with Tess, perhaps due to our common bond. Within a few months, however, I stopped returning his calls, too.

Though we haven't spoken in more than a decade, I know he's still in Boston, an anesthesiologist working and teaching at Mass General, with a husband who is also an MD. Because once in a while when I let down my guard and become consumed with thoughts about Chloe, I head down various rabbit holes online, traveling over old ground, checking on some of the players from back then.

Without giving myself a chance to think too hard, I find his office number on the Mass General website and call it. A receptionist answers briskly and when I say I'm looking for Dr. Lui, she asks if I'm a patient.

"No, but I'm an old friend. I was hoping I could speak to him if he has a free moment."

"I'm afraid he isn't available right now, but I can give him a message."

I recite my number with little hope. Because I can't imagine Dan calling me back after so many years. But twenty-five minutes later, a Boston number appears on my phone.

"Skyler, wow, hello," he says when I answer.

"Hey, Dan. Or should I say, Dr. Lui? Congratulations."

He chuckles. "Thank you, though you probably shouldn't congratulate me until I've paid off all my med school loans. . . . 917. That's a New York City prefix, right?"

"Yeah, I moved here not long after I left Boston. But you're still there, I see. And *married*."

"Yes, took the plunge a couple of years ago. He's a dermatologist I met when I was a resident. What about you?"

"Not married, but I've got an eight-pound calico cat."

"Well, that's a start. So to what do I owe this call? Don't tell me there's finally been a break in the case?"

"No, not a break. But there've been a few . . . uh, developments related to the weekend Chloe died, and I was wondering if I could run something by you. Of course, I don't expect you to remember much after all this time."

"You might be surprised. Because I've always been haunted about what happened."

"Have you, Dan?" I say, so touched by his words. "Thank you for saying that. Okay, so here goes. Remember the older guys at the party, the ones who'd apparently heard about it from Jamie and Rob's cousin?"

"Oh yeah," he says quickly. "The party crashers."

"Most of them seemed to be in their late twenties or early thirties. But do you remember a guy who was even older than that? Around thirty-seven or so?"

"Uh, no, sorry," he says after a few moments' thought. "Not anyone who struck me as that old."

"You're sure?" I say, deflated. "He would have been really polished looking. A business executive."

"If he was in the mix, I don't recall him. Frankly, most of the older guys with that WASPY, preppy look blurred together. I do remember Rob was furious about them showing up and spoiling the whole vibe."

"I know. And the party felt so *off* after they arrived. Did you ever learn anything about them?"

"Just that they worked at the same bank or brokerage company as the cousin. I assume the police interviewed them, right?"

"They interviewed everyone they could, but they were concerned a few guys might have slipped through the cracks."

He sighs. "And I remember that there were so few photos for the cops to work with—because Jamie had threatened to throw people out if she saw them taking pictures."

"Yeah, she was afraid people would post them and her parents would find out about the party."

"Well, they certainly found out in the end. . . . Could you talk to the police about that guy? See if it fits with the description of anyone your sister was seen talking to that night?"

"I don't think I have enough reason to at this point. And what would it prove, anyway? She was talking to plenty of guys that night."

"Did they ever find out whose sweater she had around her waist?"

"No, but since she was wearing it when you saw her take the wine, the police assumed the sweater belonged to the guy she went into the woods with. They never found it—or her blouse, either."

Dan is quiet for a couple of moments, perhaps searching his memory or letting the past catch up with him.

"There was always something about the sweater and the wine that seemed weird to me," he says finally. "I mentioned it to the cops when they first interviewed me, but I don't know if they paid any attention."

"Weird how?" I say, feeling goose bumps shoot up along my forearms.

"The way she grabbed the wine on her own like that. I kept wondering if the guy she was hanging with was trying to keep a low profile."

"I'm still not following."

"Okay, it seems pretty clear to us she was going out to share the wine with a guy, but why didn't anyone ever see the two of them together? And why didn't he come into the kitchen with her? Maybe he sent her inside to get it on her own because he didn't want to be spotted in her company."

My stomach twists. "You mean that he was already planning to hurt her?"

"No, not that, though I guess that's possible, too. I wondered if he didn't want anyone to notice them together because he had a girlfriend who hadn't come to the party, and he didn't want word getting back to her."

A girlfriend is a possibility. As is a *wife*.

"Yes, I see what you're saying. You've given me something to think about, Dan. Thank you."

"I'd love to see you again. Do you ever get to Boston?"

"No. But maybe you'll get to New York one day, and we could meet. I'll send you my info."

"Thank you, Skyler," he says, and it feels weirdly good to hear him say my name after all these years. "I wish you the best."

Dropping the phone into my lap, I think for a minute. C.J. might have been at the party but lying low, and that's why I never saw him. But if he was responsible for Chloe's death, why leave me the money? Out of *guilt*? And how would he have ever found out that I was Chloe's sister? Did he spot me in the lobby and recognize me from the party and then target me for a seduction? Or did he only put two and two together later? It's all so sickening, I can barely let myself toy with the questions.

I force myself up again and pace the living room, trying to figure out a next move. I need to determine why C.J. was in Boston twelve years ago and whether he seemed guilt-ridden when he returned. Asking Jane Whaley certainly isn't an option, and Bradley Kane, it's clear, will never be forthcoming. No, there's only one person I have the chance of learning anything valuable from, and that's Caroline Whaley. I certainly can't ask her if she thinks her son was a murderer, but I can try to feel her out a little, get a sense if she saw any kind of change in him.

I grab my phone from the couch and tap her number. As far as I know, she's finishing a late lunch with friends or busy doing something else to keep her grief from rearing its head too high, but to my surprise she answers on the second ring.

"Hello, Skyler," she says. She doesn't sound exactly overjoyed to hear from me, but at least I don't detect any irritation in her voice.

"I'm sorry to bother you again, but . . . but I guess I didn't know who else to turn to?"

She sighs. "Is Jane making your life difficult?"

"*Someone* is, but I'm not so sure it's her. I was hoping to speak to you again about Chris. I just feel I need more information."

"As I told you, my son and I weren't nearly as close as I would have liked. What makes you think I'd have the answers you're looking for?"

"It's more that I'm looking for a sense of him, one that I thought you'd have."

"Hmm. Well, one tries, even from a distance. What specifically do you want insight on?"

Stupidly I haven't thought this far ahead, haven't come up with any questions. And it's hardly going to be easy over the phone.

"You know what I think," Caroline says before I can fumble a response. "The two of us should sit down in person again and have a real conversation."

Yes. Though I have no desire to be in her company again, a one-on-one might make all the difference.

"That would be incredibly helpful," I tell her.

"It will have to be soon, though. I'm leaving for Palm Beach tomorrow, and I'll be gone for at least several weeks, maybe longer."

What she's saying is that it has to happen today. I quickly lower the phone to check the time on the screen.

"Depending on the train schedule, I could probably be in Scarsdale by late afternoon—and I could meet you in town for coffee."

"I'm in the midst of packing, so why don't you come here instead? Take the 4:54 from Grand Central and grab a taxi from the station. I'll text you the address. We can chat for a bit, and then get you on the train back to the city."

I think for a second. It means I won't be able to drop by the police precinct with the sketch today, but that can wait a day. I tell her I'll see her in a few hours and, after hanging up, kick my ass into gear. I purchase a round-trip ticket online, fix my hair, swipe on some makeup, and dig out my leggings, which I pair with a long, dark gray faux silk blouse that hits below my hips. When I retrieve my boots from the living room, I see that they have not been miraculously restored overnight, so I stuff my feet into an old pair of ballet flats buried in the back of my closet.

As I race to get out the door, I notice a sense of dread creeping through me, cell by cell. I'm desperate to find out if Caroline can shed light on the Boston weekend, but at the same time I'm terrified about what I might learn.

What if I discover that I slept with the man who killed my sister?

35

Now

BY THE TIME I REACH THE RIGHT TRACK AT GRAND CENTRAL, THE train is already boarding. Each car looks crowded already, and I'm almost at the end of the train when I finally just pick one. It's clear that even if I leave my coat and purse on the seat next to me, there's no way I'm going to maintain a whole row for myself, so I grab an aisle seat, guaranteeing that at least I won't be boxed in.

Moments later, two chatty, shopping-bag-laden thirtysome-thing women have slid past me to occupy the other two seats in my row. Their bags are marked with LoveShackFancy, a store I've never even heard of. As the train lurches to a start, one of them begins raving above the tuna tartare they had for lunch with the sauce she thinks might have been a ponzu, and then goes on to lament that the dress she bought might have been the wrong choice, that the one with the flutter sleeves was probably cuter on her. It's as if I'm listening to someone speak a foreign language, the words completely unfamiliar to me—*ponzu, flutter, love shack, fancy*, even the word *love* all by itself.

Ordinarily this kind of blabber would torture me, but it displaces the throbbing in my head and helps me think more rationally about the encounter in front of me. After today, I might not have another shot with Caroline Whaley, which means I have to tease out all the information I can. And do so without revealing the fears I have about her son.

Play dumb, I urge myself. *Don't show your hand*.

It's almost dark when the train pulls into Scarsdale, and the air feels much cooler than when I left my apartment. I button my coat and flip the collar up. People disgorge quickly from the train, like grains of rice spilling from a bag, and I hurry to keep up, eager to catch one of the taxis that Caroline assured me would be outside the station. But my phone rings inside my purse as I'm rushing down the platform stairs, and as soon as I reach the bottom, I step out of the crowd to check the screen.

James Tremlin. It's not an ideal time to talk, but I need to connect with him sooner rather than later.

"Thanks for returning my call," I say.

"What can I do for you?" He sounds as aloof as when we met in person.

"You mentioned you might stop by the gallery this week, and I wanted to let you know that my collages won't be there. They got— Well, they got damaged, and my part of the show is being postponed."

"Damaged? How terrible. Was the gallery itself damaged?"

"No, um, just my pieces. It's not the gallery's fault, though."

"What in the world happened?"

I'm about to say that the story is too long to bore him with, but I realize how evasive that might sound, that he might suspect that Josh canceled the show at the last minute because of a problem with my work. I'm overwhelmed with an urge to be totally honest.

"Can this be between the two of us?" I ask.

"Of course."

"A person apparently came into the gallery yesterday morning and . . . defaced them when no one was looking."

"My god. Have you contacted the police?"

"Yes. And since the pieces are all down, I wanted to make sure you didn't go to the trouble of stopping by."

Josh might be annoyed if he gets wind of the fact that I've shared the truth, but at least this way the writer won't imagine I'm on the outs with the gallery.

"Anyway, since my show is going to be postponed," I add, "I thought maybe I could email you photos of the collages. Photos from before they were damaged."

"Sure, of course. But text them to me, okay? That will be easier for me."

"Will do."

"Can they be salvaged?"

"I'm going to try."

I have no clue whether I mean that, but it seems best to stay positive with a journalist.

"Well, good luck. And I'll look out for a text from you."

The cabs have all been commandeered by the time I sign off, so I order an Uber and text Caroline to say I'll be a few minutes late. A gray Nissan pulls up ten minutes later and I climb in, verifying my name with the driver. Within a short while, the village of Scarsdale falls away, and we're on a road featuring huge homes, many behind black, wrought iron gates.

Before long my phone pings, indicating we've arrived at the address she's sent me, and the driver makes a left onto a long tree-lined drive. Based on the Tudors and jumbo-size colonials I glimpsed on the way, I assumed Caroline's house will be in a similar vein, but I'm in for a surprise. The house is clearly as pricey as anything else in the neighborhood but much different in style, more modern in design and built of stone and white clapboard. Though the rooms all appear to be on one level, there's a pitched roof in the center and one at each end of the house, perhaps as a design feature or to accommodate a very high ceiling.

The driver drops me at the end of the gravel driveway, near the attached three-car garage, and from there I follow a flagstone path that runs parallel to the house until I reach the entrance, a set of double doors. This is it, the one clear chance I have left of finding out more about C.J. Taking a ragged breath, I press the bell, and after a short wait, Caroline Whaley swings open one of the doors.

"Good evening," she says, in her deep, husky voice.

Though she'd made it sound as if she'd be home alone tonight, she's dressed like a woman expecting a small crowd for cocktails. A crisp white shirt—with the collar confidently popped—has been paired with flowy black slacks and accented with a black crocodile belt, like Barbara Stanwyck in a 1940s movie. Her hair's slicked back again, and though the day's makeup has faded a bit, it's obvious she recently retouched her bold red lipstick.

She ushers me into a simple, stone-floored foyer, which could almost be the entrance to a horse barn. But moments later I'm trailing behind her into in a jaw-dropper of a great room with floor-to-ceiling windows. The ceiling is vaulted, with two wrought iron chandeliers hanging halfway down, and the room has been decorated in various shades of gray. Clearly, no expense has been spared.

"What an amazing place," I say, trying not to sound as nervous as I feel.

"Thank you." She extends an arm toward one of the two couches. They're directly in front of a fireplace with a two-story-high stone hearth. As I take my seat, she turns and strides toward the other side of the room.

"Wine?" she asks, using the tips of her fingers to press against a dove-gray wooden panel of the wall, which pops open to reveal a mirrored bar. "I have a very nice California white chilling, but also red or rosé if you prefer."

"A small glass of white would be lovely."

What I really crave at the moment is a Diet Coke, something to keep my throat from going bone-dry, but it seems best to follow Caroline's lead. After tugging the bottle of white from a bucket and expertly uncorking it, she fills two long-stemmed glasses with liquid the color of golden straw and carries them across the room.

Since she didn't ask to take my coat, I leave it on, but I undo the buttons.

"Cheers," she says, passing me a glass. "I think you'll like this." With her own glass in hand, she lowers herself onto the couch across from me.

"Thank you," I say. I take a small sip. It's nice and buttery. "I do like it."

"Now tell me what I can do for you. I'm more than happy to listen and help if possible. And then we really need to get on with our lives."

Easy enough for her to say. Someone's not letting me get on with mine. But right here, right now, I need to focus on the point that's she's making: after this, she's done with me.

"Yes, of course, understood. As I explained the other day, I met your son in Boston. A dozen years ago this past April, to be exact. I'm just wondering if . . . if you might know why he was there that weekend."

She takes a generous sip of wine, eying me over the rim of the glass with her deep blue eyes. I hear the muted click of a door closing in another room of the house. A housekeeper moving about, perhaps. Surely Caroline would have one, and it might have been her who organized the wine in the bucket. Or maybe she's found another partner since her husband died, one not mentioned in her son's obit.

"*Why* was he there?" she asks finally, setting the goblet on the coffee table. She looks perplexed. "When you and I spoke last week in town, you said that Chris had been there on business."

"That's what I assumed at the time, but now I'm curious if there might have been another reason."

She shrugs. "Any answer I give you would be only a wild guess. Visiting friends, perhaps? I imagine he and Jane knew people in that area, though if he were there to see them, Jane would have been with him at the hotel. Which we know she wasn't."

I can't tell if she means it as a dig, but I choose to let it go.

"He did go out to meet with someone that night, but only briefly," I tell her. "By any chance do you recall him acting differently around that time? Not like himself? Perhaps troubled?"

"Are you wondering if he felt guilty about the fling?"

"Not about that, necessarily. But perhaps unsettled by something else that happened on the trip?"

She shakes her head. "I can't imagine what you mean. Besides, I doubt I'd have been aware of a mood shift on his part, and it's so long ago, anyway, that I wouldn't remember it if I had."

I sense irritation building in her now. She seems eager to have me gone.

"Right, good point," I say, realizing I have to pivot. "I know you said you thought he'd left the trust to me because of Jane's affair, a kind of retribution, but do you think it's possible he actually felt he owed me something?"

"*Owed* you?" She flips her palms up and shifts her gaze from my eyes to a point just off my face. "My dear, that's a question you'd have to ask yourself, based on the time you spent with him."

I'm totally flailing here. "Yes, you're right. Of course."

She clasps her hands together, fingers straight, and taps the edge of the steeple against her chin a couple of times. "So will that be it?"

"Um, yes." *I'm leaving with nothing*, I think wearily, not even a glimmer that might lead me to the truth. But what did I really expect her to say? *Yes, now that you mention it, Chris did seem troubled after that weekend, like he had blood on his hands.*

"Why don't I see you out then," Caroline says. "I've arranged for my chauffeur to give you a ride to the station."

"Thank you, but I'm happy to get there on my own."

"Don't be silly. It's the least I can do after you've come all this way, and he's very close by. He lives above the garage."

She snatches a cell phone from the coffee table and taps out a message. I rise slowly and pretend to take in the room again, glad at least to be saving myself the cost of another Uber.

"What a lovely house to raise a family in," I say. I don't really mean it—it's hard to imagine little boys building Lego sets on the floor of this room or racing around the lawn on tricycles—but I'm stalling, trying to come up with a more productive question than the useless ones I've spit out so far.

"No, we raised Chris and his brother in a house two miles from here," she says, rising now, as well. "It was wonderful, too, in its own special way, but after my husband died, I felt a change would do me good."

Footsteps sound behind me, and Caroline, arms akimbo, lifts her chin in greeting to the person who's entered the room from behind me.

"Ah, Carl, thank you," she says. "Ms. Moore is ready to return to the station now."

My chance for questions is over. Despairing, I turn slowly in the direction of the chauffeur, who's standing a few feet away. Last time,

I glimpsed only the back of his head, but now I see that he's tall and beefy, with short, coarse brown hair. And a mustache that's way too thin for his face.

My heart lurches.

He's the man in the sketch Alejandro drew. The man who tried to enter my studio and who ruined my collages and has been following me all over the city.

It takes everything in my power to keep my mouth from dropping open in shock. But it's definitely him, I have no doubts. I quickly avert my gaze from his face so he won't see any flicker of recognition in my expression.

Holding my breath, I force my eyes back toward Caroline. If Carl has set my life on fire, it's been done under *her* orders, not Jane Whaley's or Bradley Kane's. She's the one behind everything.

"Really, I can just order an Uber," I say, trying to swallow my fear. "I don't want to put you out in any way."

"You're not putting us out," Caroline says. " Now, please, I really do need to finish preparing for my trip."

She's got some kind of awful plan in store, that's why she invited me out here. But I can't let it unfold, can't get into the car with him. I slip my hand into my purse, fishing for my phone, and pull it out.

"I'm sure a car can be here in only minutes," I say. *Should I get an Uber?* I wonder. *Or call 911?* I'm suddenly frozen.

Caroline steps closer to me and before I know what she's doing, she's snatching the phone from my hands. "Don't be ridiculous," she says. "Carl's already brought the car around."

Terror gushes through my veins.

"Give me my fucking phone back," I shout, lunging for it. She yanks her arm away from me and steps backward, out of reach.

And then, from behind me, comes the sound of more footsteps. Not the driver's. He's standing to my right, his hands lightly fisted.

"Carl isn't taking her *anywhere*."

The words discharge like an exploding firecracker. I spin around and stare down the length of the great room. There's a man standing at the entrance, dressed in a dark leather blazer. My brain scrambles, trying to make sense of what I'm seeing.

The man in the doorway is James Tremlin, the reporter from *ArtToday*.

36

Now

I FEEL A MOMENTARY PULSE OF RELIEF—HE'S SOMEHOW FIGURED out I'm here and in trouble and come to help me—but it's quickly enveloped by a fresh rush of fear. How could he possibly have traced me to this location?

"What are you doing here?" I blurt out.

He doesn't look at me. Instead, he twists his head toward the driver. "Carl, you can leave now. Please go back to your apartment."

He knows the driver for some reason. Knows his name, knows he's got a place right here on the grounds.

The driver narrows his eyes, as if deliberating, and then trains his gaze at Caroline.

"That won't be necessary, Carl," she tells him. "I need you to stay for now."

James Tremlin shakes his head, visibly angry. "No, Mother, tell him to leave."

Mother? What the fuck? I feel like I'm in some terrifying funhouse filled with mirrors that are making everything change shape before my eyes.

"I mean it, Mother," Tremlin says, raising his voice. "This is between the three of us."

The pieces fall together. I'm staring at C.J.'s younger brother, Liam, the one who lives in Buenos Aires and supposedly flew back there last week. He's clearly in cahoots with his mother, helping her to upend my life. Which means I'm outnumbered three to one. My knees try to buckle in fear, but I don't let them.

Caroline presses her lips together tightly and then snaps her head toward the driver.

"Carl, please give us a minute," she commands. "I'll call you later if I need you."

As Carl exits the way he came, Caroline looks back at her son.

"Please, Liam, don't be a fool," she implores him, trying to force his eyes to meet hers. "Let me handle this." She's clearly been caught off guard by her son's arrival and is playing this all by ear.

Grabbing a breath, I dart toward her, snatch the phone from her hand successfully this time, and turn and race across the great room. Tremlin jerks back in surprise, but before he has time to move, I rush by him and burst into the entryway, where the door is ajar. I practically hurl myself out into the October night.

For a few seconds I'm racing through the huge pool of light cast from the house, but then I cross over the edge, into the darkened grass. I know there must be houses close by because I passed them to get here, but I can't see a single sign of life—not a light, a roof peak, nothing. My only hope, I realize, is the road and a passing car willing to stop.

By now, my lungs are on fire and my ballet flats are in danger of flying off. As I slow my pace a little, desperate for air, I swear I hear footsteps behind me, pounding on the grass. C.J.'s brother, maybe, or even the driver. Frantic, I increase my speed again. I keep waiting for a hand to grab my shoulder and yank me back, but somehow I manage to reach the road.

Up ahead a car approaches, headed in the direction of town. I flail my arms wildly and simultaneously shoot a glance behind me. There's no one there. I realize that the pounding I heard was only the blood pumping hard between my ears.

The car zooms past. Maybe the driver's unnerved by the sight of me, wondering if it's a trick of some kind. But another comes right behind it. I drop one arm to my side, hoping to look less manic. This one slows, then crawls to a stop, and the driver rolls down the passenger window halfway. He's a man of about sixty, with salt-and-pepper hair.

"Please," I plead. "Someone's following me. Can you give me a ride to town?"

He hesitates, studying me. He looks kind but wary.

"*Please*," I say, begging now. "I'm in danger."

"Okay," he responds after a beat. "Jump in."

As I yank open the door, I glance back at the house. No one is in the yard, but there's a figure standing in the doorway, backlit by the light from the entrance.

"Skyler, wait," he calls out across the grass. "Please."

It must be Liam Whaley. There's no way in hell I'm going to listen to him. I fall into the passenger seat, and, as I slam the door closed, I finally exhale in relief.

"Thank you," I say, turning my head to the driver. He's wearing chinos and a quilted olive-green jacket. Probably no one to be scared of, unless there's a senior preppy serial killer on the loose. "Would you be able to drop me at the train station? Or anywhere in Scarsdale where I can call an Uber for the train?"

"The *train*?" he says, incredulous. "You were going to walk to the train from here?"

"No, I was at a house. And someone was threatening me. I just need to get back to New York."

"Shouldn't you be calling the police?"

Should I? But what would my complaint be? All I could accuse Caroline of at this point is insisting I take a town car to the station.

"I will," I lie. "But I want to do it from home. Where I feel safer."

He nods, though he's obviously skeptical. "No problem, I'll drop you at the station."

"Thank you so much," I say, trying to sound sane and law-abiding and unthreatening. "I'm Skyler, by the way. Skyler Moore."

"Bill Townsend."

He uses voice-to-text to send a message, telling a woman named Sharon that he'll be about twenty minutes late. With his attention briefly distracted, I twist to check the road behind us. There aren't any headlights beaming through the rear window, which means Liam Whaley or the chauffeur can't be in pursuit.

As I turn to face forward again, I realize Bill Townsend noticed my action, and he glances over, looking anxious.

"Did you see something?" he asks.

"No, it's okay. I thought the person might be following me, but he isn't."

He'll know where I'm going, though, and there must be other routes to the station from the house. Does Liam plan to show up on the platform? Still clutching my phone, I pull up the train schedule. There's one to New York in thirteen minutes, ahead of the train I'd originally anticipated catching. I have to be on it.

"Good, I'll just make the train," I announce, hoping it'll spur Bill Townsend into accelerating the car. It does, and a few minutes later, he's pulling up in front of the station.

"Take care, young lady," Bill says, his eyes narrowed. He seems still unsure how to read this and happy to be done with me.

"Thank you," I say as I swing open the door. "Thank you so much."

After first checking my surroundings, I scramble up the stairs to the platform, my heart hammering in my chest. Thankfully, there are a few small clusters of people waiting by the southbound track, obviously headed to the city. I migrate toward one group while trying not to invade their space. I pretend to read something on my phone, but my eyes move back and forth between the parking lot and the stairs to the platform, on alert for Liam, or Carl, or even Caroline.

Finally, a horn sounds, and seconds later the train noses into view. As I step onboard, I shoot a final glance toward the stairs. It's clear no one's coming, which almost freaks me more. What do they intend to do next? Are they racing to New York, planning to ambush me there?

I drop into a seat in an empty row. The conductor appears, and as I show her the ticket on my phone, I notice my hand is trembling a little. Was I in as much danger as I thought? I wonder. Had Caroline intended for Carl to take me someplace, kill me, and dispose of my body?

And if so, *why*?

Maybe my theory about Chloe is just another dead end, and this all comes down to money. *Family* money. Caroline had told me to take it and run, but it must have been a lie. And I remember telling her that morning in Scarsdale that I needed to spend the day at my studio, which means she must have sent her driver to New York as soon as he'd dropped me at the station, to break into my apartment and snoop around. Maybe she was secretly helping Jane out, wanting the trust to eventually go to her grandchildren. And Liam, as part of the family, was enlisted to remain in the country and assist in her efforts.

My mind flashes back to the scene at the house. Liam's arrival. Him calling out for me to wait. There had been nothing threatening about his tone as I reached for the car door, but there was no way I was going to stop. I feel hopelessly confused, as if my brain will explode any second.

And then, as if I've summoned it, my phone rings and the name James Tremlin appears on my screen. I pick up right away. I'm desperate to know what this all means.

"Are you all right?" he asks quietly, before I can say a word.

"Am I all *right*? That's funny. You didn't seem to care a minute ago."

"You have to believe me. I came to my mother's house to make sure you were okay."

"What?"

"I need you to hear me out. As you realize by now, I'm Chris's brother, and I'm so sorry about lying to you. But I found the name of a reporter and pretended to be him so I could learn more about you and insinuate myself into your life somehow."

"You mean, so you could help your mother try to ruin it?"

"No, to protect you. I knew my mother wanted to prevent you from learning the truth, but until you called me tonight, I had no idea she'd do something as extreme as damaging your artwork."

"What do you mean by the truth?" I say, my voice nearly strangled. "What is the truth?"

"I know what happened to your sister that night in Dover. And I need to tell you."

37

Now

I LET OUT A GASP.

"Was it Chris?" I ask. Oh god, it's true after all. "Did Chris kill my sister?"

"We can't do this over the phone," Liam says. "I have to meet you in person."

"There's no way I'm going to come back there," I say, but that's not a total lie. Because I have to know, no matter what it takes.

"Are you on the train?" he asks.

I hesitate. "Yes," I say finally.

"Okay. I'm in my car now, and I can meet you in the city in less than an hour."

"All right," I say, wondering if it might be a trick. "But only someplace public, with people around."

"There was a restaurant on the lower level of Grand Central, which I assume is still there. The Oyster Bar. And there's a little bar right in the center of it. Why don't we meet there? I'll text you when I'm parked."

"All right."

After disconnecting the call, I lean my head between my knees, trying to make the world stop spinning.

THOUGH I'M STILL BADLY SHAKEN WHEN I DISEMBARK, I COME INTO the terminal and find the restaurant easily enough. It's a cavernous space with tiled, vaulted ceilings and rows of tables topped with red-and-white-checked tablecloths, about half of them full—and it's vaguely familiar. I must have been here once years ago.

As Liam described, there's a small bar area in the middle of the space, which is mostly empty except for a couple sitting side by side on one of the banquettes, maybe having a drink before heading back to the suburbs. I take a seat at a white table shaped like a toadstool and order a sparkling water.

The wait is almost unbearable. But finally, at close to eight thirty, Liam appears in the doorway. He spots me and strides in my direction, his expression stricken. In my panicky state at the house, I'd barely focused on him, and I finally take him in from head to toe. No wonder I'd thought he was European when I met him as James Tremlin. His style doesn't feel quite American. But then he's been living in Buenos Aires for years, at least supposedly.

"Thank you," he says, dropping into the chair across from me. He signals immediately for a waiter and asks for a Dewar's on the rocks.

"Was Chris at the party that night?" I demand as soon as the waiter's moved off. "Is he the one who killed her?"

"Please, just let me catch my breath."

"*Tell* me. Tell me now."

He bites his lip, looking miserable.

"Chris wasn't at the party. *I* was. I was working in Boston then, at a stock brokerage, and another broker in the firm invited a few of us—he had a desk next to a guy related to the girl having the party. I met your sister that night—and I'm the last person who saw her alive."

I can't believe it. After all these years, I'm staring at him, the guy Chloe was with, the guy with the sweater. A few days ago, we drank fucking cappuccinos together.

"*You* killed her?"

"No, I swear, I didn't. Your sister fell into the ravine, totally by accident."

"You're a liar," I say fiercely. I want nothing more than to fly across the table and pummel him with my hands or grab a knife from the table and stab him through the throat with it.

"No, please, you have to trust me. We were looking for a gazebo your sister heard about, and all of a sudden she was running ahead of me on the path. I told her to wait, to be careful, but she kept going. Finally, she stopped and turned around, told me to come on. She laughed and stepped backward—and then, God, the next thing I knew she was gone."

He presses a fist to his lips, then pulls it away. "I scrambled far enough down with the flashlight on my phone to see she was dead. I know it was horrific to leave her behind, but I knew what it looked like. And that no one would believe me that it was an accident."

I shake my head hard, disbelieving. "But she wasn't wearing her top. You *assaulted* her."

"I promise you I didn't," he says, and sighs. "Though what I did was almost as bad. I eventually got down to where her body was, and I took off her top—because I started to think there might be traces of my DNA on it."

I'm practically hyperventilating by now. Is this really all there is? And though I'm not entirely sure why—is it his demeanor, the remorse in his eyes?—I think he might be telling the truth.

The waiter appears with the scotch for Liam and silently sets it down on the table.

"I'm so sorry, Skyler," he says, after the waiter's drifted away. His eyes are watering with tears. "If it's any consolation, I haven't had a moment's peace since that night. I left the country not long after-ward and rarely come back here from Buenos Aires."

"How is it the police never suspected you?" I say, forcing my breath to slow.

"I don't think anyone ever noticed us together. I'd brought a date to the party with me, but she ended up getting smashed pretty quickly and was all over some other guy, so I went off by myself. I talked to your sister for a while outside, off to ourselves, and then circled back to her later, and that's when we went into the woods. The police questioned me a couple of days later, but I said I'd been with my date, and she confirmed it. She'd been too drunk, I guess, to notice how long I was gone."

With a jittery hand, I grab a glass and take a small sip of water.

"Something's not making sense," I tell him. "How . . . did you get all the way down the side of the ravine from the path? When I was there, it looked next to impossible."

He lets out a long, wretched sigh. "I was checking the news all Saturday, and there was nothing about a missing college girl, so really early Sunday morning I drove back to Dover and entered the woods on the other side of the ravine and made my way down from there. It was light by then, but there wasn't a soul around. I took the blouse—and a sweater of mine I'd gotten her from the car when she said she was cold."

So that answers that.

But something about his last comment lifts a thought from the corner of my mind, though it quickly flutters just out of reach.

"What does Chris have to do with any of this?" I say finally.

"He came to Boston to check on me. I'd called my mother Sat-urday morning to say I was in deep shit, that I needed help. She couldn't get the story out of me, so she sent C.J. up there. I was the problem son in those days, but also her favorite, and C.J. was used to running rescue operations on my behalf. We were supposed to meet at some point Saturday night so I could tell him everything, but I panicked and didn't show. But then just after dawn the next morning, I finally called him and blurted everything out. And thanks to some fucked-up plan of the universe—and totally unbeknownst to me at the time—you were there in the room with him."

The phone call. It had come while I was in the bathroom, and though I couldn't overhear the words, I detected tension in Chris's voice. My first thought was *wife* or *girlfriend*. When I emerged, he seemed quieter, somber even, and within minutes his whole mood darkened, chasing the magic from the room. I figured guilt might have overtaken him suddenly. Or that I'd altered the vibe by unloading my concerns about my sister.

My mouth drops open in shock. When I'd told C.J. about Chloe, I'd mentioned her name, that the party was outside Boston, and that I was worried I hadn't heard from her

"He told you what I'd shared with him, didn't he? About my sister going missing."

Liam casts his eyes down, staring into his drink.

"Yes, because it matched with what I'd just blurted out to him. . . . And because you mentioned the sweater, too."

"*What?*" I say. The thought flutters again in my mind, still out of reach.

"You told Chris your sister had a man's sweater around her waist, which I'd completely forgotten about. That's— That's the main reason I went back. And I took the top while I had the chance."

Bile rises in my throat, and I take a breath, trying to keep it down. I-I set the whole horrible cover-up in motion. If I hadn't made that one offhand comment, Liam would never have retrieved his sweater, and we would have gotten to the truth twelve years ago.

"So that's what the trust is about," I say, seething. "To ease your brother's fucking guilt over betraying me?"

"No, you have to believe me," Liam says, holding his hands up to me, palms forward. "He didn't betray you. When he told me about the sweater, he was doing it to encourage me to go to the police before they found the body and linked me to the scene. He had no idea I'd go back to the woods. Once he knew what I'd done, he pretty much banished me from his life."

"But he didn't turn you in," I say flatly.

"No," he says, looking down again. "He couldn't bring himself to do it."

"You're certainly not counting on me to keep quiet, are you?"

"Of course not. And just so you know, I'm turning myself in. I've already met with an attorney and we're heading to Dover the day after tomorrow."

"Right," I say, incredulous. "You really expect me to believe you're going to give up what I assume is a cushy life in South America and throw yourself on the mercy of the court?"

He nods, his expression grim. "There's a saying in Argentina that goes, '*A cada chancho le llega su san Martín*,' meaning, 'For every pig, it's eventually slaughter day.' Or put another way, there comes a time when you have to pay your dues. That time has come for me. My brother's death made me realize that the only way I could live with myself was to come forward."

It doesn't seem like he's bullshitting, or if he is, he's making an extraordinary show of it.

His eyes find mine. "All I ask is that you not mention my name to anyone, including your family, until I've been charged. I told my attorney I would keep it under wraps until then."

Though the crowd in the restaurant area has begun to thin out, there are still diners at scattered tables, sucking down oysters and cracking open lobster shells. What would they think if they could overhear the devastating conversation at this tiny white table?

"Okay," I say finally. "But only if you give me your word that C.J. didn't send you back for the sweater."

"You have my word, I swear. C.J. was a decent guy. The most decent guy." His voice cracks on "most."

"But if he wasn't guilty, why leave me the money?"

He shakes his head. "I think he *felt* guilty—because he'd inadvertently set certain things in motion. As soon as he found out he was dying, he called and told me he was assigning the trust to you, and I had to make sure you got it. He'd kept tabs on you, found out you'd dropped out of grad school, that you'd never married, that you lived alone. I think that even before his diagnosis, he'd been contemplating how to make up in some way for what you'd missed out on in life."

So he *did* owe me. More than I could have ever guessed.

"Explain your mother to me—because I just don't get it. Did she really think that ruining my collages would make me assign the trust to Jane?"

"No, she despises Jane, and never wanted her to have it. But once you told her you'd met Chris in Boston, she began putting the pieces together. She knew you were trying to figure it all out, too, and worried you'd learn the reason. I guess all the harassment was her attempt to keep you off-balance."

But she might have done worse than throw me off-balance, I think. She had plans for Carl to take me someplace—maybe hurt me or worse.

"I have to make her stop."

"You don't have to—because I will. I give you my word."

I drop my head into my hands. There are so many other questions, but I'm too spent to think of any right now.

"I need to go home," I say, raising my head slowly.

"I promise to call you tomorrow and give you an update," he says. "I know there's no way for you—or your family—to forgive me. But I'm going to make sure you get all the money. That's what my brother wanted."

38

Now

THE FIRST THING I DO IN THE MORNING, AFTER FEEDING TUNA and starting the coffee maker, is fold up the collage I made about C.J. and me and stuff it in my kitchen wastebasket. The work served its purpose, and I don't need to look at it ever again.

When I wash my face, I see that my eyelids are nearly the size of plums, swollen from the sobbing I finally did in bed last night as I replayed the conversation with Liam again and again. I kept urging myself to be grateful that Chloe hadn't had to fight off a sexual assault, that she hadn't spent the last minutes of her life in a state of abject fear, but, still, I knew there must have been a few terrifying seconds as she stumbled backward and felt only unforgiving air beneath her. Did she have a split-second realization that her life was about to end, that she would never be a TV host or anchorwoman or famous war correspondent? Had her head exploded with pain as she hit the ground and her neck snapped in two?

Finally, close to dawn, a small swell of relief joined the sadness—because, as selfish as it sounds, I now know for certain there was nothing I could have done to save my sister that night. I fell asleep at last around five.

I'm nursing a second cup of coffee when my buzzer rings, startling both Tuna and me. But then I remember it must be Nell, and it is. I buzz her in and open the door to her a minute later.

"Cute place," she says, panting from the hike up the stairs. She sounds sincere, though maybe she's still feeling sorry for me. She explains she has a guy helping her and the plan is for her to stay with the van while he lugs the collages up the three flights. I shut Tuna in the bedroom and wait by the front door until the bearded, twentysomething helper arrives with the first batch. He makes three trips in all, sweating by the last one. The pieces are encased in brown paper and bubble wrap, with the name of each collage written in black marker across the bubbles.

"Thank you," I say as he leaves, closing the door behind him and locking it again. All ten pieces are now leaning sadly against my small bookcase. It hurts to look at them, and I'm tempted to toss a blanket on top, like a tarp over a dead body, but I decide it will only make me more aware of them.

As soon as I let Tuna back into the living room, I summon the nerve to text my mother, David, and Nicky and ask if they can be available for a Zoom call at seven tonight, a time when I'm pretty sure they'll all be home from work. I give no explanation—I'm certainly not going to say it's about Chloe and leave them in a state of anguish all day. Besides, my mother will probably assume I'm planning to come clean about why my show was canceled. Sure enough, they all respond without any questions.

I spend the rest of the day doing as many mindless chores as I can drum up: washing my kitchen floor, scrubbing the bathroom tiles, lugging towels and sheets to the laundromat. Anything to keep my mind off the Zoom call ahead, as well as Liam Whaley, and whether he's really en route to Dover, Massachusetts. I dread the thought of breaking the news about Liam and Chloe, but my family needs to hear it from me, not the police.

Just before seven, I carry my laptop to the table and click on the Zoom link I forwarded to everyone. Soon after I see my face on the screen, a window opens showing my mother and David sitting side by side on the nubby green couch in the den, a room I'll never set eyes on again since they're moving next month. And then suddenly Nicky slides into view on the couch. She's obviously decided to join them there, rather than calling in from her own place.

"Thanks for doing this," I say. "Sorry if I threw off anyone's plans, but I have something pretty serious to share."

The three of them bunch a little closer together, perhaps from an instinctive desire for moral support. Do they assume I've fucked up my life beyond repair and am about to dump the details into their laps right now?

"Is this about the other night?" my mother asks coolly.

I don't feel even a moment's satisfaction from knowing I'd read her mind correctly.

"No, Mom, it's not about the other night. It's about Chloe—I have some news."

I force myself to get to the point immediately—that a man, knowing I was Chloe's sister, reached out to me last night with information. He confessed that he was the one who was with her in the woods that night and that her death was an accident.

Both my mother and David emit moans of despair, and Nicky bursts into tears. Before any of them can pepper me with questions, I fill in all the blanks I can, emphasizing Liam's claim that he hadn't assaulted Chloe.

"He simply confessed all this to you out of the blue?" David says, sounding fairly dubious.

"Not out of the blue. He said he's been tortured for years and finally decided to turn himself into the Dover police, which is supposedly happening tomorrow."

"What's his name?" David demands. "Where is he now?"

I explain why I can't give the name yet, but David looks unconvinced.

"What makes you think he isn't some nutjob?" my mother snaps. "Or that he's lying about what really happened to cover himself?" Her eyes are wild with grief and anger.

"I don't have any proof," I say, "but I sense he's telling the truth."

She shakes her head. "There's something you're not telling us. I can feel it."

"I've shared every detail he gave me, Mom," I exclaim, feeling my own anger flare and not bothering to disguise it. "You have no right to accuse me of withholding anything. I didn't then, and I'm not now."

"Okay, okay," David says, tamping down the air with his hands. He turns to my mother. "Margo, what possible reason would Skyler have for not telling us everything she knows?"

"None," I say, not giving my mother time to respond. "The bottom line is that Chloe went out into the woods with a stranger and a bottle of wine without telling me where she was going and ended up slipping over the edge of a ravine. It seems it was a terrible accident, and there's nothing I could have done to save her." I choke back a sob. "I know you prefer the version where I didn't tell you the full story, or the one where I'm somehow to blame, that she could have been saved if I'd only thought of summoning the National Guard to look for her that night or something else of that magnitude, but I know now for sure that I did everything I could."

My mother jerks back as if she's been slapped, but she says nothing. David exhales a long, rough sigh. I can tell from his face that he knows that what I've said about her is all true.

They clearly need some time to process this together, so I say quickly that I'll be in touch as soon as I have more information, and that I'm still so sad for all of us. Then I tap "end meeting," leaving them to comfort one another on the nubby green couch.

I realize that this is the way I'm always going to be in this family: the girl on the outside looking in, now and forever. Lately I'd been telling myself that something might change once my mother saw my opening and discovered I was starting to make something new, but no collage in the world could thaw her heart. I see that now.

And oddly, there's a certain peace in accepting it. For the first time in years, that dull sensation of dread I've always lugged around with me seems to have dissipated.

As I head to the fridge a little while later for a Diet Coke, my phone pings with a text from Nicky.

> Oh my god, Sky. It must have been so hard for you to hear what that guy had to say. Thanks for sharing with us.

> Yeah, so hard. But at least we can stop the endless wondering now.

> Right. Mom's really upset of course, but I think this will be better fr her in the long run. And maybe you cn call her later, so just the two of you cn talk this out.

I read her last message a second time as I sip my soda, mulling over the words. And finally I send off a reply.

> Skip the Dr. Phil shit, okay? Things aren't going to change
> btw mom + me, and you need to finally accept that.

There's no follow-up ping, and it doesn't surprise me. I've never talked back to Nicky like that, and she's probably smarting. I love her and I want her in my life, especially if I manage to bring a baby into the world, but I'm no longer going to pretend that we're part of a happy, functional family.

By the time I'm dressing for bed, I still haven't heard from Liam, and I'm starting to despair. What if he's chickened out? But as I'm pulling back the duvet on my bed, he finally calls.

"I'm in Boston now," he says. "My lawyer's spoken to the district attorney for Dover, and it's all set for me to turn myself in tomorrow and talk to the DA myself."

"Okay," I say, barely believing that we're finally getting some closure. "Will you go to prison, do you know?"

"I'm not sure what's in the cards for me, but anything will be better than the last twelve years."

"I want to forgive you," I tell him, "and maybe someday I can, but I'm not there yet. But in the meantime, thank you for letting me know the truth."

"I haven't forgotten my other obligation, by the way—to make sure you end up with the trust. My mother has committed to calling off the dogs and ceasing any harassment. I've told her if it starts up again, I'll drag Chris's name into this, which would kill her. She's having a hard enough time anticipating the fallout from what I'm about to do."

"What about Jane, though?"

"That will stop, too. My mother has agreed to tell Jane that if she tries to block you from receiving the trust, she'll disinherit Mark and Bee. Jane wasn't a good partner to my brother, but she's not a monster. She'll back off."

"Thank you. Good . . . good luck tomorrow."

We sign off, and before setting the phone on the bedside table, I text Mikoto.

> I figured everything out, all thanks to something you said.
> And I mean EVERYTHING. Can I treat you to dinner?

A minute later, once I'm already snuggled under the duvet, Tuna appears from the other room and hops into the bed with me.

"Guess what?" I say as her eyes bore into mine. "We're millionaires."

In a way, it's blood money, and it doesn't make me any less heartsick about Chloe. But I'm going to use it the way C.J. intended. To start my life again.

39

Six Days Later

AFTER A COUPLE OF DAYS OF REALLY CHILLY WEATHER, IT'S fairly mild out, which is nice. Using bubble wrap and twine, I carefully swathe the first collage I've repaired, lock up my studio—where I've started working again—and take the elevator to the lobby. I'd originally planned to hail a cab to the gallery but decide to walk instead.

The collage I'm carrying is *Daydream*, the one that Josh has a buyer for—as long, that is, as the collector approves of its new iteration. I removed the damaged image and, after a couple of days of searching, added something else that I hope works well. The overall result is bold and compelling, I think—maybe even more so than the original.

That doesn't change the fact that it was unsettling to repair the piece, to briefly look at that ugly word and also alter what I'd worked so hard on, but I'm okay about it now. My plan is to salvage as many of the collages as I can. They're going to be slightly new and different creatures from what I first envisioned, and I'll just have to make peace with that.

And starting the repair work has actually been a nice distraction during a crazy week. Once Liam turned himself in, the media swarmed around the case. Mostly in the Boston area, but according to Nicky, who's gotten over our text exchange, my mother and David also have been hounded at home.

I kept the appointment with Rebecca Rosenbaum, the attorney, the other day, and plan to use her if I have to, but I don't think that's going to be necessary. Bradley Kane called yesterday to say that Jane Whaley is no longer challenging my status as the beneficiary—the result, no doubt, of Liam's efforts. It will take a while for the money to land in my account, but it's coming. This means that after my exam at the fertility clinic, I can commit right away to the first IUI.

The idea makes me both nervous and giddy at the same time. I have no second thoughts, though. Not a single one.

The one thing I didn't do this past week was drop by the police precinct and file a report about the vandalism. Since Caroline has called off the dogs, it seems best to let that sleeping dog lie.

Nell is at the front desk when I arrive at the gallery, reading a catalog. She looks up and smiles. I greet her and ask if Josh is around.

"He said he might not make it back by the time you got here, and that you could just leave the collage. . . . Oh wait, here he is."

I turn and spot him through the plateglass window, striding toward the door, radiating his usual Upper-East-Side-meets-boho vibe. As he crosses the threshold into the gallery, I see he's hand in hand with a blonde who can't be more than twenty-five. She's wearing tan pants, flared at the bottom, with an oversize, luxe-looking cable pullover, and she's carrying a white purse with the word *Dior* in big letters. Instagram-ready.

"Hey, Skyler, hi," he says. He turns to the girl. "Kelly, why don't you head back to the office for a few minutes. There's an espresso machine in there. Just help yourself."

She nods, looking a tiny bit unsure, and then disappears. Not a girlfriend. I guess. But they're something.

Well, he wasn't for me, anyway.

"Can I take a look?" he asks, returning his attention to me.

I still don't love the idea of having to watch him react, but I'm less bothered than I was the last time I brought him a piece. As soon as I nod, he grabs a pair of scissors from the drawer of the reception desk and carefully removes the wrapping from the collage, then asks Nell to hold it while he steps back for a good look.

"Wow," he says after a couple of seconds. "It's fantastic, Skyler. Different, yes, but as riveting as the original."

"Do you think your client will still want it?"

"Yeah, I'm sure of it."

I feel my shoulders relax. Yes, the money will be great, tiding me over until the trust comes in, but this was also a test for me, a chance to see whether the collages could still work with changes.

"And how about the rest?" Josh asks, an eyebrow cocked. "Are you still thinking you'll be able to repair them?"

"Yup. I'm going to be taking a break from graphic design jobs for a bit, so I'll have the time."

"Tell you what," he says, flashing me one of his best sales-guy grins. "Let's pick a date for the show and see if it helps spur you on."

He goes behind the desk and taps a few keys on the computer.

"Does February twenty-seventh work for you?"

"Yeah, it does," I say, not needing to check my calendar. "Three months should be enough time to get everything done."

"Great. And we'll do another party. I promise a crowd as big as we had last week."

I almost tell him to skip the party, but then I bite my tongue. After speaking to Dan Lui last week, I found my thoughts pulling me back to the day we found Chloe—searching the house, searching the woods, standing at the edge of the ravine with him, Jamie, and the two Dover police. I started to wonder if my anxiety about being in groups of five or more, which started after Chloe's death, is somehow related to that moment, a post-traumatic reaction. And maybe knowing that could help me to finally conquer it. With the help of a good shrink, of course.

I bid farewell to Josh and Nell. It's only three o'clock, so I decide to drop by my studio before going home. I'll organize supplies for repairing the next collage on the list, and maybe sip a cup of tea at my worktable before heading home. Tonight's the night I'm taking Mikoto out for a celebratory meal.

When I step off the elevator to my floor, I find that the corridor is quiet, though I can hear muffled conversation coming from behind one of the doors. As I approach my own studio door, my heart skips. There's a piece of paper poking out from beneath it, clearly the edge of a note someone's left for me.

I approach cautiously, both fear and anger spiking inside of me—has Caroline decided not to cease her efforts, after all? As soon as I unlock the door and flick on the light, I reach down for the note. My anxiety immediately quiets when I see that the name scrawled at the bottom is Alejandro's.

I'd messaged him the other day to thank him for coming to the opening and apologize for the show being canceled. I told him, too, that his sketch helped me identity the man who'd been prowling around, and that the guy was no longer a threat. He wrote back saying he was glad he'd been able to help.

But the note has nothing to do with any of that.

I heard you in your studio earlier, but I must have missed you. I was wondering if you'd like to have dinner with me some night this week.

Is it simply a friendly offer? I wonder. No, it seems like he's asking me on a date, something I never saw coming. From the little I know of him, Alejandro seems interesting and thoughtful, and from the glimpses I've gotten of his work, he's clearly very talented. But why complicate my life any more than it already is at the moment?

But maybe . . . maybe there's no harm in saying yes.

ACKNOWLEDGMENTS

There are times in life when I cringe at the thought of doing research, but when it comes to my novels, I adore that part of the process. Research is essential for making sure the facts (about everything from crime scenes to people's jobs) are accurate, but so often when I'm researching, I turn up little nuggets that spark ideas for amazing plot points.

As expected, I do a lot of research online these days, but I also talk to experts on various subjects, and the details they provide can make all the difference. For *Between Two Strangers* I'm incredibly grateful to those in the know who gave so generously of their time: Susan Brune, Brune Law; Barbara Butcher, consultant for forensic and medicolegal investigations; Paul Paganelli, MD; Joyce Hanshaw, retired captain from the Hunterdon County Prosecutor's Office; Jim White; Cheryl Brown; Jonathan Santlofer; Randy Abood; Jodie King; Betsy Fitzgerald; and Elias Isaac.

Thank you, as well, to my wonderful, brilliant editor, Emily Griffin, for all her incredible work on the book, and to the awesome team at Harper, including Amy Baker, Lisa Erickson, Robin Bilardello, Olivia McGiff, Stacey Fischkelta, and my terrific new publicist Heather Drucker.

A huge thank you, as well, to my agent, Kathy Schneider of the Jane Rotrosen Agency. How fantastic it is for me to be working with her.

I have to give a special shout-out, too, to my own team: website editor Laura Nicolassy Cocivera; social media manager Imani Seymour; and website tech director and designer Bill Cunningham.

Finally, to my readers: How did I ever deserve such a fabulous group of people in my life? Thank you immensely for reading my books; giving me the chance to be a full-time author for more than ten years; taking the time to review my books on Goodreads, Bookbub, barnesandnoble.com, and Amazon.com; and sharing snippets of your own lives with me via my website (katewhite.com), Facebook, and Instagram. I absolutely love hearing from you, so please, never stop.

ABOUT THE AUTHOR

Kate White, former editor in chief of *Cosmopolitan* magazine, is the *New York Times* bestselling author of the standalone psychological thrillers *The Second Husband*, *The Fiancée*, and *The Secrets You Keep*, among others, as well as eight Bailey Weggins mysteries. White is also the author of several popular career books for women, including *I Shouldn't Be Telling You This*, and the editor of *The Mystery Writers of America Cookbook*.